THE THINGS WE DO FOR LOVE...

IT WILL END IN DISASTER

PATRICK MORGAN

For Her

CHAPTER 1

Beginnings are always the tricky part.

Coming in, there's only so much information available. Between character limits, unoriginality, fear, and the dumbed-down digital parlance of our times, you're lucky if there's enough to go off that might generate an hour of acceptable conversation, at best.

Tell me about your job. Any passions or hobbies? What's your family like? Are you close to your parents? Do you have any siblings? Do you have any tattoos? How about pets? What brought you out to L.A.? Would you consider yourself spiritual, religious, or neither? Are you into politics? What about sports? Who's your favorite band? What's your favorite TV show? What's your favorite color? How about your favorite food? What's your star sign? Do you have a spirit animal? Beer or wine? Beach or mountains? Yes or no?

Twenty fucking questions, over and over and over again. Who cares?

Like, honestly, who cares? What's the point?

"Let me see her."

I smirk in mock indignation, though I have no idea why I

do this since I fully expected the question.

"Come on, Lance. Pass it over."

This isn't the first time this has happened. And as much as I might wish otherwise, I know it won't be the last time, either.

I open the right app, find the right message, click on the right girl. I'm about to slide it across the bar top when I pause just long enough to swipe so the first photo he sees is the bikini one. I hate myself even as I do this, but it gets the desired result.

"Woah. Hello, there, Caroline."

I don't blame Jared for reacting that way. He is me a week ago. Truly, he is most men most of the time.

"Jesus. She's sexy, man. And this is your first date?"

He takes one last wistful look at the screen before passing it back to me. I close out of the app before I pocket the phone back in my jacket.

"Yep. Why do you think I brought her here?"

"So you could take advantage of the free drinks and my exceptional service while still looking like a boss?"

"Bingo."

Jared lifts his shot glass.

"Same as it ever was."

I lift my shot glass.

"Same as it ever was."

Clink.

We throw back the Ketel, and then he clears our glasses and moves off down the bar to help someone else.

God, I fucking hate myself sometimes.

CHAPTER 2

It stopped being fun right around the same time it stopped being about the chase. I'm sure that's no coincidence.

I can remember exactly when it happened and who it happened with. It was December, because this place was done up in twinkly lights, and my buddy Jared the barback had on an ugly Christmas sweater with real silver jingle bells sewn into the wool. Her name was either Cara or Clara, she had a nose ring and sleeves, and I knew I had it in the bag from the word 'go.'

I'll never know for sure, but I'm fairly positive she showed up drunk. Her breath smelled like peppermint schnapps, though it could have been just peppermint gum, which obviously makes it hard to tell these things for sure in retrospect. But her whole demeanor that night was so aggressively forward, so abundantly flirtatious and suggestive, that the mystery just vanished like smoke before either one of us really even said hi. We both knew what was going to happen from the moment we locked eyes and that initial hug lasted just a few seconds longer than it should have.

That was over a year ago now, but I remember it well as

being a turning point in my dating life. Because when you take away the question of 'will they or won't they,' you're just left with 'when will they.' And as it turns out, that question's not nearly as much fun to answer.

From there, it was a steady bleed of boredom, like a contagious disease that spread out to all other frontiers of my sexual psyche, robbing me of adventure, intrigue, and joy. 'Will they/won't they' lost its luster even when it was still there, alive and well, between us. Nothing was organic anymore. The chase revealed itself for what it always was and always will be: just a pre-ordained pattern, some prehistoric ritual hardwired into my DNA to make me and all the other apes waste our time and hard-earned money on such trivialities.

And for what? Sex? Love? The survival of the human race?

"So, would you consider yourself more a religious person, a spiritual person, or neither?"

Caroline's big brown doe eyes shine playfully in the candlelight as she zeroes them in on me from across her upturned rosé. She wears the instantly-recognizable expression of someone who believes they've just introduced a spicy, new, unexpected ingredient into a familiar conversational dish. I smile the way I know I'm supposed to smile as I slowly run the tip of my index finger around the rim of my whiskey sour.

"Ooo, we're really getting into it now, huh?"

Her laugh is coquettish and feels a tad bit embarrassed, a notion that's quickly confirmed when the dimples in her cheeks redden to match her wine.

"Sorry, we don't have to. I don't want to make you uncomfortable."

If only she knew that the true source of my discomfort lay more in her nervous backpedaling than in the initial question itself.

"No, don't apologize. Never apologize."

She looks like she's about to say sorry for that now, so I cut her off before she can.

"There's nothing you could do or say that would make me uncomfortable. You can let go of that concern right now."

It comes out harsher than I intend it to, so I soften it with just the wisp of a smile. She tentatively reciprocates, and I wait for the flush to fade on her collarbone before answering.

"I was raised Catholic, but I stopped going as soon as I got the chance to in college. The priest at my church back home used to slip his hand down the back of my pants waistline every time I worked as an altar boy, so that kind of permanently soured me on the whole religion thing I think."

Improbably, Caroline's eyes can get bigger.

"Oh, my God. Are you serious?"

"Unfortunately, I am. Those stories you hear about in the news? That could have been me."

Caroline's face is a portrait of genuine empathy. She's particularly beautiful like this, with her pouty lips drooping open and her eyes wide and white. I'm sure many men would love to be the personal recipient of such a picturesque reaction. It's almost enough to make me feel guilty that it's absolutely lost on my emotional person.

"That was you. Did you ever tell anyone?"

I reach for the whiskey.

"I'm telling you now."

"No, but I mean… back then, did you ever tell your

parents? Or the police?"

I drain what liquid is left in the glass and shake a couple ice cubes into my mouth to chew on.

"No point. This guy was beloved by the community. Besides, it's not like he ever grabbed my dick or exposed himself to me or anything. It could have been worse."

Caroline still looks positively stunned.

I don't always venture up this particular kernel of personal history on first dates, but it's also not exactly uncharted territory for me, either. If it comes up, it comes up. Frankly, I don't think it's a big deal, though it never fails to come across as a big deal to whomever I reveal it to. And Caroline is no different. Surprise, surprise.

"Well, I'm so sorry that happened to you. That is not okay at all, whether he… touched you there… or not."

It's hard not to wince at the way she says 'touched you there.' Any encouraging signs I may have gotten up to this point—her subconscious habit of reapplying lip gloss after every other sip of wine, her decision to wear a tight coral-colored sweater that conspicuously bares her shoulders and collarbone, or the fact she's repeated twice already that she doesn't have to work tomorrow—suddenly feel fatally offset by the way she just said those three words. If she was pink before, she's definitely red now.

I need another whiskey, but Jared is all the way at the other end of the bar, blissfully preoccupied with a small bachelorette party that appears to be drinking quite literally from the palm of his hand. The two other bartenders working right now know that I'm associated with Jared, too, so they've long since made a habit of ignoring me every time I come in.

"I appreciate it. How are you doing on that rosé? Ready

for another one?"

Caroline's cocoa saucer eyes blink with surprise and glance down at her glass on the counter. It's still probably half-full, but I'm hoping that won't matter.

"Oh. I think I'm okay for now, thank you."

You can't really blame someone for not wanting to do shots with you on a Tuesday night, especially on a first date, and I suppose especially when that someone is thirty-five years old. I have a harder time sympathizing with someone who's still working on their first drink though—and wine, no less—when I've just finished my third. My watch lets me know we're already over an hour into this thing, too.

Fuck. This isn't going as expected. And now that I know that and I'm self-aware of the situation underway, it's not going to get any easier. I'm going to have to ride this out to an utterly unsatisfying conclusion for the both of us.

Which, of course, begs back that age-old question I can't seem to satisfactorily answer for myself: why am I even here? What am I doing with this girl? What am I doing... period?

If I just wanted sex, I could have gotten it so much easier than this. But I knew that. I know that. I'm no fool. For some reason, I made the choice to engage in this stupid ritual once again tonight. But why?

"Are you all right?"

"Huh?"

Caroline knows how to care, I'll give her that. If there's any shred of annoyance, boredom, or fatigue, she's hidden it all well behind an expression that emits true unbridled sympathy. She should have been a shrink or a nurse. Come to think of it, maybe she already is one of those things, since I can't seem to recall anymore what she does for a living.

"Are you okay? You got quiet all of a sudden."

It finally dawns on me that she must think I'm reliving some personal hell caused by a pederast priest from my childhood. And maybe it's all those shots Jared and I did before she got here, but that thought alone makes me laugh out loud.

Right away, the confusion and concern on her face lets me know she neither gets it nor thinks anything is remotely funny.

"Yeah, I'm good, thanks. Maybe we should just change the subject."

I tack that last bit on because it seems to make sense for me to say given what I think she thinks this situation is. Ever the empath, Caroline nods slowly, then genuinely surprises me by leaning forward on her bar stool and taking my hand without any warning or preamble.

"Is this a Claddagh ring?"

Here we go. This is also well-traveled date terrain.

I look down at the silver band on my finger and study the converging hands holding their heart with the crown on top. As much as I love the ring for its sentimental value, it's probably sending out the wrong signal, leading even the most casual observer to mistakenly believe I'm out here desperately offering my heart up to the first person who shows any interest. Sometimes I wonder if I should just turn it around to face the other way, but then again, that might also put out some confusing first date signals to those in the know with Claddagh rings.

"It is. My last name is Lonergan, and we're a very Irish family, as you might expect from the name. It was my grandfather's ring. He willed it to me when he passed."

"Oh, I'm so sorry."

It takes me a second or two to realize what she's talking

about. We're definitely slipping further and further away from each other in terms of our frequencies.

"No, don't be. He's been dead a long time now."

Caroline blushes and abruptly snaps her hand back from mine, which definitely adds to the growing sense of awkwardness.

"Oh. Well, still. It's a beautiful ring. I'm sure it means a lot to you."

"Thanks. Yeah, it does."

We both look anywhere but at each other. Seconds pass in silence before she speaks again.

"You know, when I was younger, I also had an incident like your experience with the priest."

Oh, Christ. How are we on this subject again? Speaking of priests, the space between us now suddenly has the air of a confessional booth. It's borderline suffocating.

"I had an uncle try to kiss me at my sweet sixteen. He's not in my family anymore, thank God, but I'll never forget it. It's a terrible feeling, being that young and unaware, but also so very aware at the same time. You know that something's not right, but you also don't trust yourself enough to say or do something about it, because an adult's an adult and you're just a kid. You know what I mean?"

Not really. I mean, I understand what she's saying, but that just wasn't my experience. I've never felt like a victim, and I don't carry around any emotional baggage or trauma because of some lonely old man in a tablecloth. But to each their own, I guess.

That drink. I need that drink.

Jared's still schmoozing all the way down at the end of the bar. I stand and lean forward over the sticky marble countertop to see if it will get his attention. When it doesn't,

I slurp down the fresh sliver of liquid that's newly formed in my glass from what's left of the melting ice cubes, then I toss back those remnants in my mouth, too, and slide away from the bar and from Caroline.

"Be right back. Just gotta use the bathroom."

She mumbles something that sounds an awful lot like a dejected 'okay,' but I'm already a man in motion now, so I have no time for second-guessing.

Putting one foot in front of the other, I glide past a row of background characters until I reach the bachelorette party. They're still enraptured with whatever dumbass parlor tricks Jared's started peddling now, and I grind my teeth when not a one of them looks my way as I pass them by. Shooting my friend the most murderous glare I can conjure up while still keeping my feet moving, I finally round the end of the bar and dip into a darkened hallway.

This is one of those fancy, progressive bathrooms you see popping up more and more frequently in liberal-leaning cities across America. On my left is a black countertop lined with sink basins, faucets, blow dryers, towel dispensers, mint jars, candy dishes, and candles. On my right is a shallow row of four wood-shuttered doors, unlabeled yet utterly innocuous, each leading to a small, closet-sized, gender-neutral, politically-correct room with a toilet, a toilet paper roll, and a metal bin for disposing of feminine hygiene products and other non-flushable refuse. Let's just say this isn't the place, the town, or the time period to bring your non-woke parents to if they originally hail from the Midwest or the South.

Things have gone awry with Caroline, I think, as I duck into an empty bathroom cubicle and unzip my fly to relieve my bladder. There was promise there once; though even then, I'm not sure what my ultimate end-goal was. She's a sweet girl. They usually are. Unfortunately, that just makes me feel all the more like an asshole for not knowing what I'm doing here.

A grim smile pulls up the corners of my lips. I'm reminded that I'm doing precisely what I'm supposed to be doing. What my parents want me to be doing. What they practically beg me to be doing every time I give them the occasional rare call to check in and they ask what's new in LaLaLand and then playfully-but-not-actually-playfully lament their current lack of grandchildren. Because they know as well as I know that they don't really give a damn about the auditions, the workshops, the rat race. When am I going to settle down? That's the million-dollar-question and the only one that matters to them.

And because of that, I'm trying to do what every fucking kid in my po-dunk problematic hometown already did years ago: they dated, they fell in love, they got married, and they started squirting out more little people to overrule and overrun this fair planet.

Genetic programming. Manifest destiny. How we get there doesn't matter. The end result is all anybody cares about.

So long as I eventually find my way to settling down with some sweet girl and we produce a couple mewling babies to carry on our line—whatever the fuck that means—I guess my life will have been a success in the eyes of the people who claim to love me for me. I could win a fucking Oscar and it wouldn't mean shit to them. But give them an heir to the family name? Instant standing ovation.

My mood has gone sourer than the whiskeys. Despondent and pissed, I'm about to shake my dick when my ears prick up at a new sound.

At first, I think I'm imagining it. But when I quiet my mind and concentrate on listening, it's obvious and identifiable. I know that sound even if I don't know who is making it or where it's coming from.

Because the sound itself… that is the unmistakable, unforgettable sound of a woman in pleasure. Somewhere between a moan, a hum, a gasp, and a whisper. Maybe all of them at once or each of them in turn. It's not entirely clear since it's not exactly right there in the tiny room with me, but it's still close enough that I can hear it.

My eyes follow my ears up to the ceiling. Is it coming through the vent up there? Now that I've stopped peeing and I'm only listening, it's louder. Just loud enough to make out the words, soft and breathy, but full of feeling. Full of zest. Full of life.

"Fuck… FUCK… yeah… fuck yeah…"

The words are punctuated by light masculine grunts, and now that I'm still and silent and trained on it, I realize the wall to my left is shaking slightly every now and then, a persistent rhythm of vibration. I sense it before I hear it or see it, but it's confirmed when I reach out and lay the flat of my palm against the cool wood.

If they heard me come down the hallway, open the door, or use the stall next to them, they sure don't seem to give a damn. The wall thuds again and again, picking up speed and intensity, as all the while I listen to her muffled voice coming from the other side. Even though I know I shouldn't.

"Fuck… don't stop…. there… right there… harder…. HARDER… fuck… fuck YES… fuck ME…"

I can feel the reverberations coursing through my fingers, down my wrist and forearm, and into my shoulder socket.

The sheer force of these unseen strangers colliding over and over again into one another on the other side of this flimsy wall sends shockwaves through my sensibility.

Do people really still do this sort of thing? Fuck in cramped public places like bar bathrooms and airplane lavatories? This isn't a college fraternity party. I'm as sexually experienced and open-minded as they come, but even I have to admit that I find myself surprised by the brazenness of what's happening less than five feet away from me. This isn't that type of bar, that time of night, or that part of the city.

"FUUUUUUUUUUUCKKKK……."

The thumping and shuddering both come to an abrupt halt, and now there's only the faint sound of breathing coming from the other side of the wood, coarse and throaty. That begins to slow and soften too after a while, and all of a sudden, I remember that I'm still standing here in the dim bathroom stall light with one hand pressed against the wall and the other hand on my dick—which, I notice, has long since switched gears on me and currently stands at full attention.

What am I still doing here? And how long have I been gone for?

I draw my face close enough to the watch face on my wrist to realize it's been at least ten minutes since I left Caroline alone at the bar. Even if this makes for a good story because it's not exactly something you experience in real life every day, she just doesn't seem like the type of person who's going to get it. Maybe that's why I feel a sort of mild letdown as I depress the flush lever with the sole of my shoe, unlatch the door, and amble over to one of the sinks along the opposite counter.

I'm too tipsy not to watch the stall next to the one I just

exited in the mirror. Some people would probably just wet their hands and then get the hell out of there, but not me. I'm not the one who should be embarrassed by this situation, so I'm going to take my time lathering up and scrubbing beneath the hot water.

Besides, it's not like they're going to come out anytime soon. Not when they can hear someone out here who's clearly using the facilities. Someone who could catch them in the act and potentially report them to the staff or the bouncers.

But the door does open. It's not just a timid crack, either—it swings wide open.

Out from the darkness emerges the most beautiful woman I've ever seen.

Her eyes burn. Rings of green-grey with flecks of gold, they catch candlelight from the countertop as she draws closer in the mirror's reflection. I'd swear her eyes are actually on fire.

She stares me down unabashedly, to the point where I actually am suddenly embarrassed to be here, even though my feet are rooted to the ground and every muscle in my body has turned to stone. Someone has physically severed the wires in my brain that allow me to move, to speak, to close my jaw, to fucking breathe.

The woman doesn't blink as she moves further into the light of the mirror and the dozen candles flickering beneath it. There are three open sinks, but she chooses the one right next to me, closing what little space was left between us.

What color is her hair? It looked black as obsidian when she first materialized, a glowing shadow swathed in darkness. Now that she's physically closer, I see brown, blonde, red, even silver. Her hair shifts and shimmers like something alive, falling in thick, wild waves that perfectly frame the kind of face even a supermodel would kill for.

Cool as hell, this exotic apparition reaches into a sequined clutch and produces a silver tube, all the while without blinking or breaking eye contact. There's such an easy, practiced fluidity to her every motion, as if she's been doing all this for centuries now.

It's not until the tube has found its way like a homing missile all the way up to her mouth that she finally shifts her eyes to her own reflection in the mirror. Even still, I am all locked up. There's nothing I can do but stand there and stare like a fossilized fool as she slowly glides the stick along and around her lips, tracing their full wet contours in the deepest shade of red imaginable.

Smooth, slow, and steady, she takes her time. Only when she's fully satisfied does she kiss the air without a sound, cap the stick, and return it to the clutch at her side. Her eyes— those eyes—flick over to me without warning in the mirror, and now my heartbeat goes into overdrive.

"You're wasting water."

Seconds pass. Maybe minutes. Could be hours, honestly. She has cast a spell over me.

A hot flush creeps up the back of my neck. Little pins and needles dance across the nerve endings throughout my body, a tapestry of pain and pleasure that fires with reckless abandon, like a meteor shower raining down upon the earth.

So slow it's nearly imperceptible, her lips curl upward at the ends into a wicked smile.

"Give a girl a hand?"

She rotates and gives me her back. I see it all unfolding in slow-motion in the mirror because I still can't figure out how to do anything else but look on in a stupefied awe.

There, in the glass reflection, I trace the curvature of her naked spine as it spouts out from beneath her waves of iridescent hair. Down it goes, unobstructed by undershirt or bra strap, until it finally disappears beneath the glittering black sequined horizon of her dress waistline. Even in the dim candlelight, her skin glows a soft lustrous luxury between her shoulder blades and along the small of her back, and I don't think I've ever wanted anything more in my life than to know what it feels like to not only look now, but touch. Christ, I need to touch her.

Maybe she finally gives me permission, or maybe the sheer potency of my desire finally unblocks the paralysis, because first my eyes move, then my head and neck, and lastly my whole body turns in an awkward pirouette. Now, I'm not just seeing her in the mirror, I'm also taking her in for real, in the flesh, right in front of me.

She takes a couple steps backward until there are only inches separating us. I'm not sure I can bear it anymore. The flush has grown into a raging inferno that threatens to swallow me up in a blaze of want. Every muscle fiber I'm made of is shaking me from the inside-out and from head to toe.

"Let me help you."

Her right hand floats up behind her and comes for me. I can only hold my breath and vainly brace for an impact I could never, ever be prepared for. It comes all the same as her fingers find mine without looking or searching, and I'm ashamed that she must feel me trembling violently inside her, but there's nothing I can do to stop it.

Tidal waves crash there again and again. I remember all too late that my hand is still soaking wet and hot from being under the sink all that time, but there's nothing I can do about it now, and she doesn't seem to care. My knees threaten to buckle altogether as she guides me, until I feel something new against my burning skin. I realize belatedly that she has released me, maybe hours ago, and her hand is back at her side, but my arm is out and my hand is a ball of liquid fire, and it's melted and fused now to some small bit of metal wedged between my finger and thumb.

"Up we go."

Her words are like magic, and I'm convinced they're the only real reason anything is still operational on my end. Bit by bit, the zipper climbs along its jagged tracks, sewing sparkling folds of fabric back together again.

Even though I know I'm the one holding it, squeezing it for dear life between the bones of my fingers, there's some kind of reverse gravitational force happening here, a kind of perverse unnatural magnetism that pulls my fist up along the path. Every square inch of skin I lose sight of beneath the glittering black feels like another little death, over and over again. But there's nothing I can do about it all except soak it in and pray to God I don't wake up suddenly and realize that none of this is real.

My heartbeat peaks with the zipper as it finally runs out of real estate to climb. There's a breathless moment where I wrestle with an overwhelming urge to reverse course and drag the zipper back down the way it came, if only so I can see her one more time for what she truly is, before she steps out of this space and walks out of my life forever.

Profoundly, I know that I've seen something, I've breathed something, borne witness to something I'll never forget, no matter how hard I might try. Not that I would ever want to.

And because I know it's fleeting and it's already dissolving before me, there's the brutal sensation of sudden loss, so staggering and painful I can feel it in the basin of my blood. I want to cry out in thirst or in terror—I don't know which is which—and then reach out and pull this woman against and into me and never let her go.

"Perfect."

She truly is.

The zipper slips away from my fingers as she rotates her lithe body around to face me, and there she is again, in all her power. She's so close to me now that I'd swear the gold sparkles in her eyes are moving, swimming around in circular whirlpools meant to draw in and drown onlookers like sirens in the sea. But I am mesmerized, as captivated a captive as there ever was.

Slowly, she begins to lean in toward me, and it's all I can do not to faint. My knees knock against each other as I feel the hot air of her breath tickle my earlobe. Pressure builds within me as I struggle not to give in. This radiant being is so, so very close now, right here beside and up against my body, her cheek grazing mine as I breathe in the shared cloud of her essence. She smells like cinnamon and sex, and her voice drips warm molten honey into my brain.

"Good night, my love."

A violent ripple cascades through my body as she glides on past. Currents of ecstasy rock me again and again in her dizzying wake. I am floating in the air, both inside and outside of myself, as thick ropes of electricity shudder and shake my organs and veins. Basic motor functions are still long gone, but at least I have enough primordial instinct left to reach out a hand and break my fall as I topple sideways toward the bathroom counter.

The world is spinning. I can feel my heart thumping all

the way up in my skull as I continue to surf on this experience like a masochistic lunatic. That gasping sound I hear has got to be my lungs coming back to life as they finally remember they only ever had one job to do, one simple job, and where they were these last five minutes or five hours, I might never know. It's a miracle I'm still alive. Actually, I'm not convinced I really am yet.

With a slow, delayed reaction, I become aware there's something wet and sticky on my inner thigh. Christ. How is that even possible? Nothing happened.

And yet, at the same time, what didn't just happen? That was… amazing? Mystifying? Horrifying? I don't know what that was.

But, fuck. I could do it again. I want to do it again. Hell, I think I might need to do it again.

I know that she's long gone before I look up in the mirror, but I do it anyway, because I'm just that delusional in this current state of bewitched stupor. Some infantile, reptilian part of my brain wants to will her back into existence, as if simply wishing her to return enough times might actually conjure her back. It's the same kind of visceral craving I imagine drug addicts must possess when they're in the most fervent throes of their addiction.

And though I know it makes no sense since I don't know who she is or what she just did to me, my God, I feel that intense pang of longing right now for whatever the fuck it was.

"She's something, isn't she?"

It's a man's voice that snaps me out of the dream. I see him in the mirror's reflection step out from the very same place that the woman came from. Tall, muscular, and impeccably dressed, he approaches the counter with a friendly smile on his face, his pale blue eyes twinkling as he buttons up his shirt.

I'm not surprised that he's classically handsome, albeit in a worn-down, weathered sort of way. His gelled hair is more silver than black, and salt-and-pepper whiskers cover taut but craggy cheekbones. The man's shirt and blazer are obviously tailored to fit him just right, but there's still no denying that this is a person who knows how to take care of himself at his age. Even if he's past his prime, there's something solid, polished, and monolithic about his appearance that I know women of all ages and backgrounds must find attractive.

What does surprise me is just how jealous I find myself of this rugged stranger, for no reason other than the fact that I know she was with him. But the knowledge doesn't make me angry so much as envious, and I can do little more than gawk slack-jawed at his reflection as he reaches across me to rinse his hands beneath my faucet, which I'm only now realizing has still been running this whole time.

"You're wasting water, mate. You know we're in a drought, right?"

I was too discombobulated to pick up on it earlier, but there's no mistaking it now that he has an accent. Because of course he does, the fuck. Australian, it sounds like. Motherfucker.

He finishes washing up, all the while with that same sunny disposition and those pearly whites gleaming at me in the mirror, before cutting off my water and grabbing a couple paper towels to dry his hands. He's about to toss them in the trash when he pauses and seems to really consider me for the first time.

"You're a lucky one, you know that? She hasn't done that in a long, long time."

That? I want to ask him what is that, but he's moving again now as he gives me a hearty slap across my shoulders on his way out.

"Good for you, mate. Good for you."

And just like that, he's gone.

What… the… fuck? What just happened?

Drought be damned, I turn the sink back on so I can splash a few heaping handfuls of water on my face. I need it to get my shit together.

There's hot water streaming down my face when I hear a third voice in here now.

"Lance?"

I glance up in surprise because I don't know how this new person could possibly know my name. But then I see in the mirror that it's Caroline, standing just at the edge of the bathroom hallway, her left wrist clutched awkwardly in her right hand, looking for all the world like she couldn't be more embarrassed to be here right now.

She just keeps standing there holding herself like that and watching me in the mirror. I'm sure I'm supposed to say something, just like I'm sure I'm supposed to have not disappeared entirely from our first date for who-knows-how-long. But honestly, I completely forgot she was here. I know that doesn't make it any better, and I'm sure she thinks I'm the biggest asshole on the planet right now, but what she doesn't know is that I'm still reeling from my earlier encounter with her… whoever she was.

"Lance? Are you okay?"

This poor thing has no idea.

"Hey… hey, Caroline. I just…"

I glance at my watch and quickly do the mental math. I've been gone for more than twenty-five minutes.

"Fuck. I'm so sorry. I just…"

I just… what? What could I possibly say to her in this situation? There's no earthly way to make this right.

"Hey."

She takes a few halting steps forward and lays a hand on my shoulder. I turn around to face her, and she gives me a sad smile.

"Don't apologize. Never apologize. Right?"

I grimace.

"Seriously, though… I'm so sorry."

She shakes her head.

"Listen, it's fine. It's my fault, really. I shouldn't have pressed you on that stuff. I'm the one who should be apologizing. Even though I know it's not allowed."

Caroline half-chuckles at her half-joke.

I'm suddenly overcome with a profound sense of pity for her. That, combined with my shame, makes me feel unexpectedly tender. Gently, I grab hold of the hand she's rested on my shoulder and bring it between my own.

"It's allowed. You can—you should do whatever you want. Seriously. I'm the asshole who left you by yourself at the bar this whole time."

Those great big brown eyes turn downward at the floor for just a few seconds before finding their way back up to me again. When they do, there's a brand-new expression percolating behind them.

"You know how you can make it up to me?"

"How?"

Her smile isn't remotely sad this time. If anything, it's seductive.

"Buy me another drink?"

Say what you will about Caroline, this woman continues

to surprise me. It's not every day a person displays this kind of patience and compassion, especially in Los Angeles, and especially after everything I've put her through tonight. If I were her, I would have ducked out of here after ten minutes of waiting. Fifteen, at most. But Caroline is still here.

Even if she is not. Although… maybe she is.

"Of course. It's the least I can do."

I hold my elbow aloft as an offering, and Caroline loops her own arm through it. There was a day and a time where such physical contact would have been exhilarating for me, but now I'm convinced I'll never appreciate the true nature of intimacy again unless it's with…

Her. She is nowhere to be found. I take every opportunity I can to scan the bar, scouring every stool, every booth, every table, every single foot along every single wall for a glimpse of black-sequined magic. It's a kind of sick, desperate insanity that possesses me, since I knew full-well she wouldn't be here when I came out of the bathroom, just like I knew full-well her Australian lover would be gone with her as well.

Still, though, I can't help myself. In between sentences, in the lulls of silence that punctuate my conversation with Caroline, I sweep my sights across the nocturnal landscape, blindly holding onto hope without rhyme or reason for some kind of miracle.

Even after the lights have begun to come up, we've finished our drinks, and I've closed out my 'tab' with Jared, I keep searching for her. Even after Caroline invites me back to her place and we move hand-in-hand toward the door, I keep looking behind me, expecting to see her materialize from the shadows with that wicked grin adorning her perfect face. And even after we've climbed into a rideshare vehicle and started making out in the backseat, I keep peeking my eyes open every few seconds, gazing wildly through the back window as if I'll actually find my mysterious stranger out there watching me intently from the dark.

CHAPTER 3

"What were you doing last night?"

My fingers pause for one second, two seconds, and then continue slowly buttoning up my dress shirt from the bottom.

"What do you mean?"

"You didn't come home last night."

"I told you. I had to work late."

"All night?"

"Yeah, all night. I slept in my office."

Even though my eyes are fixated on what I'm doing, I can feel Sarah staring at me from across the room.

"You didn't want to sleep here?"

"I didn't want to wake you. I know you have your big exam today, so I thought I was being considerate."

"By sleeping in your office all night, only to wake me up early this morning when you come sauntering in through the back door?"

I give Sarah my full attention.

"'Sauntering in through the back door?' What is this? Some kind of interrogation? I told you: I thought I was being considerate."

"You thought you were being sneaky is more like it."

With a heavy sigh, I return my concentration to the last couple buttons.

"I really don't want to do this right now. You can think whatever you want to think. I have to finish getting ready."

"You missed a button."

My chin dips as I check to see if she's right.

"Here. Let me help you."

Begrudgingly, I hold still and do my best to mask a grimace, allowing a few seconds of space and silence for her to properly fix my shirt. After the beat has passed, I examine her handiwork below me and let out another sigh.

"Thanks."

"So, tell me: when did you stop loving me, Jason?"

I look up at Sarah, utterly dumbstruck.

"What?"

"You heard what I said. Stop playing dumb and give me a straight answer."

"I really don't have time for this—"

"Well, you need to make time for this, Jason!!!!!"

Her voice booms across my small bedroom, and it's loud enough to make me wince. Even if the choice feels more than a little forced on her end, it's enough to get an authentic physical reaction from me at least.

"I have to be at work in half an hour."

"I don't give a good god-damn when you have to be at work, Jason! You're there all night, you want me to believe, and now you slink in here for a shower, a change of clothes, and a cup of coffee, and you're telling me you don't have time for your eight-months-pregnant wife because you already have to get back there now?"

"I didn't invent the modern American workday, Tonya.

Late nights, early mornings… this is part of the bargain you made when you married a lawyer. You knew what you signed up for when you said yes."

"Attorney."

There's a brief second where I have no idea what's happening before I finally find my tongue again.

"What?"

"It's actually 'this is part of the bargain you made when you married an attorney.' Not lawyer."

"It's the same thing."

Sarah shrugs and holds up the page as proof.

"I know it's the same thing, but you told me you wanted to be verbatim. 'Word-for-word,' you said."

I can feel all the energy and momentum we've cooked up together slipping out from under us. If I don't move quickly, there won't be any hope of getting it back. At least not for this pass.

"Okay, got it. Thank you. Can we just take it back a few lines before that, then?"

"Of course. But do you still want me to stop you if it's not verbatim?"

The magic is almost completely dissipated now. I grit my teeth and remind myself that she's the one doing me the favor here and that I need to remain patient with her.

"You know what? I think it's fine actually. The audition's in less than an hour, so as long as I'm not like egregiously off-base or anything, let's just keep going."

"You sure?"

"Yeah."

I shake out some of the tension in my arms and shoulders while bouncing up and down on my heels a few times.

"You ready?"

"Yep. Let's do it."

Sarah turns her attention back to the script.

"Well, you need to make time for this, Jason!!!!!"

Her outburst is even louder and more abrasive this time, and I can't help myself from literally jumping back into the wall and tripping over my own two feet.

"Jesus Christ, Sarah."

She seems genuinely surprised and confused.

"What?"

"You don't have to scream it at the top of your lungs. We're just talking in our kitchen at home."

"There are five exclamation marks at the end of this sentence here. Five. Plus, we're not just talking—this is a full-blown argument. She thinks he's cheating on her."

"I know that. I'm just saying that maybe it doesn't have to be such an enormous explosion. If I were Jason and Tonya just shrieked bloody murder at me like that this early in the morning, I think I'd just turn around and walk right back out the door. There has to be a reason he stays to have the rest of their conversation."

Sarah puts her hands on her hips and scowls at me.

"He stays because she is literally carrying his child inside of her. And because deep down, despite his workaholic nature, he's not a cheater, he's actually a good husband, and he's going to make a great dad. So even if she really lets him have it here, he's not going anywhere. Besides, it says so right here on the page. So, you're wrong, and I'm right, no matter what." She winks at me to punctuate her argument. "Five exclamation marks, Lance. Five."

"All right, I think I'm good. Thanks for helping out."

Sarah looks crestfallen as I gather up my own copy of the sides from my bed.

"Wait… are you serious? You don't want to finish the scene?"

"I think I've got it from there. The first half is what I really wanted to run a couple of times, so thank you for that."

"You swear you're not just being salty? I can do it with less intensity. It's your audition, not mine."

Now she says that, of course.

"I swear I'm not being salty. I need to hit the road anyway or I'm gonna be late. Thanks again for running lines with me. You're the best."

I give her a quick peck on the cheek and a little sideways hug while simultaneously glancing down at my watch.

Fuck. Knowing traffic, I might be late regardless. This is what always happens to me. I allow myself to get caught up in the moment and then I completely lose track of time. My agent's going to have my balls in a glass on her desk if I'm late to another audition.

"All right, then. You're going to do great. Just don't forget that you're an attorney, not a lawyer."

"It's the same thing."

"You know what I mean."

There are few things I hate more in this world than arriving late to an audition. Not only is it my agent's biggest personal pet peeve, but it's also just a horrible look in general.

And to make matters worse, I've never read for this particular casting director, Selene Blackwood, and I know she's a big shot in the industry, so this is my one and only first impression. I cannot afford to blow it.

Sarah is following me around our 'cozy' two-bedroom apartment like a shadow as I gather my car keys from the counter and pluck a couple water bottles from a shelf in our fridge. I love my best friend and roommate, but I don't have time for this. Not today of all days. It's as if she wants something, but she's too afraid to come right out and say it. I can tell by the way she's been hovering around me ever since I got up today, like she's a moth on a light or a puppy with severe separation anxiety.

Getting grilled by her for details about my date with Caroline last night was no surprise, but that was hours ago now. She hasn't left me alone since this morning. Although I guess it did work out in my favor when I decided I wanted a scene partner to rehearse a bit.

"Lance."

"What's up? I really have to keep moving."

She runs one hand through her hair. It's her trademark tell that she's uncomfortable with whatever it is she's about to say. I have half a mind to ask her to wait until I get back, but she spits it out before I get the chance to even open my mouth.

"My therapist says I need to be more direct, honest, and communicative with you when it comes to money. So, this is me asking you if you think you'll be able to Venmo me your portion of the rent for the past two months by this coming Friday."

Christ. Now? She picks now of all times to lay this on me?

"What's happening on Friday?"

Sarah combs through her hair with her fingers again.

"My therapist also says I need to establish firmer deadlines with you."

Is this really happening right now?

"Jesus Christ, Sarah. Look, I can't do this right now. I'm already late enough as it is."

"I'm sorry. I just—if not now, then when? You know?"

I shake my head at her as I walk toward the door.

"Not now. Definitely not now. We can talk more about this when I get home, okay?"

She sinks down to the couch.

"Okay. I'm sorry. I shouldn't have said anything."

"No, it's okay. Let's just talk tonight, all right? I've got to go."

"I know you do. Sorry. Break a leg. You're going to do great."

"Thanks."

And then I'm finally out the door.

CHAPTER 4

Ask Angelenos which freeway is the worst and you're bound to inspire a passionate debate. With the obvious caveats that it all depends on time of week, time of day, and what part of the city you're in, the general consensus is that The Five, The Ten, The One-Ten, The One-Oh-One, and The Four-Oh-Five are the highways that most locals hate the most. Which one is worst depends on whether or not you're willing to go to great creative lengths to avoid it during the peak of rush hour.

For my money, The Four-Oh-Five is the biggest, baddest, most wicked bitch of the west. Unfortunately, it's also the only real option for me coming down from Reseda to Brentwood on an early Wednesday afternoon. I just have to hope and pray a route that's primarily—and somewhat shockingly—currently shaded in yellow on Google Maps remains that way instead of turning red at any point. Barring that kind of unfortunate development, my phone predicts I'll actually make it to this audition in time.

Of course, parking is a whole beast in and of itself. Finding free, easy-access parking was never an issue while growing up in a flyover state. Here in California though—

and specifically in L.A.—it's a wonder they don't charge you just for walking the sidewalks or breathing the smog-infested air.

Home sweet home, though. Every place has its problems, and at least this one's pretty to look at. Plus, no matter what my parents might think, you can't become a working actor in Hobart, Oklahoma. It's actually a minor miracle you can become a working anything in Hobart, Oklahoma.

As if I didn't have enough problems already, I'm running on empty by the time I exit Wilshire Boulevard. I know my car well enough not to fear coming to a complete stop before I make it to the audition, but there's no way I can get back up to the Valley afterward without filling up somewhere along the way. Though gas is exponentially more expensive down on this side of the hill, I'm not sure I have the luxury of a choice anymore.

Fuck my life. Why does everything have to be so exceedingly difficult for those of us just following our dreams? Is it not enough I have to use the calculator app on my phone every time I visit a discount grocery store just to stay alive? Let's not forget that I also now sleep in a room the size of my parents' bedroom closet at home.

Memories of the earlier argument with Sarah bubble up inside my mind as I search in vain for that mythical open parking space on the city streets. Sarah's patience is the stuff of legend, and she's easily one of the nicest, most chill human beings I've ever come into contact with, but I had to know this day would come sooner or later. Everyone has their breaking point, and if I'm being honest with myself, she probably should have cut into me a whole lot sooner than she did.

Still, she knows I'm not trying to hoodwink her or

anything. If I had the money, I'd pay her. I'm not some degenerate liar or freeloading conman. She knew what I was when she agreed to rent out her spare bedroom to me, so she can't say that any of this must come as a surprise.

I'm an actor in Los Angeles. That means I'm also a waiter in Los Angeles. And as anyone who's ever worked in the hospitality industry out here can attest, income is anything but steady when you're living off tips and the generosity of people who are notoriously not known for their generosity.

Because of time, I'm forced to dump my car at a valet stand outside a swanky café. The bad news is that I absolutely cannot afford to pay for parking, let alone valet parking, given my financial woes. The good news, however, is that this café is only two blocks away from the casting director's office, so I should have no issues making it there in time… if I run.

Here's where the acting comes in early. I grab the claim ticket from the attendant, thank him, and then hustle up the front steps into the bustling restaurant as if I'm running late for an important social engagement. Because I came here once upon a time for a brunch date, I know for a fact that I can beeline through this place to the back patio and then escape through a garden gate that leads out to the alleyway behind the building, all with no one inside left the wiser. A quick turn, and now I'm sprinting past dumpsters, graffiti-decorated walls, and homeless encampments. All the while, I'm watching the blue dot on my phone that represents my body close in on its intended destination.

In a breathless, sweaty rush, I catapult around the side of a brick building that must house the particular office I'm looking for. If only I'd been here before, I'm sure I would have known where to park and how early I needed to have left home to avoid all this mess. Too late now, though.

Next time. Provided there is a next time.

The business directory on the wall inside the front door informs me I have five floors to climb. Because of course it's five floors off the ground. Fuck. Surely, there's an elevator somewhere in here, but the staircase is right in front of me and it's literally four o' clock on the dot according to my phone. Taking the stairs two at a time, I leap and bound my way up as quickly as I can without tripping. The last thing I need to do is break a bone or chip a tooth.

I arrive at long last in a narrow hallway littered with lookalike human beings. As much as this shouldn't still surprise me, it never fails to dishearten my psyche and twist my stomach up in knots when I come face to face with so many faces that look just like mine. I know it's the nature of the industry and it comes with the job, but that doesn't mean it's not incredibly demoralizing at the same time. Moments like this one make me want to build a time machine, visit my past, and tear down all those stupid 'you are special' motivational posters plastered on every schoolroom wall in America.

"Lance? Lance Lonergan?"

In what world does a casting office actually run on time? Did I make a wrong turn somewhere and enter The Twilight Zone? These places never stay on schedule.

"Last call for Lance Lonergan?"

I wave my arm in the air and frantically shuffle past the doppelgänger cyborgs until the woman calling my name finally spots me coming and nods in annoyance.

"Lance, you're with Donna Goodwin, is that correct?"

"That's correct."

"Superb. Well, we're ready for you. That is, if you're ready for us."

There's a healthy dose of skepticism and maybe even outright contempt coming through strong in the way this complete stranger speaks down to me and leers out from behind her half-rim glasses. I want to launch into a long, impassioned soliloquy about all the hoops I had to jump through just to arrive here on time today, but I know it's of no use. Every other sad sack in this corridor of anxiety probably has a similar story, and I'm sure she's heard them all over the years and she couldn't care less.

"I'm ready. Let's do it."

Never mind that I'm not even remotely close to being ready. Anyone with eyes and ears can see my heavy perspiration and hear my ragged breathing, put two and two together, and deduce that maybe it might be a kindness—no, a mercy—to give me just a few meager seconds to compose myself. Or surely it wouldn't upset the great acting gods in the sky too much to let the person scheduled after me go first while I have a moment to stick my sweaty forehead under an air blower or mop my pit stains with some toilet paper in the bathroom.

But no, this is Hollywood, time is money, and the show must go on. I remind myself that I am prepared, and that I am worthy of greatness. Good things can and will happen for me, because I want this more than any of those other brainless sycophants outside, and I'm willing to do whatever it takes to get to the top.

This is the familiar mantra running through my head as I take a deep breath, steady my nerves, and slide past the woman holding the door open for me so I can step fully into the room.

Ho… ly… fuck. It's her.

I can't believe it. I just… I can't believe it. How is it possible? How is she… who is she?

"Selene, we have Lance Lonergan from Donna Goodwin. Lance, you'll be reading with Stephanie over here. Do you have any questions for us before we get started?"

I have so many questions, but none of them are for 'us'—they're only for her. For… Selene? Is that her name? Is that who she is? Selene Blackwood… the casting director?

How is it possible that the same woman from last night—the same mythical goddess that held me utterly enraptured beneath her spell—is now in the same room with me once again, and that we're breathing the same air?

She's traded in the short sequined dress for something more professional yet no less alluring: a long black jacket, buttoned tightly across her ample chest, that fits snugly at her shoulders and then falls all the way to the floor beneath the tabletop she sits at the center of. Her lips are a paler shade of red today but no less full and plump. Even done up in an elegant ponytail, her hair has that same lustrous, kaleidoscopic quality to it where it seems to change color and move on its own behind her neck, as if tickled by a soft yet persistent breeze. And her eyes. They don't need the magic of candlelight to flicker and flame, all those dazzling flakes of gold peeking out from within wheels of aquamarine.

Selene's smile is every bit as enticing and suggestive as I remember it being from the bathroom last evening… and from my dreams all last night, too, if I'm honest. Right now, every part of my being wants to be the one and only thing responsible for that smile, and I willingly surrender my entire brain to that idea with the pure and absolute conviction that it cannot be false. It has to be true.

A new movement demands my full attention beneath the

table. I bite my tongue and immediately taste blood, because my good God, there are her legs, long and toned and shapely, on full naked display, each dead-ending in a black spiked heel at her foot. She's just crossed one of those perfect legs over the other at the knee, and I follow them further up with my thirsting eyes until her thighs disappear altogether beneath a black leather skirt, and now I'm lost there in the beautiful abyss, and I couldn't look away to save my own life.

"Lance?"

I swear to Christ, it's like a fucking tractor beam.

"Lance!"

The assistant with the glasses has to shout to snap me out of it. At some point, she must have taken a seat next to Selene, because all three of them are in a row now at the table, and they're all observing me with varying expressions. The assistant looks agitated, Stephanie the reader looks bored, and Selene looks... amused? Aroused? Predatory?

"I said: do you have any questions for us? If not, please begin. We're trying to keep a strict schedule today, which I'm sure you'll understand."

I'm not sure I understand anything anymore.

"Okay. Just go ahead, Stephanie. Maybe this is some part of his performance or something."

The reader clears her throat. Improbably, it does just enough to disrupt my trance and momentarily divert my attention away from Selene. Or maybe she just decided to release me finally.

"What were you doing last night?"

I turn to the one named Stephanie.

"What do you mean?"

"You didn't come home last night."

Selene draws me in again. I need to know what she's

thinking right now. Does she remember me from last night? She has to.

Stephanie clears her throat again.

"You didn't come home last night."

My fingers tense on the papers in my hand. I'm aware my palms are sweating. My palms never sweat.

I've completely forgotten my line. I had everything perfectly memorized, and now that I'm actually here in the office doing the damn thing, I can't for the life of me remember my second line. Am I having a fucking heart attack right now? I can feel it hammering against my sternum.

Am I about to faint? I've never fainted before. Is this how that happens to a person?

"You didn't come home—"

There's no choice left to me; I have to steal a glance at the script.

"I—I told you. I had to work late."

"All night?"

"Yeah, all night. I slept in my office."

"You didn't want to sleep here?"

"I didn't want to wake you. I know you have your big exam today, so I thought I was being considerate."

"Let's skip ahead."

It's a new voice that cuts in: Selene's voice. I recognize it from last night. Does she recognize me?

"You've seen enough?"

That's the assistant.

Selene snaps her neck sharply in the woman's direction.

"No. I said, let's skip ahead. Lance…"

She knows my name.

"…start at: 'Just tell me. What do you want from me?'"

Something flutters at my side. It's the papers. A few of

them have fallen from my trembling hand and now lay splayed out on the dark carpet.

Everything is either happening much too fast or much too slow. Time seems to be hiccupping and unsure of itself, despite all laws of nature, history, and physics.

Stephanie clears her throat again. Is she doing that intentionally because of me? Am I blowing it?

"Do you want me to lead him in?"

Silence. My knees crack loudly as I bend down to retrieve the fallen sides.

I have to get it together. No one else here seems to be experiencing a full-fledged panic attack. Like it or not, this isn't a dream or a hallucination. No matter what happened last night, no matter who this woman is sitting not twenty feet away from me, this is all really happening in the here and the now. This is my career, my livelihood, my very life at stake, and I'm making a fool of myself.

I just can't get over it though. She's here. She's real.

The assistant sighs impatiently.

"I think you'd better."

Stephanie the reader clears her throat for what feels like the millionth time.

"I should have known better. My parents warned me from the start. They told me then that you were no good for me. Maybe I should have listened. They said this would happen. They told me you would hurt me, but I didn't want to believe them. Maybe I should have, though."

It takes more mental fortitude than it should suppressing the urge to glance down at the copy in my hand. I know these words. I've spent long hours rehearsing them silently, over and over again, until they were tattooed on my brain and on the tip of my tongue. There's no logical reason why I should feel like my cranium has been vacuumed completely dry.

"Maybe I should have—"

"Just tell me. What do you want from me?"

"What do I want from you?"

"Yes."

"Jason. I want everything from you. I want you to look at me again like the way you first looked at me, like I was the only person in the world that really mattered to you. I want you to listen to me, truly hear me, as if your whole life depended on what I might say or not say. I want you to hold me like you're drowning. I want you to touch me like you're discovering God. I want you to kiss me like you're poisoned and only my lips hold the cure. I want you to make love to me like it's the first time and it's the last time, but every time, and always."

Selene slides her chair back and rises.

"It's not working for me."

The casting assistant also begins to stand.

"Me neither. Should we move on, or did you want to take a break?"

Selene glowers at her.

"Stephanie's not working for me. I'm going to step in."

The blood rushes to her assistant's face as she fumbles her way back down to the chair.

"Of course."

She and Stephanie both look shocked. For that matter, I bet so do I.

Selene gracefully steps out from behind the table and walks toward me. My legs feel like jelly, and I'm aware once again that I'm physically shaking. I never do that. Christ, I never do any of this.

She stops not five feet away from me. Selene Blackwood is close enough that there's no denying that already-familiar yet flaky, amorphous feeling again: this all-encompassing, violent desire to touch her, to sort of mold into her, so that every part of us is pushed against and into the other until we can become this one perfect thing. It's such a strong feeling that it suffocates me internally to the point where I'm not sure I know how to breathe. But for some reason, I'm also not sure that I need to anymore. All I really need is just to be here, now, with her.

First, the smile washes from her face. And then other things do, too. The shining flecks of gold in her irises sputter out as her eyebrows narrow, and new lines are drawn across her forehead. Inch by inch, her chin lowers toward her neck. Selene has let her hair down from the ponytail, though I'm not sure when, and it now runs out wild in waves on either side of her head. This isn't the same woman I saw last night at the bar, but it's also not the same woman I saw just a minute ago seated behind the table.

"I should have known better. My parents warned me from the start. They told me then that you were no good for me."

This new woman shakes her head slowly from side to side and places her hands on her hips. I'm reminded again of that tight black leather skirt and those delicious thighs that it's wrapped around, but not for long. With a snap of her fingers, she summons my instant focus higher up on her body, and now she's pointing at me as if in warning, though there's just a gleam of mischief in her darkened eyes.

"Maybe I should have listened. They said this would happen."

Her chest rises and falls as she breathes.

"They told me you would hurt me, but I didn't want to

believe them."

Selene tilts her head to the side. Her expression changes again, this time into something hurt, something suffering. Seeing it, I feel as if I might suddenly weep. Have I wronged her? Oh, God, tell me I haven't wronged her somehow.

"Maybe I should have, though."

I have to do something to win her back. If she remains like this a second longer, I think I'll explode. Sweat is streaming down from the pores along my hairline. If I was quivering before, I am positively vibrating now from head to toe, a thrashing bundle of energy and emotion.

"Just tell me! What do you want from me?"

Can she sense my desperation? Does she know that she, alone, is the cause? Is she aware of what she does to me?

"What do I want from you?"

"Yes!"

Selene's chin dips toward her chest.

"Jason."

Her voice is much lower now.

"I want everything from you."

She lets her words fully register with me before she takes one step, and another, and then another, closing what little distance was left and defusing what defenses I still had operational against her. Selene is so close now that I can smell her, an intoxicating combination of rosemary, spice, and bonfire.

"I want you to look at me again like the way you first looked at me, like I was the only person in the world that really mattered to you."

As if I had any other choice. She makes me afraid to blink in case I might miss her.

"I want you to listen to me, truly hear me, as if your whole life depended on what I might say or not say."

Selene reaches for me as I hold my breath and brace for impact. For some unknown reason, I expect her hands to be searing hot when they finally find mine, but they're not. Strong and warm, sure, but not painful like I fantasized they might be only seconds before.

"I want you to hold me like you're drowning."

Slowly, she brings our hands to her body and places mine on her hips. The papers drift down and away as my fingers dig deeper into the leather, savoring the tactile daydream of what lies beneath. She feels soft yet strong, like every woman should feel there. I cannot get over the wondrous revelation that I am standing here with my hands on the hips of this sublime deity.

"I want you to touch me like you're discovering God."

Selene gently guides my hands further up and in along her stomach muscles beneath the jacket until they meet just below the curve of her chest. She holds my gaze intently as she pulls them up further, and even though I might burst, I try not to lose myself, because I know even now that if I forget what this feels like one day, I'll never forgive myself.

I survive in a kind of blissed-out suspended animation, categorizing how round and full each breast is beneath my roving palms, noting with a delirious silent joy how she intentionally maneuvers my thumbs so there's no mistaking her nipples are hard even underneath the layers of her jacket and whatever other materials she wears beneath it.

"I want you to kiss me like you're poisoned and only my lips hold the cure."

She brings my hands up along her collarbone until they fan out on either side of her neck. I am holding her but she is also holding me, and together, we are so much stronger because of it, I just know. Selene's chest swells with her breath as her tongue flickers out between her lips and wets them like an invitation. My face drifts toward hers on the gravity of expectation and unrelenting desire, wondering what might happen if this actually happens, a dream I never knew I needed until last night.

Her voice is a whisper just inches away from my mouth as she guides me in.

"I want you to make love to me like it's the first time and it's the last time, but every time, and always."

She moves my hands up higher still behind her ears until they're buried deep within her hair, and I can feel the back of her skull throbbing against my fingertips. The space closes between us in a breathless rush, but then she pulls back right at the last possible moment, right before it's gone altogether. There's an aching pause where she teases me there on the precipice, her eyes closed and her mouth just centimeters away from mine, and I'd swear she sort of smiles because she knows exactly what she's doing and so do I, even though I'm powerless to say no—not that I'd ever want to in a million fucking years.

At last, she gives me exactly what I need to survive. I can breathe again because she's here and I can taste her, sweet and sharp and exotic. Her lips make mine numb. My eyes close and roll back inside my head, lost in senseless ecstasy, as I meet her tongue with my own.

Vaguely, I feel her hands leave mine as my fingers clamp on tighter to the roots of her hair, pulling her closer into me. Her arms glide up around my throat until I feel her fingernails trace along the vertebrae in my neck and then burrow up into my hairline, and we are pushing ourselves into each other now, desperate and hungry and exploratory.

The world falls away. I could be in this moment forever. She is all there is now. I forget who I am entirely, and I care even less. All that matters to me is that she wants me for her own; I can tell by the way she kisses me. Bit by bit, I surrender more parts of myself to this woman, becoming putty in her hands, blank and formless, but all too willing to be transformed into the divine by the sheer power of her genius. So long as she wants me, I am hers to do with as she wishes.

It's for those reasons that when she finally does release me, I'm left feeling a confusing mess of contradictions. Deeply satisfied yet utterly unfulfilled. Profoundly relieved yet achingly unreleased. She has filled my cup to the brim but cut the faucet right there at the exact moment of overflow. I'm left trembling a different kind of tremble—this one no longer a physiological byproduct of carnal thirst, but rather, a reminder of the magnitude of what has just passed between us. The aftershocks that follow an earthquake.

I open my eyes to a strange but beautiful new world the way an infant might, and the first thing I see is Selene. Even physically detached from my person, she holds me firmly in her gravitational aura, trapping me with her mind. I stand and breathe in the space between us, thanking every lucky star there ever was that she chose me for this moment in time and that I could be in her orbit.

She blinks, and the astral specks of light return to her eyes.

"That's not too much to ask now, is it?"

Another second passes where she keeps me suspended within her gaze, and then she blinks again, turns, and circles back around the table.

Both the assistant and the reader immediately stand.

"My God, Selene, that was incredible—"

"Wow. I can't even... all I can say is wow—"

"Let's take fifteen."

Selene lifts a hefty stack of headshots and resumes piled high on the table to unearth a carton of cigarettes. She glides right on past her fawning associates toward the exit, both of whom now scramble to accommodate this new directive from their leader.

At the door, Selene pauses ever so briefly to look me up and down. The effect is unnerving, as if she's seeing me for the last time. I wonder why it feels that way to me, even as I wonder why such a thing should cause me such a sudden and terrible dread.

"Better. Good, not great. But better."

She leaves the room, followed closely by her two minions. I can hear the assistant's shrill voice on the other side of the door announcing the fifteen-minute break to the assembly of actors gathered there.

Apparently, I have been left to my own devices.

The casting room now feels unnaturally quiet and devoid of life after their exit. It's not just the disappearance of three human beings that I feel in the pit of my stomach; it's the disappearance of her energy. The sheer magnetism and power she held over me... that couldn't be an accident. That wasn't just acting. There was something there, something real and hot and otherworldly, something that neither one of us could resist or deny.

And yet, she just ripped me out of it without warning, and with a sort of detached, cruel, casual disinterest the very moment she walked out the door.

What am I supposed to do now?

Follow her, you fool. Isn't it obvious?

CHAPTER 4

I'm halfway out of the room when I remember I've left my sides strewn out on the floor. I do a quick awkward dance back and forth by myself while my mind deliberates what's actually important in this situation, before finally electing to pick them up and then to hurry out the door.

What is happening with me right now? Why am I so discombobulated and out of sorts? This isn't me.

She's nowhere to be found in the hallway; it's just a sea of faces that look like minor warped distortions of my own. Surely none of these other men are destined to receive the same kind of special treatment I just received in the other room, right? There's no way she does this with everybody she encounters. Both the assistant and the reader seemed genuinely surprised when Selene announced she'd be stepping in as my scene partner.

Besides, I've been to hundreds of auditions, and never once has a casting director actually gotten up from their chair to do the scene with me. It's their job to observe and to consider, not to actively participate. And even if she's the first of her kind to buck that industry standard, there's still no way she goes around kissing every guy that reads for her.

That had to be a one-time, spur-of-the-moment inclination she just couldn't control.

Despite all my logical protestations and ramblings, I can't deny a growing sense of jealousy over these thoughts as I maneuver my way past the queues of handsome young wannabe television stars. The very idea that one of these hacks might find himself in a similar situation to the one I just found myself in… no, there's no way. Not possible.

Selene isn't down in the lobby. But then again, why would she be? She grabbed a pack of cigarettes from the table on her way out. It should have been obvious to me much earlier than it is now just where she was going and what she was planning to do on her break, but I'm all out of sorts. My brain is still stuck in a sultry fog, smothered in between my baser animal instincts and something more magical and inexplicable I can't quite put my finger on.

She's nowhere to be found out on the sidewalk in front of the office building. I retrace my steps from earlier, rounding the corner and hugging along the side toward the back alleyway, trying (probably unsuccessfully) to look like I'm just a perfectly normal guy going about a perfectly normal order of business, rather than some crazed lunatic with a manic, hungry gleam in his eyes.

It's frankly alarming just how crestfallen I feel when I whirl around a corner into the alley and find that she's not there. I'd convinced myself that's exactly where I'd find her, leaning up against the bricks, a cigarette in one hand and maybe her phone in the other, looking all cool as hell with one leg probably bent and propped up against the wall and that black leather skirt riding dangerously high as a result.

But it's not to be. The alleyway is mostly deserted, and I don't have better luck on the other side of the building, either. Before long, I've made a complete circle around the structure, and I'm still coming up empty.

She probably went for a walk. This is her place of business, after all; it's her casting office. She probably knows this area like the back of her hand. Maybe she walked over to a coffee shop or a newspaper stand. For all I know, she just went for a stroll around the block to get her steps in and soak up some California sunshine.

The dawning realization that I might not be able to physically locate her right now is nothing compared to the dawning realization that I might never see her again.

'Better. Good, not great. But better.' Stranger things have happened, but that's not quite the kind of glowing endorsement that makes a person think they'll get a callback after an audition. Normally, I'd be dismayed at receiving such an overtly lukewarm reaction to my work. Right now, though, there's only one true reason why I desperately need to get a callback, and it has nothing to do with my professional aspirations.

A part of me wants to take another lap around the building, but even as worked up as I am, I know deep down that it would be useless. She's not going to magically appear out of thin air in any of the places I've already checked, and there's even less sense behind taking off in a random direction down the street when I have no discernible clues as to which way she might have gone. Who knows… maybe she hasn't even left the building yet; I only assumed she did because she grabbed that pack of smokes. Maybe she got held up inside somewhere before she had a chance to take her cigarette break outside.

It's a long shot, but it's all I've got. The more I replay our parting moment after the scene ended, the more I'm convinced she has no intention of calling me back. And if I don't get a callback, I'm probably not stumbling into her at Jared's bar anytime again soon. Just as I have a hard time imagining Selene Blackwood goes around making out with all the actors who audition for her, I also have a hard time believing she makes a habit of fucking Australian hunks in Studio City bar bathrooms.

Not that I know anything about this woman, really. It just all seems like particularly unusual, extraordinarily risky behavior for a person in her position. That being said, I guess she did do both of those things. I don't know…

I'm only about halfway up the first flight of stairs on my way back to the fifth floor when I finally spot her. Thank God.

Down in the center of the main entry foyer, there's a courtyard that's surprisingly lush and inviting for a Brentwood office building. I suppose just the presence of a courtyard inside an office building is surprising as well. It's boxed off all around in glass walls and doors, but it's either open air up above or there's a glass ceiling there, because sunlight showers down on the area with generous abandon. Numerous palm trees and ferns line the short concrete sidewalks that crisscross and connect the courtyard doors, and there's even a modest running water feature and a couple of wooden park-style benches scattered about.

Selene has chosen the bench nearest the small fountain pond as her throne. She sits languidly on one end, leg crossed at the knee, with one arm stretched out along the back of the bench and the other arm bent and holding a cigarette to her lips. Though she now dons a pair of fashionable black sunglasses over her eyes, she's abandoned her spiked heels below the opposite end of the bench and is presently barefoot.

Her head is cocked up at one of the palm trees. I wonder if she sees something there or if she's simply staring into space. Hopefully, she's lost in her own memories of what just transpired between us five minutes ago and five stories above.

It's impossible to ignore the 'ABSOLUTELY NO SMOKING ALLOWED' warnings etched into the glass beside every courtyard door. What kind of woman not only chooses to disobey those rules, but also chooses to do so in the very place she comes to work at every day? She can't not be aware of those signs. What does that say about her as a person, then? All I know is that I want to know more.

She doesn't even glance my way as I swing the door inward to her garden sanctuary. Whatever it is that she's focused on, I'm either not loud enough or not worthy enough to divert her attention away from it. I close the door gently behind me and take a few cautious steps in her direction, but she still doesn't seem to notice me.

It's not until I've drawn fully level with her bench that she finally tilts her head toward me and exhales a long plume of smoke. I get the uncanny sensation that she's been expecting me.

"Lance Lonergan. What are you still doing here?"

She knows my name. Not only that, she knows my full name. Selene Blackwood remembers me. She knows who I am.

"I—I just wanted—to thank you. For reading with me back in there. That really helped me."

It's difficult to know for sure because of the sunglasses, but Selene appears at least mildly amused.

"Did it now? You felt like that was a strong pass?"

Why am I blushing?

"What did you think?"

"I'm asking you, Lance Lonergan."

I'd swear she's not wearing sunglasses the way she always seems to freeze me in place with her eyes.

"I think the second part was definitely stronger than the first. I'm not sure why I stumbled a bit there in the beginning. That's not like me."

"Is this why you followed me out here? To plead your case for a callback?"

Now I'm definitely blushing.

"I didn't follow you out here."

"Really?"

She blows another plume up at me and smiles.

"I just came out here to see if I could bum a smoke."

"Uh-huh. Is that so."

Even still, she leans forward to retrieve the pack of cigarettes wedged between her shoes beneath the bench. I find it next to impossible not to look at her legs every two seconds, but especially now while she's bent over and focused on something other than me.

Selene passes a cigarette between our fingers. Once again, I'm briefly overcome by the oddest sensation: a flash of panic where I fear her skin might scald my own when we make contact, even though of course it doesn't. She snaps her fingers to sever me from this irrational fantasy, and after she does it, there's a flame now where once there was nothing. It takes me longer than it should to realize she's simply produced a lighter and she's waiting on me to use it.

I'm not a smoker, but today I am. Selene strikes me as the kind of woman who can make a lifelong vegan go halfsies on a rare T-bone steak. I lean forward to accept the light from her hand, nod, and murmur my thanks.

"Well, now you have your smoke. Are you satisfied?"

I can't even begin to answer that question. I'm immensely relieved to be in her presence once more, but I'm not sure I'll ever be satisfied until I'm kissing her again.

"You do recognize me, don't you?"

Selene bends down to put the lighter and cigarettes back near her shoes. When she's done, she swings both legs up on the bench in front of her and crosses them at the ankles. In another world and with another woman, maybe I'd be offended that she hadn't asked me to sit down yet, but I'm truthfully just happy to be back in this particular woman's orbit again.

"Are you asking if I've seen you in something in particular?"

She's not making this easy, is she? A part of me wonders if Selene's really being earnest or if she's just toying with me. I know I'd prefer the latter, obviously.

"No, I'm talking about last night. Royalties Tavern in Studio City."

Selene takes a long drag from her cigarette. Again, I can't tell if she's genuinely stumped or if she's just getting off on watching me squirm. Either way, she's in no great rush to respond.

After a solid ten seconds of silence where she just sits and smokes and watches me, I finally cave.

"In the bathroom. You came out of a stall and asked if I'd zip up the back of your dress for you."

Selene basks in the rays shining down from above, her pale skin a luminous glowing white like the moon in a starless night sky.

"What if I told you I had no idea what you're talking

about? Would you be devastated?"

My heart drops.

"No… of course not."

"That would be cruel though, wouldn't it? Even if it were true, that's the sort of thing that's better off left unsaid. Wouldn't you agree?"

"No. Not necessarily. I can handle the truth. I'm thick-skinned enough."

"Because you're an actor?"

"Sure. And… and because I'm a man."

"Uh-huh. And because you're a man." She sighs. "Well, don't you fret, Lance Lonergan. I remember you well from last night. You were the bad boy who kept wasting all that precious water."

I smile for what feels like the first time in ages. It's stupefying just how ridiculously relieved I am to hear her words right now. But stupefying or not, all that matters is that she remembers me.

"That's right. That was me."

Selene stubs out what's left of her cigarette on the bench handle, flicks the butt into the fountain pool, and begins to gather her things.

"Thanks for giving a girl a hand. I guess we're even now, huh?"

She gestures at the cigarette I'm holding while sliding both heels back on over her feet. It's nearly burnt out now, and I've probably taken two or three drags at most from it. I'm sure she's smart enough to have long since realized that a smoke isn't what I really came out here for, assuming she ever bought that lie to begin with. Still, I'm not about to blow my own cover.

"I guess so. Thanks for the cigarette."

In one fluid motion, she rises up from the bench and begins to walk over toward the door. I realize with a startling desperation that I absolutely cannot let her get away.

"Is that it?"

Selene stops, arches her back, stretches her arms out luxuriously, and faces me again.

"Well, what more do you want from me?"

I'm not prepared for the question, just as I wasn't prepared for her to get up and leave so suddenly. Even if she's on a fifteen-minute break that's long since expired, I can't let this be the end of us. I need to know I'll see her again, some way, somehow.

"Will I… do you… will I see you again?"

Her smile widens, feline and flirtatious.

"Are you asking if you got a callback?"

I swallow hard.

"Sure."

She makes me stand in the sun and sweat.

"We'll see, Lance Lonergan. We'll see. Lots more talent to see today. You were good at times, but I've certainly seen better. I wonder how much you really want this, this career. It isn't for everyone, you know."

"I want this. I want it more than anything."

"Do you?"

"I do."

"I'm not sure you have what it takes."

Something stirs inside me. I've felt heat this whole time with her, but this is a new kind of hot.

"You don't know me."

"No, but I know your kind. Young, rash, haughty, arrogant. You're from the Midwest, I bet? Or the South? You were a big fish in your small pond, but now you're a little piece of plankton in a great big ocean. Are you ready to fight for your own survival? Are you ready to give everything, give up everything, do anything, do whatever it takes to make it? Do you even know what that means? Do you have any idea what it costs? Are you prepared for any of this? Or did you just come out here with your palms outstretched and your dick limp between your legs, another pretty-boy beggar who wants the world for himself but who wouldn't even begin to know what to do with it?"

Bile ruptures upward in my chest and lungs until it has to get out.

"You don't know a goddamn thing about me."

I'm shaking again, but this time it's rage that holds me within its quivering grasp. I can feel my temperature rising internally from head to foot as the blood boils beneath my skin. It's taking all my self-control just to keep my temper in check and not really say or do something I'll regret.

Selene just stares on, impassive.

"We'll see."

And then she leaves. I watch her turn and walk through the glass door, back into the lobby, and up the stairs. At no point does she stop or spare me even the slightest backward glance. For the second time, she leaves me feeling not just dismissed, but rather vacated and almost abandoned somehow.

The anger doesn't subside, but it does calcify quickly into a new feeling: a growing desire to prove her wrong. There's a swelling vengeance there, a motivation to show her who I really am and illustrate in no uncertain terms just how wrong she is for judging me at face value. Especially based on one stupid audition for a TV show that's not even remotely well-written either if we're being honest.

I also need her to know who I am, though. Not just as an actor or an artist, but as a person. Because as much as she may have gotten under my skin just now by inflaming my every private insecurity and hidden morsel of self-doubt, I also can't deny there's a part of me that feels bizarrely… turned-on somehow.

I never would have dreamed that someone calling me out on my fears or raking me across the hot coals of amateur psychoanalysis would actually excite me, rev me up, and energize me. Maybe if that someone was anyone else, my instinctual response would be to fight or flee. But not with her.

Her, specifically—Selene—she makes me want to fuck.

She makes me want to fuck her until she knows the real me, the true me, the me she can no longer deny, refuse, or resist.

I need to make her know who I am so that she can never forget about me, so that every single man she meets after me will feel insignificant to her, just a hollow formless shadow of what she once foolishly misjudged and took for granted.

She needs to know in every cell of her body and in every corner of her brain that I'm forever worthy, and not just of this profession or this industry.

She needs to know that I'm worthy of her.

CHAPTER 6

I wake up bright and early the next morning after a restless night of dreams and hallucinations.

In one dream, Selene and I were roommates rather than Sarah and I, and despite our best efforts to remain professional, stick to the script, and rehearse the scene together, we could not stop ourselves from throwing the pages down and ferociously fucking like rabbits in my bedroom. As a result, I never made it to the audition, and though I was vaguely aware there would be consequences for that, I remember not caring, especially not while in the throes of sexual ecstasy.

Another dream also involved a role reversal and re-write of history. In this one, I found myself in a dark, unrecognizable place. I tried to reach my hands out to discover where I was, and to my increasing horror, I realized I was in a coffin. But then I felt first the energy presence and next the physical presence of another person there, a woman who laid a finger to my lips, wrapped an arm around my shoulders, and calmed me in my nervous disquiet. She hugged me into her body until my calm became lust, and it wasn't until I slipped myself inside of her that I realized it was Selene, and that rather than a coffin, we were actually in the wooden restroom stall of the bar I first met her in.

Not all the dreams were sexual. On more than one occasion, I heard my phone ringing and looked over at the screen to see my agent calling. I'm not sure how many times I was too slow to pick up the phone, but it seemed like it happened throughout the night. Even if I did pick it up, there wasn't always a voice on the other end, and when there was, it was never good news. I didn't get the callback, the voice would say, and I'd be left wondering when or if I'd ever see Selene again.

These last types of dreams were the most fitful ones, and understandably, they were also the ones I'd often wake myself up from in a cold sweat, desperate to check my phone and to see if there actually was a missed call or a text there from my agent's office. And of course, at one or three or five in the morning, there never was.

"Have you heard anything yet?"

Sarah slowly depresses the plunger on the French press. Bless her for making coffee. I need it badly after such a fitful night.

"Not yet. It's probably too early though. I don't even know if anyone's in the office yet."

"I don't know why I assume these people are always just awake and working and on their phones at all times. Maybe you've forced me into watching too many episodes of Entourage."

I laugh and accept one of two mugs she's prepared.

"Donna's certainly no Ari Gold. Though I guess I'm not exactly Vincent Chase, either."

"Not yet, at least. Give it some time."

Sarah's patience: the stuff of legend. She's even been kind

enough not to bring up the rent I owe her yet. I'm hoping that she's either forgotten or she's at least decided to wait until my next payday to ask again about it.

"What about you? Any big plans for the day?"

My roommate crosses over to the corner of our living room and nestles into one of those oversized egg-shaped armchairs that everybody seems to love so much. She sets her coffee mug on an end table next to it, kicks off her slippers, and retrieves a blanket and her laptop from the floor beside her.

"Just another day in paradise, my friend, livin' that sweet, sweet, work-from-home life."

It's hard not to be envious of her situation. Here's a woman in her early thirties that gets to spend every workday in her pajamas. For Sarah, there's no such thing as a commute, all the watercooler gossip takes place over Slack, and if she doesn't feel like working, she can just flex her unlimited PTO policy and take it easy.

How the other half lives. Sometimes I wonder why I had to ever fall in love with acting. Surely, it would have been more sensible to fall head over heels into coding or crypto, but the heart wants what it wants, I guess.

My phone buzzes in my pocket, and when I check the screen, it's either a dream or a nightmare come true: Donna Goodwin.

This is the moment of truth. It's the moment I've been waiting for since Selene Blackwood threw the gauntlet down at my feet yesterday afternoon and challenged me to show my true colors. All last night and into the wee hours of the morning, I've been dreaming of this phone call. As high as the stakes normally are in these situations, obviously in this particular scenario, they feel all the more like life-or-death.

"Is it them?"

I nod quickly and answer the phone.

"Hello?"

"Lance, it's Brian."

My heart plummets. Brian is Donna's assistant. If this were a good phone call, Donna herself would be the voice I'd hear on the other end. Since it's Brian's voice though, I know already that the worst of my suspicions have been confirmed. It's a no.

"Brian. How are you?"

"I'm well, thank you. And you?"

"Great."

There's an uncomfortable silence that follows. Why is he drawing this out? Is he some kind of sadist who gets off on torturing struggling actors that are down on their luck? Just rip the band-aid off, Brian. I can take it. Even though I'm not entirely sure that I can this time, to be honest.

"What are you doing right now?"

"Um… I'm standing in my living room having a cup of coffee with my roommate. Why? What are you doing right now?"

"I'm calling one of our clients to let them know that they have a callback today, that's what I'm doing right now."

Everything changes.

"What?"

"That's right, Lance-y. Twelve o'clock noon, on the dot. And get this… are you ready?"

I can barely nod and whisper into the phone.

"Yes."

"The location is at a private residence out in Malibu. And you know who lives there?"

"Selene?"

"Even better: the showrunner. Marty Schwartzman."

This time, I'm actually speechless. I sink into one of the barstools at the kitchen counter and stare off into space.

"That's right, Lance-y. Your callback today is at the beachfront home of one Martin Schwartzman. Now, please God, tell me you don't have some catering thing at the same time."

"I don't have some catering thing at the same time. I'm off today."

Brian purrs into the phone.

"Perfect. I'll let them know you'll be there, then, and with bells on. Break a leg, okay? This is a big one. Don't 'f' it up."

"I won't. Thank you so much, Brian."

"Ciao."

Sarah is waiting expectantly for me.

"Well?"

"I got a callback!"

"Fuck yeah, you did! Congrats!"

She bounds up out of her chair and envelops me in a tight squeeze.

"Thanks."

"Today?"

"Yeah. Twelve o'clock. Apparently, it's at the showrunner's private residence, if you can believe that. Out in Malibu."

"Wowza. Very Harvey Weinstein vibes. You better be careful."

I laugh and drain what's left of my coffee.

"Don't worry. I can hold my own."

Sarah situates herself back in her cozy work-from-home setup.

"This is a big deal then, I take it?"

"Absolutely. They bring in the episode director, it's a big

deal. They bring in the showrunner? That's a huge deal."

"Wow. Well, knock 'em dead. Let me know if you need to run lines or something."

"Thanks. I think I should actually get a move on. Last thing I want is for them to think I make a habit of being late, you know?"

Sarah nods and puts her headphones on.

"All right. Go get 'em, tiger."

"Thanks."

It's slowly starting to hit me what this means. A callback is one thing; a callback with the showrunner is another. And if Martin Schwartzman wants to see me, I'm assuming that means Selene Blackwood will also be there. She'd certainly be present in normal circumstances if the callback was at her casting office. Though I guess these are far from normal circumstances, which means there's no guarantee she'll be there at his house.

But if she is there, then today just became one of the most important days of my entire life. Just like that. Not only does today represent my best chance yet at breaking into the industry I've been trying for years now to infiltrate, but it also represents a chance to see Selene again when I wasn't sure that was a given after our conversation yesterday in the office atrium.

Even more importantly, it represents a chance to wow her, to dazzle her, to draw her in and leave her wanting more. It's telling that she decided to call me back in the first place, given my wayward performance and all that blistering rhetoric she threw at me in the courtyard. Clearly, I must have done something right to make an impact on her of some shape or kind, whether it was two nights ago at the bar, yesterday at the audition, or even right afterward outside.

Sarah removes her headphones and flags me down with her hand from the egg chair.

"Lance, you're still good to come to Macho's though, right? For my party?"

"What time is it happening again?"

"Five o' clock. The one on Ventura and Van Nuys. Remember?"

Now I do. Today is her ten-year anniversary of moving to L.A. It's not the kind of thing I'd feel the need to celebrate personally, but Sarah's different than I am. She's the type who finds any excuse to organize a social outing or get-together, and preferably one with a theme.

"Of course. I'll see you there."

"You'd better. No flaky bullshit this time, okay? This is important to me. Okay?"

"Of course. I get it. Don't worry, I'll be there."

Sarah throws her sternest look yet at me before returning the headphones to her ears and diving back into the world of online marketplace customer support.

There's something about the way she said 'no flaky bullshit this time' that bothers me, particularly since I can't remotely begin to put my finger on what she's referring to. Sometimes it's just difficult to live with someone whose patience and memory both far exceed my own, though. I'm not sure why it's even a concern for her, given the fact that my callback's at twelve, her anniversary thing is at five, and I already said I don't have to work tonight.

Whatever, though. Onwards and upwards. I have a date with destiny to attend.

CHAPTER 7

It's 11:30 a.m. when I pull up at the address Brian sent me via email. Nothing like showing up half an hour early when you're bound and determined not to show up late. Given the uncertainties of L.A. traffic though, I'm just glad I got here on time.

There aren't any other cars on the street. It's the first thing I notice after I clock the time on my dashboard before cutting the ignition to the car. And while I wouldn't be the least bit surprised if the Ferraris, Porsches, and Bentleys that belong to these obscenely wealthy homeowners are all stowed safely away in carport driveways or four-car garages, I'd be lying if I said I wasn't just a bit unnerved by the total lack of vehicles out here on the road. There's no reason why I should feel like I just rode into a ghost town.

But a ghost town is exactly what I find this early afternoon a couple blocks off the Pacific Coast Highway. No cars, no people, no nothing. Just a slew of fancy sprawling beachfront properties precariously situated along a ridge overlooking the ocean, each separated from the other by an inordinately unnecessary amount of space.

I doublecheck the email from Brian and the Google Maps

information on my phone just to make sure everything's in proper alignment. Unless someone or something made a serious mistake, I'm supposedly at the right place.

With so much time to kill, I figure I may as well do a little exploring. I want to save at least ten minutes or so to practice the scene again in my head before going in, but that still leaves me with plenty of time right now to mosey around and check out the scenery. Walking is probably good for me anyway; it will keep my nerves at bay and help me stay relaxed and loose before this callback.

This is the dream. Malibu on its own merits would be impressive enough, but after spending decades languishing in southwestern Oklahoma, every time I come near this area it feels like I've just entered the gates of Valhalla. And though I'm obviously grateful to Sarah for letting me live with her and for being so flexible and understanding about money sometimes, Reseda's not exactly a California paradise.

But Malibu… Malibu is what people think of when they think of California. Blue waves crashing endlessly against white sandy beaches. Shiny sports cars whizzing along serpentine roads that cut right through the mountains. Cool, misty mornings spent idling around at farmers' markets or on hiking trails until the sun finally breaks through the marine layer and summons every golden-haired surfer out to the break. The landscape is gorgeous, the people are gorgeous, the weather is gorgeous. It's a little slice of heaven on Earth.

The houses are nothing to sneeze at, either. I come from a brown and barren land that's freckled with trailer parks, camper vans, and cookie-cutter one-story townhomes. You know you've made it in Hobart, Oklahoma, when you can buy an above-ground pool from the hardware store and set it up yourself. Here, even with the Pacific Ocean less than half a mile away, you just know that every single one of these places comes with its own in-ground swimming pool, just like you know that not a single one of these homeowners ever cleans or maintains it themselves.

Each of these homes looks different than the others, as if the designers all made a concerted effort in shaping this street to represent a cross-section of architectural variety. Astoundingly, though I suppose not surprisingly, no house is less than three stories tall, despite the presumed danger of erecting these magnificent towering domiciles in an area of the country that's famous for its mudslides, earthquakes, and wildfires.

In this day and age, it's fashionable to make-believe like the trappings of fame and fortune aren't a motivating factor in becoming an actor. I've met dozens of my contemporaries in classes, workshops, and showcases who claim they only got into this career purely for the love of the artform itself. They all swear they'd be content to spend the rest of their mortal existence surviving off peanut butter and jelly sandwiches and ramen, so long as they stay true to their bohemian selves and never compromise their ideals.

I call bullshit. These concepts are not mutually-exclusive. You don't have to turn in your 'true artist' card the day you're lucky enough to sign a multi-picture contract with Disney where you play some Marvel character in a cape. And while there's no denying that 'making it' means different things to different people, show me the starving artist who says they would never trade in their east Hollywood studio for a mansion in the Palisades if it meant sacrificing just a bit of their artistic integrity, and I'll show you a liar.

My nostrils prick as they catch a whiff of a new odor that is decidedly different from the familiar smells of salt and brine accompanying me on this stroll so far. It's immediately unpleasant, even though I can't quite put my finger on what it is I'm picking up on. Some people hate the smells of the beach—all that fishiness and sunscreen—and while that's never been me, this new scent doesn't register as belonging in that same aromatic realm. It gets stronger and stronger, until my eyes start to water and I can feel my throat gagging up.

Finally, my eyes catch up to my nose as I spot the source. Just up ahead along the sidewalk, two large seagulls squawk and squabble over a furry lump, pecking and clawing at both the mass and at each other. They beat their wings and flutter around noisily, fighting for dominion over their newfound bounty. Neither one seems particularly concerned by my presence as I draw close enough to identify what it is that's got them so worked up.

At first, I thought it could be a rabbit or even a possum, but there's no mistaking it now as a dog. The breed is unclear. It looks larger than a chihuahua but smaller than a bulldog.

Based on its size alone, I find it doubtful to believe the seagulls could have killed it, though I'm sure stranger things have happened in the animal kingdom. Gulls can be vicious, and they've lived around people and domestic animals long enough to have become fearless creatures out here. This dog looks like it's suffered a much more gruesome death than these birds could have possibly delivered, though. Maybe it was just at the wrong place at the wrong time when one of these millionaires decided to go out for a joyride.

I've seen and smelled more than enough, so I spin on my heel and start doubling back the way I came. I wouldn't consider myself a 'dog person' or really even an animal lover in general, but that doesn't lessen the disturbing nature of what I've just experienced, especially on a sensory level. Every time I hear one of the birds behind me shriek, I get another clear image in my mind of the mutilated carcass getting torn apart and ravaged, to the point where I begin to find it difficult to think about anything else.

The scene; I can think about the scene. I should be thinking about nothing else anyway, as my watch unceremoniously reminds me I have just eight or so minutes left until go-time. I've wandered too far along this street, allowing myself to get caught up in my outer explorations and inner musings, and now I've paid the price for it. Not only did I stumble upon a grisly tableau that was better off left undiscovered, but I also mistakenly forfeited most of the time I'd planned to set aside for prep work.

Reality sets in. In less than ten minutes, I'll be reading for the great Martin Schwartzman, the creative mind and driving force behind at least half a dozen TV shows in the storied history of Tinseltown. And as if that weren't enough, I'll be reading for him in his home. Unconventional as that may be, it has to be a very, very good sign as it relates to my chances of booking the part. Selene must have seen something she liked in me after all to send me straight through to this late stage of the process.

I pull up level with my car and grab the sides from the floor of the passenger seat. In a perfect world, I wouldn't have even brought them with me. While it's certainly kosher to bring the script with you to a callback, I'm not sure the same can be said for a screen test or a final read with the showrunner, as this is uncharted territory for me.

To be honest, I'm not even clear what this is to begin with. Brian called it a callback, and while that's what usually follows the initial audition, I've never heard of a callback occurring at the showrunner's private residence.

Then again, what even is 'usual?' This whole industry has been turned on its head due to the advent of the internet, smartphones, web series, and streaming services. Perhaps there's no such thing as a uniform procedure when it comes to booking a role anymore.

I'm confident in my memorization, but after yesterday's showing, I'm also not about to take any chances. Those were extraordinary circumstances, of course. I could not have known Selene Blackwood would be the selfsame stunner from the bar. Anyone in my situation would have reacted similarly.

Today should be much more straightforward since there won't be any surprises here at Martin's house.

And what a house it is. The closer I get to it as I walk up the front sidewalk toward the door, the more spectacular it becomes. What this structure lacks in height, it more than makes up for in sheer width; you could fill it with maybe ten or twelve full replicas of the apartment I share with Sarah, each stacked side-by-side. The roof swoops up from the ground at a lazy rounded angle all the way up to a stone chimney before dramatically ending and then falling in a straight, ninety-degree perpendicular line back to the lawn below.

Thick wooden shingles cover the walls and nearly all of the surface area along the curved front of the house, broken up only here and there by small circular windows inset with tinted glass. If you squint, it's not hard to imagine you're staring at the side of an ancient weathered galleon that's run way too far ashore and now remains marooned here amongst the rocky cliffs, slowly decomposing and rotting away in the moist sea air.

That's not to say it's rundown, though. Rather, the house just looks old, austere, and imposing, like it's been here for a very long time. I'm surprised the windows aren't larger or more numerous, given that's the overwhelming trend out here along the coast, but maybe the builder saved them all for the back side of the house that comes with the ocean view.

I still have two or three minutes to spare, but it feels like the opportune moment to knock and announce that I've made it here on time. As is my ritual, I go through a silent mini-mantra first to remind myself that I deserve to be here. I've worked hard, I've come a long way, and I've made many sacrifices to get to where I am today. So why not me? Why not now? I deserve to have my every dream come true.

Martin Schwartzman surprises me with just how quickly he answers the door. No more than three seconds have elapsed after I rap my knuckles lightly against the wood when suddenly the knob turns and the door swings in. Unless he was on his way out or just so happened to be in the foyer of his lavish home, it's almost as if he's been watching me from inside and he knew exactly when I'd get here.

The man standing before me in the entryway is much larger and also much hairier than I expected. He's got to be at least six feet and change, and he looks like one of those people who will refer to themselves as being 'big-boned' even though there's little doubt he's also probably allowed himself to enjoy a bit too much of the finer things in life. Martin is definitely broad-shouldered and barrel-chested, but he also has a sizable paunch between his chest and his thighs that can't be as readily explained by genetic disposition.

He has a thick head of messy black hair that continues down into a long, unkempt curly beard. I'm pretty sure I see small drops of some kind of liquid caught in there around his lips and below his nostrils, but I can't tell if it's water, sweat, or wine. Martin also has an abundance of hair on his arms and his legs—a fact I'm keenly aware of because he's wearing a patterned silk kimono and absolutely nothing else, it appears.

"You must be Lance!"

He goes in for a handshake that somehow becomes a hug before I know what's really happening. Everything about this meeting is disarmingly unexpected.

"Come in, come on in."

Thankfully, the hug ends just as quickly as it begins. He's off and actually running down the hallway now, bare feet padding along and without so much as a backward glance to see if I'm following him.

What a loony-bird. I have half a mind to walk back out, get in my car, and drive away, if only because I have no idea what just happened. This whole scenario keeps getting weirder and weirder by the second.

But then I remind myself that this is LaLaLand, after all. Bring me all your crazies and your eccentrics, your egos and your personality disorders, because all are welcome here where the world falls off into the sea. It takes a certain type of person to go into this industry to begin with, and those who have attained the highest echelon of success like a Martin Schwartzman type no doubt have also paid for it psychologically in spades. I decide to close the door and follow him in.

Martin's house is every bit as luxurious and envy-inducing on the inside as it is on the outside. It's all one big open floorplan connected by white marble floors, and each room I move through dwarfs the one that preceded it, either in size or splendor or both. Vivid Renaissance paintings adorn the walls at every turn, and despite the armada of chairs, tables, couches, sculptures, and other expensive-looking artifacts I come across, the home somehow never manages to feel cramped or closed-in around me. I may as well be touring through an art museum or a treasure galleria rather than strolling through a stranger's house.

"We're in here, Lance. Come on in."

Following the sound of his voice, I come around the corner of a hallway and find myself in a wide, sunken den that must be his living room. The overhead sconces are dim and there surprisingly isn't much for natural light in here, but at least there's a crackling fire burning in an impressive stone hearth that's anchored at the far end of the space across from me.

Martin is nowhere to be seen, but a familiar figure stands in front of the fire and gazes downward into the flames. Even from behind and even from a distance, I'd recognize the shape of that woman anywhere.

Selene. Of course she's here. I'd both expected and hoped she would be, but I also knew that nothing was a given. Now that I see her here in front of me, I am relieved and also amazed, as always, by what her very presence does to me on a cellular level.

My eyes drink in her voluptuous figure, framed and silhouetted picturesquely against the fireplace. Dark as this room is, the firelight provides just enough illumination for me to note with a breathless thrill that she, like Martin, appears to be only wearing a silk kimono or robe of some kind. The thought alone gets my heart racing and sends extra blood rushing to a region of my body I did not expect would need it today.

Martin has re-emerged from who-knows-where, only this time he comes armed with a black bottle and a clear stemless glass. He crosses the den and comes up a few steps to stop just in front of me, then swirls the liquid in the bottle and grins mischievously through his wet bristly beard.

"Wine?"

Am I dreaming? Is Martin Schwartzman offering me wine at a callback for his TV show? What is going on here?

"What?"

He lifts the bottle to his mouth, pulls the cork out with his teeth, and spits it behind him onto the floor.

"Would you like some wine?"

I turn to look at Selene. She's still staring into the flames with her back to me. Does she even know that I'm here? She must know. There's no way she's not hearing all this right now. What the fuck is going on here?

"Don't worry; she's having some too. We're both having some. Why don't you join us?"

"I… I'm sorry. I thought I was here for a callback?"

Martin laughs uproariously and pours a generous portion of red wine into the empty glass.

"You are! Of course, you are. But come on, Lance. We both know this is a little… unconventional, wouldn't you say, for a callback? Getting invited out to the showrunner's home address? The day after the initial audition? Come on, now."

He hands me the glass, descends into the den, and collapses luxuriously atop a white sofa, kicking his furry legs out until his bare feet rest up on a coffee table. Martin reaches to the side and retrieves his own wine glass from an end table to refill it from the bottle.

When I look over at Selene again, she is facing me. I'm not sure when she turned around, but she stands there now in front of the fireplace with her arms folded across her impressive chest. It's hard to tell for sure in this lighting, but I think she might be smiling.

"Not what you expected, I take it?"

Selene's shadow stretches out abnormally far along the marble floor, flickering and dancing in the firelight cast from behind her body. It shifts in my direction and Selene follows, slowly stepping down into the sunken den and gliding past Martin and the furniture until she rises once again before me.

Like clockwork, my organs short out and malfunction the closer she gets to me, and then my breath catches in my lungs and freezes there. The sensation is both painful and pleasurable all at once.

"Cheers, my love."

There's a soft clink as she taps her wine glass against mine and lifts it to her lips.

Those lips. I've never seen such undeniable, plump, perfectly kissable lips. The tiny golden flakes in her irises sparkle as blood-red liquid rolls lazily back into her mouth. I watch the skin around her throat pulse as she swallows once, twice, three times, before she finally lowers the glass. Her lips are stained and still wet, and she runs the tip of her tongue out between them to gather in every last drop as she watches me watch her with my insatiable need. She's clearly enjoying herself.

"Drink."

I do. Her word is a command I can't help but obey.

The thought crosses my mind that this is both absurd and wildly inappropriate, standing here in a Malibu beach house drinking wine at twelve o'clock in the afternoon on a weekday with the casting director and showrunner of a TV series that I'm supposed to be auditioning for.

But it's also what they wanted and what they asked of me. I'm only doing exactly what I'm told. No one could say any different.

I'm far from a connoisseur, but this wine has a funny taste to it. It's not necessarily bad, and I'd even go so far as to say it's probably one of the better wines I've ever tried. It certainly tastes expensive. But there's also just a hint of an aftertaste that stands out as different from the rest.

After I've finished sampling the drink and lowered the glass back to my side, Selene reaches across what little space still separates us and lays her thumb at the corner of my mouth. I try not to tremble as she drags the pad of her finger across my lips, dips it in between her own, and sucks. For the life of me, I cannot look away.

"What do you think?"

Mustering all my willpower, I finally break eye contact with Selene and turn to Martin. He swirls the dark wine in his glass and grins at me like the Cheshire Cat.

"The wine. What do you think?"

It's hard to think of anything right now other than what just happened. I can still taste where Selene has been, right there on my lips and in my mouth. She tasted me too, lest I forget. Not that I ever could, would, or will.

"Great. I'm not much of a wine expert, but this tastes great."

Martin scoffs between sips.

"You're not much of a poet, either. 'Great?' This wine costs more than your car payment. I would hope it tastes a whole lot better than 'great.'"

There's a quick flare-up of anger within me at the man's casual condescension, but I allow it to pass, especially since I know nothing good can come from it. I remind myself where I am and what I came to do. Martin, Selene, the wine… I can't let any of this get to me or derail my opportunity. So many people go through life without ever getting their one big shot, and I'm not about to miss mine.

"My apologies. Like I said, I'm not nearly as cultured as I should be when it comes to fine wine, but I'm very appreciative you're letting me try this. It's fantastic."

Martin scratches his thigh beneath the kimono, which is riding a bit too dangerously high on his thick furry legs for my liking.

"Relax, lad. I'm just fucking with you. He's a bit high-strung, Selene. Was he like this yesterday?"

Selene tilts her head and studies me. I suddenly get the very real impression she can read my mind, so I focus all my attention elsewhere in the room, bouncing my thoughts like a ping pong ball from object to object—chair to table to rug to window to fireplace—desperately doing everything in my power not to think about what I want to do to her when she looks at me like that.

"You're nervous."

She reaches out and places a hand on each of my triceps, giving my muscles a small but firm squeeze.

"There's nothing to be afraid of."

Her voice goes from a coo to a whisper. It's just her and me now.

"You said you have what it takes. Now's your chance to prove it. Cheers, love."

Selene clinks her wine against mine again and raises it to her lips. But just before the glass meets her skin, she pauses, and her eyes smolder as she waits, challenging me.

She's right. This is what I wanted. It's all I've ever wanted.

Whatever it takes—that's what I have to be willing to do to make my every wish come true. And I'm willing.

I lift up my glass and drink it down, and she follows me.

Martin claps his hands together loudly to break the spell. "That's the spirit!"

He clambers up to his feet from the sofa and prances over to us with the bottle, evenly emptying what's left between their two glasses before finishing with the most generous portion in my own.

"You know what I think the problem is?"

I honestly haven't a clue, but thankfully he doesn't leave me waiting very long. Martin pinches my shirt between two fingers.

"It's your clothes, man. How are you supposed to get relaxed when we're in here like this and you're standing there like that? No wonder."

My heart quickens.

"Oh, yeah? Sorry. Brian—my agent didn't really specify if there was a certain look or wardrobe you were after for the character—"

"Not the character. You! I'm talking about you! We gotta get you into something more comfortable."

He ropes a meaty arm around my shoulders and pilots me away from Selene, and now we're moving off down another marbled hallway through the shadowed labyrinthine corridors of his estate.

"I appreciate it, but this really isn't necessary—"

"It's absolutely necessary. You're stiff as a two-by-four."

"I'm sorry about that. I guess I just wasn't expecting—"

"You weren't expecting any of this. Yes, yes, I get it. How old are you, anyway?"

"Thirty."

Martin stops us so fast I nearly spill my wine. His dark eyes are manic and intense, but I'm still having a hard time focusing on anything other than the dewy spiderweb of wine and spittle droplets hanging throughout his beard and mustache.

"I get it. This is your first time. You've gone further than you've ever been before. You're terrified you're going to say something or do something that fucks it all up, and it will all come tumbling down. Let me let you in on a little secret though…"

Martin Schwartzman leans in close enough that I can feel his whiskers tickling my earlobe.

"So is everybody. That feeling never goes away. You think just because I've won a couple Emmys and made a few million I don't still shit a brick waiting on the Nielsen numbers to come out on every new pilot I produce? You think I'm Mr. Cool Cucumber every time the phone rings and it's the studio? There's always a bigger fish; just remember that. This business will eat you up and spit you back out if you're not careful. You gotta play the game right. So, fuck fear, fuck cowardice, and fuck impostor syndrome. Fake it till you make it. Do whatever you have to do, because if you don't, I guaran-fucking-tee you somebody else will. You got that?"

I resist the urge to wipe my cheek dry of all his verbal spray and choose to simply nod instead.

"I do. I appreciate the advice."

Martin slaps my shoulder and propels us into motion once again.

"Good boy."

We enter upon a room that's small-ish by the opulent standards of the rest of his home. One whole wall is hidden by a long, ornate room divider that's covered in what look like Egyptian hieroglyphics and drawings. There's also a large Oriental area rug that nearly swallows up all the marble floor beneath it, and ringed around the rug on all sides is an eclectic collection of vases, urns, and pots, each of varying size and material. The three walls without the dividing screen are completely concealed in floor-to-ceiling mirrors that run end to end, giving the space the feel of a dance studio at best and a carnival funhouse at worst. High above us hangs a dimly-lit chandelier composed of gold, crystal, and flickering electric bulbs that are made to emulate candles.

I have absolutely no idea what purpose this room could possibly serve.

"You'll find the wardrobe on the other side of that screen. Help yourself. I'm sure you'll find something in there that suits your fancy. It's quite the collection, if I do say so myself."

Martin gives me a light push into the center of the room, then detaches and spins back toward the way we came. With his long legs and hulking frame, he's already practically vanished by the time I realize he intends to leave me alone in here.

"Don't take long though. Confidence, intuition, and decisiveness; that's what separates the 'haves' from the 'have-nots.' Remember that, lad."

His voice lingers long after he does in the echoing chambers.

What a basket-case. This guy must be on more than just wine. Probably coke, Adderall, or speed. Who knows these days.

What I do know, though, is that Martin Schwartzman is a living, breathing stereotype made real: the cracked-out

Hollywood fat-cat, larger than life, richer than God, arrogant as all get-out, and yet still a man who knows how to turn on the charm when he wants to.

CHAPTER 8

Why am I in here? What do they expect me to change into? Does this man just own a whole menagerie of silk robes? I guess that concept isn't nearly as farfetched as it should be, given everything else I've already experienced since walking through the door.

Liquid courage; that's what I need right now. I've already committed myself mentally to seeing this through. If Selene and Martin mean to test my dedication, then the first step is proving I can be one of the gang, that I can both talk the talk and walk the walk. I gulp down a couple generous swallows of wine before ducking around the end of the room divider.

On the other side, there's a gaping hole in the wall that's illuminated from within by a row of sconces, each modeled after a similar fashion to those fake candle electric bulbs I saw in the chandelier. It's a closet, I guess, though I've never seen a closet without doors before.

I step inside and find myself wedged between all manner of elaborate clothing items. It's far more than just an impressive collection of robes and kimonos. There are shawls in here, capes, cloaks, gowns, feathered boas, tuxedos, fur coats, and all kinds of elaborate costumes for men and women. Everything feels less like a millionaire's home wardrobe collection and more like the contents you'd find in an exotic Halloween store or a vintage clothing shop on Melrose.

It's also a remarkably long room, maybe twenty feet deep in here or so. I drag my fingertips along the assorted textures, enjoying the tactile adventure while sipping leisurely from my glass all the while. Velvet, cashmere, wool, sequins, rhinestones, polyester, leather, lace, nylon, fleece, rubber… there are so many odd materials and surfaces to touch, smell, and take in. Time slows and then sort of bends as I savor this feast for the senses, as unexpected as it is surprisingly delightful.

The wine has started to loosen me up, but I'm still unsure as to why I'm being asked to change into 'something more comfortable' when Jason, the role I'm auditioning for, is a lawyer. Even with Martin making it clear he's referring to me and not the character, I'm still confused as to what kind of choice he wants from me right now.

I'm wearing a button-up shirt, slacks, and leather shoes— far from what I'd consider to be 'stiff' or 'high-strung'— especially given the nature of the part. If anything, I wondered this morning whether I was under-dressed, and even briefly debated donning a necktie and blazer. So how do I reconcile Martin's desire to see me more comfortably attired with my own desire to properly convey this character?

The compromise I come up with is to wrap myself in a luxurious red-and-black satin smoking jacket that drapes all the way down to my knees. I step out from the closet space and move around the room divider to examine my appearance in all the mirrors.

Not bad. Not bad at all. It's definitely a bit large for me, which makes sense given that it belongs to Martin (I assume). The shoulder area is baggier than I'd like it to be, and I have to double-knot the belt to cinch it shut at the waist, but overall, I don't hate it. Standing here in the center of this weird little room ringed with antiquities and odd treasures, I'm struck by how much more I fit in thanks to this new look. I toast my own reflection and polish off the wine.

Even though I'm alone this time, for whatever reason, it feels easier to navigate my way back through the hallways of Martin's beach house. Whether it's the familiarity of having already come through here once before or it's because my eyes have adjusted more to the low light conditions of these corridors, I move smoothly and with a languid, graceful confidence.

There's even a part of my brain that starts playing make-believe, and I allow my imagination to run with the idea that this is all mine and that I'm a powerful millionaire who wears satin smoking jackets, drinks expensive wines, and entertains high-profile industry elites here at home in my mansion.

Selene and Martin are seated next to one another on the sofa when I re-enter the sunken den. She's leaning over and whispering into his ear while he stares off into space with a tranquil but vacant expression. Her eyes follow me as I step into the room and stop at the stairs.

I gesture down at the jacket.

"Will this work? I wasn't exactly sure what you had in mind."

They ignore me. Martin's still not looking anywhere near my direction, and though she's zeroed-in on me with her eyes, Selene continues articulating in a hushed tone that only Martin can hear. Only when she's good and ready does she finally stop, sit back in the cushions, and nod.

"What do you think, Marty? I think he looks rather dashing, even if it's not quite what we had in mind."

Martin snaps to attention and examines me from the couch.

"Mama mia! It's the ghost of Hugh Hefner. The only thing missing is a pipe."

Selene's eyes sparkle.

"Our boy needs a refill."

Improbably, I've managed to outpace them, as both of their wine glasses are still half-full. Unless, of course, they finished and replenished while I was gone, which actually seems like a pretty valid possibility given the mood and scene I stumbled upon in here.

I fidget with the glass in my hands.

"I'm okay, actually, but thank you."

Martin rises to his feet with a huff, shaking his head and swatting his fingers through the air.

"No, no, knock it off, son. We're all friends here."

Like the kind of exotic European sports car he probably owns one or two of, Martin Schwartzman can go from zero to sixty in a flash. One second, he's practically comatose nestled between his couch pillows, and the next, he's a big blur of motion, streaking up the stairs out of the den and back to his kitchen, wet bar, wine cellar, or wherever it is that he keeps his stash.

Left alone, the air between Selene and I crackles with electricity.

"Am I still reading for him?"

One of her eyebrows raises slightly.

"Are you worried you won't? Is that why you're so wound up today?"

"I'm not wound up. I don't know why you both keep

saying I'm tense. I feel just fine."

She crosses one knee over the other, and I try not to fixate on the silken fabric as it shimmies ever higher up her leg.

"If you're not nervous and you're not tense, then what's the harm in having a little fun this afternoon?"

Selene starts massaging her calf… because of course she does.

"No harm at all. Trust me, I love to have fun. I just thought this was a callback."

She smiles flirtatiously.

"And it is, so you've got nothing to worry about. You can have all the fun you want."

"That's the spirit!"

Right on cue, Martin dashes back into the room with a freshly-opened bottle of wine.

"You can have all the fun you want! Isn't that wonderful? Isn't she wonderful?"

He tops off her glass and then dances over to refill mine.

"Another 'great' wine for you to try, monsieur."

Resistance is obviously futile, so I just nod appreciably as the potent elixir flows.

"Thank you so much, Mr. Schwartzman."

"Egads! Call me Marty, for fuck's sake. Social cues, my boy, social cues…"

I grimace and toast him.

"My bad. Thank you, Marty."

This wine is fruitier and juicier than the first. The peculiar aftertaste is still there, though: that kind of faint chalkiness that's almost indecipherable. I take a second sip just to explore it further and consider that maybe I'm more of a wine guy than I originally thought—or maybe I just have expensive tastes, and I don't know what I've been missing all these years drinking boxed, bagged, table, or cooking wines. This is damn good.

Martin situates himself back on the couch and tops off his own glass. He appears nowhere near as distracted by Selene's legs as I am. She continues to make gentle circular massaging motions with her fingers up and down both calves, only now she's also begun moaning softly and closing her eyes while she does it too.

My brain is forever forgetting not to stare and want.

Martin smacks his hands together in a boisterous clap.

"All right! Now that we're all properly liquidated, shall we get started?"

It figures that he's finally ready to get to work when work is now the furthest thing from my mind. I'm profoundly, helplessly mesmerized by the tiniest crease on the side of Selene's right knee where the skin of her calf meets the skin of her thigh. With every roll of her thumb, every squeeze of her palm, every caress of her fingertips, I study with amazement the way this shadowed intersection stretches, shifts, and reforms again. I've never been so envious of a person's hands before, but nonsensical as it is, that's exactly what I experience: a burgeoning jealousy that it is Selene, not I, who can give Selene pleasure like that.

"Ahh… I see it now: the focus, the intensity, the desire."

Martin leans forward and stabs his index finger into the air at me.

"There it is. That's what Selene told me about. That's what Jason is all about."

He clambers up to his feet again, bounds up the stairs, and grasps me by the shoulders.

"Desire. Jason is a man who desires everything. He wants it all. The world is not enough for this man. Jason wants—

no, Jason needs to be the best attorney that's ever lived, the best husband that's ever lived, the best father that's ever lived, the best man that's ever lived. This is his greatest strength, but it's also his greatest weakness. He is a perfectionist's perfectionist, but none of it is based in neurosis or in a fear of failure. It's all just desire—a burning, scorching-hot desire—and a drive to have everything that he's ever wanted. Do you understand what that feels like, Lance?"

"Yes."

With every bone in my body and every fiber of my being, the answer is yes.

"Good boy. Then show it to me."

Martin pats my shoulders and circles behind me.

"Show it to both of us."

Selene's eyes open. Slowly, she leans back into the sofa cushions, drawing her hand up against the hem of her robe so that it slides higher and higher toward her waist. Every new centimeter revealed of her thighs is a revelation, an invitation to not just look, but to absorb and to never forget. I want to memorize every pore and every contour, to search for freckles and birthmarks and dimples, to rove not just with my eyes, but also with my fingers and my lips and my tongue along every single perfect molecule of her body.

There's a soft pressure on my shoulders again, though now it's more distant, almost dreamlike.

"That's it. Now go to her."

He gives me a light push that I don't need because I have more than enough motivation on my own. As I step down into the den, Selene uncrosses her knees, puts both feet flat on the floor, and lays her palms on the kimono flaps covering her thighs. Her lips pout, and her chest lifts up and down with every breath. Slow… rhythmic… deep.

"Lance."

I love the way she says my name, like she's already claimed me.

"Do you want me?"

Her elbows pull backward and her robe slides up further.

"Do you want me, Lance?"

"Yes."

She curls her fingers under the hem, teasing me.

"How bad do you want me?"

My tongue feels thick in my throat. My heart is on fire.

"So… fucking… bad."

Selene tilts her head.

"Yeah?"

She brings one hand up higher and tugs downward slightly at where the kimono covers her collarbone. Her eyes never leave mine.

"What do you want to do to me?"

When my ability to speak simple words falters, my body thankfully answers for me, propelling me nearer and nearer until I'm standing just in front of her, an object caught helplessly but willfully in her gravitational magnetic field.

Selene drags her nails lower along her neckline.

"Do you want to touch me?"

My legs buckle and I fall on my knees, but there's no pain, only a willing surrender and a rush of pulsing energy now that I'm even closer to her.

Selene's tongue slides out between her teeth and wets her lips.

"Do you want to taste me?"

Her voice drips with a tantalizing proposition I could never ignore or resist, not that I'd ever want to. She moves her hands to the knotted belt at her stomach and plays with the loose ends, wrapping them casually around her fingers.

"Lance."

I'm trembling all over. I can't stop shaking. There's a dam inside me that's about to burst.

"Tell me what you want to do to me."

"I—"

Again, my speech fails me. She's untying the knot now, slowly but surely, and the anticipation alone might actually be the death of me.

"Lance."

The knot comes apart.

"I—"

Selene, and Selene alone, is all that holds the sheer fabric of her robe as well as the sheer fabric of my existence together.

"Tell me what you want to do to me."

"I want to worship you."

The words finally come tumbling out in a wrenching gasp, hoarse and thirsty and desperate.

Selene pulls apart the kimono as the corners of her lips curl into a smile. Her voice is both a whisper and a command.

"So worship me."

Selene's body takes my breath away. Despite all the fantasizing I've done in recent days and sleepless nights as I've replayed mental movies of our every interaction, nothing could have prepared me for the stark wondrous truth of what actually lies beneath. It's almost too much to take in, and I can feel my brain short-circuiting as my attention zigs and zags from one delicious viewpoint to the next, feverishly surveying and claiming and emblazoning on my eternal memory in case this momentary glimpse of heaven is all I ever get.

How perfect it is that I'm already on my knees, a suppliant disciple come to temple for devotion and transcendence, a ravenous explorer all too eager to map out new terrain and taste of forbidden fruit.

My fingertips reach out to graze her ankles, and there's an electric pop when skin meets skin. I can feel the raised places where veins intersect below the surface and above her bones and tissue, and I wonder if I get her blood racing down those runways the same way she always knows how to get mine.

I take my time. Not because I want to, but because I need to. Against all probabilities and laws of the universe, the most ravishing woman I've ever encountered has laid herself bare before me. Unthinkably, she has actually invited me to revel in her own perfection and to take some of it for myself. I cannot be greedy and I cannot be fast.

It wasn't so very long ago when all I could do was stand and look on, from an unforgiving distance and with a hungry curiosity, at the soft spot behind each knee where calf meets thigh. Now, I'm here and I'm holding that hidden place in my hands, feeling the warmth and soaking in the smooth silken splendor of her legs… and I need more.

I hook my hands around her knees and lean my body forward and down until I'm low enough that I can press my lips against the toned supple softness of her calves. From somewhere up above, I hear Selene emit that same low moan she made earlier when she was massaging her own legs.

Only now, she's unequivocally making that sound as a reaction to every kiss I plant up and down between her ankle and her knee, first on one leg, and then the other, moving back and forth to shower each limb equally with all the tenderness and affection I can give her. After all, these are the sacred towers responsible for propping up every bit of glorious goodness that comes above, and they deserve my unfettered attention and adoration.

Selene reaches forward and glides her fingernails across my scalp as my lips climb above her kneecap for the first time. It's the perfect complement to the sensory rush I feel as I move my hands along the sides of her thigh muscles, kneading the flesh there between my fingers. I meander my tongue across her skin in long, lazy, winding stretches that are punctuated by deep, savoring kisses. All the while, she moans her approval and rakes her nails in my hair and all over my skull, pulling me not just along her, but through her and into her.

As much as I fundamentally crave the carnal knowledge of what she feels like and tastes like inside, I also have just enough remaining coherence left to want to save the best for last.

That's why I place my forearms on either side of her hips on the couch and glide my face up along her lower rib cage, kissing and nosing my way around the loose folds of sheer fabric to uncover more and more of Selene's torso. I feel her stomach muscles contract gently as I press the tip of my tongue in her navel, and a smile forms on my lips as I make a mental note of where she might be ticklish. Somewhere in the back of my muddled brain, I vow that though this is the first time, I cannot let it be the last.

I'm suddenly overcome with a singular, all-powerful need to feel her breasts in my hands. Everything up until now has been a slow, steady burn of succulent discovery and sensual tenderness, but coming level with her perfect chest has ignited a newfound, frenzied curiosity in me that must be slaked, so I relinquish myself entirely to this new demand

and grasp for Selene as if my life depended on it.

Inconceivably, she is even more perfect to the touch than she is perfect to behold. If she's startled by my sudden change in focus, speed, or intensity, she doesn't show it at all in the way her body responds. There's no flinch or whimper, just more of the same as before: low, decadent moaning, as well as massaging of my scalp between her fingernails.

I trace the full circumference of her breasts with my fingers, my palms, and with the heels of my hands. When I cannot bear it any longer, I fall forward and wrap my lips around her left nipple, sucking and kissing and flicking the soft hardness of it with my tongue.

I could do this forever, I realize with a crystalline sense of clarity. This is heaven. There's nowhere else I'd rather be, there's nothing else I'd rather be doing, and there's no one else I'd rather have now here in my mouth.

As it turns out, the only thing in the whole wide universe that can pull me away from her left breast is the desire to spread my love equally with her right breast, which I do now.

Eventually, I find that my mouth has a mind of its own and has moved of its own accord between her breasts, raining slow kisses in her cleavage there as I slowly make my way up her sternum and then back and forth along her collarbone.

My hands have minds of their own as well. I'm not sure when it happened, but they've somehow fanned out on either side of us and taken hold of her hands. Our fingers are intertwined and our arms are outstretched along the width of the back of the couch, but my mental focus doesn't stay there for long, because now my mouth is moving up the nape of her neck to her chin and finally to her lips, where she meets me with an enthusiastic fervor.

Kissing Selene is unlike kissing anyone I've ever kissed before. None of those previous kisses and none of those women seem to even exist for me anymore. They were all just a speculative prelude, the kind of daydream a boy has when he's still a virgin and he has only his limited juvenile imagination as a way to mentally fumble at what real passion might be like and feel like. Just as he has no clue or concept of what will one day await him in the moment, I had no way of knowing I'd never really kissed anyone, not really, until I kissed Selene.

In the midst of it all, my hands leave her hands and fall down along the sides of her body until I dig my fingers beneath her ass cheeks. She's firm and strong yet soft and smooth. I find myself deeply wishing I could see her ass displayed in front of me the way I now see her chest, but I also know on some profound, instinctual level that I should just be thanking every lucky star in the galaxy that any of this is even possible and actually happening right now.

Selene slides forward on top of my hands, lifting herself and giving me more of her weight. She arcs her body back and forth, rolling her spine in such a way that makes it impossible for me to think of anything right now other than her riding me.

Is that what her face would look like? Would her hair whip back and forth like that, shining and shimmering and changing colors like a rippling iridescent flag in the wind? What would it feel like to have her move like that on my cock? How would it feel to have my fingers wrapped around her hipbones as she gyrated, or to twist her nipples between my fingers as she circled round on top of me, or to cup her ass with my palms as the muscles there flexed with each and every downward thrust?

These kinds of thoughts and fantasies threaten to push me over the edge just in my mind alone. That realization is enough to convince me it's time to give in to what we've both been waiting for. I could spend eons charting myriad paths all over her body with my mouth, but right now, there's only one place I want and need to be.

Selene must be telepathic, because she melts deeper into the couch, widens her legs, and wraps her hands around the back of my head once again. She purrs with pleasure and anticipation as I sink lower and lower until my face is fully between her thighs.

"Worship me, Lance."

As if I needed any invitation. I grip her ass and plunge my face into her pussy.

It's everything I ever could have asked for… and more. She's already wet and warm, but I waste no time in working her up even further with my lips and my tongue. Selene tastes divine in my mouth, like she's magic and I'm drinking from the fountain of youth or lapping up some fabled nectar of the gods. On the one hand, I am simply not worthy to be here with my head pressed between her inner thighs, tasting this magnificent angel's hidden sex. And on the other hand, she is the one who put me here, and that has got to count for something.

Selene squirms on my mouth and my hands, her moans building with her mounting orgasm. She rocks herself forward and presses me in deeper by the skull until I'm even more immersed in her than I ever could have dreamed possible. I'm not just tasting her anymore; I'm breathing her in and swallowing her whole so that my every sense is overcome with her body and her being.

I want her to come and I want her to come on me, so

I take no chances. As much as I've loved eating her out while gripping her ass from below, I pull my hands out from beneath her now so I can make better use of them. I keep my mouth and tongue on her clit, but I dip one finger and then two into her body, and I move them until I feel her start to shudder above me. She's almost there now, so I reach up with my free hand to grab her by the hip and pull her in closer until I'm fully submerged in the first waves of her climax.

The world falls away. There is only her and only me and only us together right now in this moment. She screams out her pleasure, digs her nails into my scalp, squeezes my head tighter between her legs, and convulses wildly as ripple after ripple shakes her down.

It's only when my lungs start to burn that I realize I can't breathe, and as much as I don't want to, I finally have to wrench myself free from her with a heaving gasp for air.

She's waiting for me, panting and dripping, but staring me down from above with an indescribable expression on her face. We lock eyes and struggle to catch our breath, both hot and wet and vulnerable.

"Wow. Now that was really something."

I turn with a start toward the voice, and that's when I remember for the first time in what seems like hours that Selene and I are actually not alone in here. Martin Schwartzman sits behind me on the other side of the den in a leather armchair and rubs a small towel between his hands.

"Seriously. Bravo, young man. Bravo."

He tosses the towel to the side, stands, and adjusts his kimono.

"I wanted desire, and boy oh boy, did you give me desire."

My head is swimming. There's a whirling, swirling

hodgepodge of emotions and thoughts trying to find solid footing in my brain. I'm still caught up in the religious sexcstasy of everything Selene and I just experienced together, but little pinpricks of surprise, confusion, shame, and even nausea are now threatening to dismantle it from the inside out.

I was so absolutely lost within her in the best way possible that everything else ceased to exist, including natural laws of time and space. And though I'm still riding that high and savoring the delicious, fertile aftershocks that accompany it, the nagging, insistent awareness of where I am, what I've done, and who I'm with is becoming increasingly difficult to ignore.

Martin yawns, stretches, and scratches at his hairy protruding belly.

"Selene has all your info of course, so we'll be in touch. I am going to have to ask you for that jacket back, as nice as it looks on you."

He lumbers over to me with an outstretched palm and waits patiently until I remove the jacket and turn it over to him in a kind of daze. Martin folds it with a weird reverence before tucking it under his arm, and then he nods to me solemnly, makes his way up the stairs, and finally disappears down a darkened hallway without another word.

When I turn back to Selene, I'm surprised to find her shockingly composed. Her kimono is knotted shut, her breathing has steadied, and she's not even glistening anymore. It's actually remarkable how put-together she now appears, considering just seconds ago we were both wet, flushed, and out of breath.

"I'll show you out."

She stands and calmly moves around me, even as I

continue to struggle to get my bearings.

"Wait… what?"

Selene pauses at the mouth of a different hallway than the one Martin just went down.

"I said that I'll show you out."

I'm still on my knees, but my mind is scrambled eggs spilled out all over the floor.

"What… wait. What just happened?"

"What do you mean what just happened? You got the callback you wanted."

Is she kidding?

"What? What are you talking about?"

Selene places her hands on her hips and gazes down at me.

"You seem to be in a stupor. Thank you for coming out today. We got everything we needed. I'll show you out now."

I stutter out an incredulous laugh.

"Are you serious?"

"I'm deathly serious."

"But… I didn't… we didn't even do the scene."

"It wasn't necessary. Like I said, we got everything we needed. I'll be in touch."

What is going on right now?

"I don't understand—"

"What don't you understand? You wanted a chance to show us what you got, and that's exactly what we gave you. But it's time to go now. Marty and I are expecting our next guest any minute."

"Next guest? You mean, your next actor? Or what do you mean by that?"

Selene is silent.

"How many guys are you seeing?!"

"Careful, Mr. Lonergan. Careful. Let's not ruin a good thing. Jealousy doesn't become you."

"I'm… I'm not jealous. I just thought that I was—"

"The only one? Come on, now. Surely you understand what a big decision this is. We have to be absolutely certain. That's why I can take no chances. It's the nature of the game."

I suddenly feel very foolish down here on my knees in this strange man's living room, having done the things I've done and said the things I've said.

How the hell did any of this happen? Sure, I'm drunk, but I've been drunk before. I've done some crazy things in my life under the influence, both sexually and non-sexually. But this whole situation feels exponentially more absurd, hazy, and dreamlike, almost as if I've had an out-of-body experience.

Even now, I'm struggling to ascertain the boundary between reality and fantasy. It's incredibly difficult to believe and accept that I just went down on a casting director in front of a showrunner in his own house. How did I get here?

"Lance."

She says my name in such a way that I physically cannot ignore her or look away.

"I need you to listen and obey me now. It's time to go. I'll walk you out. Follow me."

I'm still dazed and mentally muddled, but I clamber up to my feet somehow and move in her direction. Selene waits until I've climbed up the steps from the den, and then she turns and leads me down the hallway. Silently, we move through the twists and turns of all the passageways and rooms I first encountered when I arrived. Each is vaguely familiar but also different, with new shadow placements along the walls and paintings. At last, we reach the front door, which Selene opens for me.

Something isn't right here. The sky is a different color than it should be, a deeper blue with tints of gold that don't add up. I stop dead in my tracks to fish my cell phone out of my pocket and check the time on the screen: 6:53 p.m.

But that's impossible. I stare down at the numbers in disbelief. There has to be some kind of mistake. I click the phone on and off a couple of times, thinking maybe it's just short-circuiting or being weird. Stranger things have happened with technology. The thing probably just needs to be rebooted. Maybe I've left it on for too many days without restarting or turning off.

Yet there's no denying the color of the sky. And the sun—the sun was high above me when I first arrived on this street, about half an hour before noon. Now it's nowhere to be seen in front of or above me. The only place it could possibly be is behind me and behind the house, but that would mean that it's over the ocean, which would also mean that it's setting, which… which just doesn't make any sense.

I turn to Selene as if she might have the answers. She's leaning against the open door with her knee bent and one bare foot pressed against the wood. Smoke drifts lazily in my direction from the cigarette perched between her pouty lips. I have no idea when she lit it or where it even came from.

"What time is it?"

The ember glows red as she inhales deeply.

"It's time for you to go, Lance."

"No, I'm serious. My phone says it's almost seven, but that doesn't make any sense."

She shrugs.

"That's technology for you."

"Seriously, though. Do you have the time?"

Selene's eyes squint.

"It's sunset."

"But… but that doesn't make any sense. My callback was at noon."

She shrugs again, utterly unfazed and unbothered. What doesn't she understand?

"How could it be 6:53 if my callback was at 12:00? How is that possible?"

"Time flies when you're having fun, I guess."

She starts to move back inside.

"Hey, wait a second—"

I catch her arm with my hand just before she can close the door. Selene's head whips around with a hiss as she clocks the exact place on her body where I've detained her, and there's a flash of fury across her face as the skin tightens around her lips and cheeks. I retract my hand quicker than if I'd just touched a hot stovetop.

"Woah! Sorry. I just… I'm just confused, that's all."

Slowly, her face settles into a more natural expression, calm yet calculating. She considers me silently as she smokes, and the fire in her eyes dwindles until it finally transfers over exclusively to her cigarette.

"You're a bold one, aren't you?"

I don't know how to respond to that.

The faintest whisper of a smile forms as Selene steps backward into the doorway.

"I like that."

She's not done with her cigarette, but she's done with me. The door closes in my face.

I stare at the wood blankly for a full ten seconds or so, wondering if that's really the end of this conversation, and by extension, this whole crazy experience. There's a part of my brain that keeps thinking she'll open the door again any second now, laugh, and tell me that it's all been a dream, a hallucination, a prank, or even some kind of bizarre, half-baked reality TV program they're trying out. My phone will reset to the proper time, the sky will reveal itself to be an elaborate and realistic set on a studio soundstage, and all mysteries will be revealed.

But that's not what happens. The door doesn't open, Selene doesn't reappear, and the clouds rolling by overhead are too vivid and realistic to be fake. All I have to do is walk out further into the street to get a glimpse of the sun and confirm that it truly is setting out over the ocean. And my phone, even after the hard reset, still chooses to brazenly defy me by displaying the numerals 7:18 on the screen.

As bad as this headache is fast becoming, the nausea I felt earlier is even worse. I haven't thrown up while drinking in years, but I remember all the warning signs well, so I decide not to take any chances. Hunched over, with one hand over my mouth and the other pressed firmly against my solar plexus, I rush around my car until I can crouch down next to the driver-side door, presumably well out of sight of the Schwartzman abode and anyone inside it.

Spasms rock my body as I hurl my guts out onto the Malibu street. It's all liquid, which isn't surprising considering the amount of wine I drank in there. Ruefully, I recall I didn't have much this morning by way of breakfast—just a smoothie and a protein bar. Of course, I didn't expect to be drinking so heavily, either, and I also didn't expect to be here for seven hours somehow.

Thinking of food makes me remember with a sinking revelation that Sarah's L.A. anniversary is tonight—and that it started over two hours ago. I was supposed to be at Macho's at five, and I promised her that I would be there. She hasn't called or texted me, but I know better than to assume that means my absence hasn't gone unnoticed.

I wipe vomit residue from my lips with the back of my hand. How the fuck did this happen? It just doesn't make sense. Seven hours couldn't possibly have passed by that quickly. Not without me noticing, and not without something happening along the way to make me realize just how much time was slipping away. I should have gotten hungry, or thirsty, or tired. My phone should have rung or buzzed, and I have no missed calls or texts.

At the very least, Brian or Donna should have checked in with me around one or two. They know better than anyone what a big deal this opportunity is, so it doesn't track that they wouldn't call afterward to see how the callback went. Even my email inbox hasn't seen any new action over the past seven hours.

It's as if the whole world went on pause when I stepped inside Martin Schwartzman's house and then rapidly fast-forwarded the second I came out of it. That, or maybe I got sucked into a black hole or an alternate dimension. There's just no wrapping my brain around how something like this happens. It doesn't make sense.

I try calling Sarah but it goes abruptly to voicemail in the middle of the third ring. Not a good sign. In the midst of the automated recording telling me to leave a message, I cancel the call and hang up. Best to just get there as fast as possible and make it up to her in person. Maybe I can buy her forgiveness with a couple tequila shots, a hug, and an explanation as to why I'm so late.

But what on Earth can I possibly tell her? That I got

invited to drink two bottles of wine and play dress-up in a stranger's Malibu beach house? That I lost track of time and somehow spent nearly seven hours in that house without actually doing any acting or even discussing the true purpose of my visit? That I inexplicably decided it was okay to perform cunnilingus on the casting director right in front of the showrunner with absolutely no sense of shame or common human decency?

These are the thoughts tumbling around my polluted cranium when another wave of nausea forces me into more puking out on the street.

When every last bit of bile has exited my body, I drag what's left of that body into my car, collapse in the seat, and recline violently backward. Even after all that puking, I feel worse than I did before. Maybe I'm not quite as nauseous, but my headache has intensified, and now I have the full-blown spins. There's nothing I can do except lie back, wrap my arms around my chest, close my eyes, breathe shallowly, and wait it out.

Wait for the sickness to subside, wait for the pain to recede, wait for the alcohol to wear off, and most importantly, wait for normalcy to return. That, or wait to wake up from this dream. One or the other.

But until then, there's nothing I can do except to wait and hope that somewhere along all that waiting, I fall asleep, and when I wake up, I'm right again.

CHAPTER 9

As the warm, late morning light streams in through the blinds onto my face, the first conscious thought I have is that it's Friday, and that it being Friday should be significant to me for some reason.

After racking my brain for several seconds, I finally have my answer: today is the day that Sarah not-so-subtly insisted I pay up my portion of the rent for the past two months. Shout-out to her therapist for emboldening Sarah to make such a long-overdue, absolutely-justified demand—but Christ, it comes at a difficult time for me financially.

It's only natural that this revelation also sparks a painful reminder that I missed her L.A. anniversary last night. By the time I woke up and realized I was even asleep to begin with, alone inside my car on a dark Malibu street parked outside Martin Schwartzman's house, it was well past midnight. Even if Sarah and her friends were still partying at Macho's—a long shot, to be sure—I was in no fit state to make my first appearance of the night, more than seven hours after the fact and with no clear concept of an excuse for my extraordinary tardiness.

So, I did the only thing I could do in that situation: I drove home to go to sleep and cut my losses for the evening. I wasn't surprised to find Sarah's car parked at our apartment and to find her door closed and the lights off inside her room. It was a weeknight, after all, even for someone who works remotely from home. I was also relieved to find her asleep, since I knew it meant I'd have just a bit more time to formulate my excuse for not making it to Macho's.

What I did not think about last night or remember until this very moment this morning was her request for me to Venmo her the rent today. Any scenario in which she might forget about that ask, or even take mercy on me and give me an extension, seems like it could be utterly unrealistic now after I effectively stood her up last night at the party I pledged to attend.

I groan and reach for my cell phone on the nightstand. It's 10:03 a.m. I have a catering gig in six hours; it's a corporate dinner party for some Silicon Beach tech startup in Venice. The pay is good, and the fact that it's on the West Side means it probably won't last all night the way a Hollywood Hills party could. But still, it's the last thing I want to be doing with my time today. I'm nursing an unexpected hangover from an unexpected amount of heavy drinking yesterday.

Worse, I'm already battling all manner of demons this morning. The rent and Macho's stuff with Sarah would normally be bad enough, but I also have to contend with whatever the fuck yesterday was at Martin Schwartzman's house. While sleep came quickly in my car outside his house, it was much more evasive once I returned home and slipped under my own bedsheets last night. Because as hard as I tried, I could not stop replaying the events of the day and wrestling with all the hazy inconsistencies I experienced.

Even now after getting a bit more rest and placing a decent number of hours between me and that callback, it still doesn't make much sense. I don't understand where the time went or how I got so inebriated and uninhibited that I did the things I did. The only logical explanation I have is that Martin must have put something in the wine, like roofies or some other powerful narcotic, that lowered my defenses and made me act completely out of character.

Still… it doesn't explain the time. I've had time slip away from me while drunk or on drugs before, but not like that. Seven whole hours don't just evaporate in the blink of an eye.

My phone vibrates on the nightstand next to me. It's actually a relief to hear the sound and to see the screen lighting up, considering there was that abnormally long period of time yesterday where absolutely nothing happened on it by way of calls, texts, emails, or anything. It was almost as if I found myself in a dead zone somewhere out in the middle of nowhere, even though I was smack dab in a wealthy, densely-populated area of Southern California. Another thing that makes no sense.

My heart skips a beat when I recognize the number calling: Donna Goodwin. I fully expected this call to take place yesterday after I finished my callback, so the fact that they're calling me now this morning comes as a bit of a surprise.

This is a good thing, though. Despite all the weirdness and debauchery, a call from my agent the day after a callback with a casting director and a showrunner has got to be a promising sign. If this is it—if this is my 'big break,' the one monumental phone call that changes my life forever—then everything that happened yesterday will obviously have been well worth it.

I take a deep breath and answer the phone.

"Hello?"

"Lance, it's Brian."

Reflexively, my heart dips at the realization of hearing Brian's voice rather than Donna's. But then I remind myself that it was actually Brian, not Donna, who called yesterday to give me the good news about getting the callback in the first place. I shouldn't rush to any premature judgments.

"Hey, Brian, how are you?"

"I've been better, honestly. You know my dog, Yorkie? She has some kind of fungal infection."

There's a pause on the line because I think he's going to keep talking, but he doesn't.

"Oh, no. I'm sorry to hear that."

"Thank you."

"I hope she feels better soon."

"Thank you so much. You're a sweetheart."

Another lengthy pause. Come on, Brian, spit it out. You didn't call me to talk about your dog's fungal infection. Or at least, I really hope you didn't.

"Anyway, that's not the only bad news I have to relay. I just got off the phone with Selene Blackwood's office, and unfortunately, it's a no. They're going with Taylor Lautner instead."

It's as if someone just opened an airlock door in outer space on my fucking soul.

"I'm so sorry. Selene's assistant said you did a good job and that it was a really tough decision, but ultimately, they had to go with a more proven commodity."

"I… I don't understand. I thought your email said they wanted an unknown for the part?"

"That's what they told me as well, but you know how these things work. The network probably came in at the last minute and insisted on a name. I'm sure it had nothing to do with your performance."

What. The. Fuck.

I'm at a loss for words. How could this happen? After all of that? Whatever that was…

"I know this is tough, but on the bright side, you need to remember that this is the furthest you've gone. Plus, now you have a legit casting director who's a fan of your work. I'm sure their office will keep you in mind for future projects, and that means everything."

I just don't understand how they could do this to me. After everything that happened yesterday, after everything they put me through… they went with Taylor Lautner? The fucking wolf-guy from Twilight?

"Lance-y? You still there?"

"Yeah. I'm here."

"Okay, well, I'm sorry to be the bearer of bad news, but I also have to get back to work now. We'll get the next one, okay? Keep that chiseled chin up. Talk soon. Ciao."

"Bye."

What was the point of all that yesterday if they were just going to turn around and give the part to a celebrity? I bet he didn't even have to read for them.

And the turnaround time here—it just doesn't add up. Less than 24 hours ago, they bring me in to read for the showrunner in his house, in his fucking Malibu beachfront estate, and now they're going with Taylor Lautner?

I throw my phone across the room against the wall. Shock and dejection are fast mutating into cold rage. I can't stop replaying yesterday's events in my head and marveling with a mad, delirious incredulity at my own participation in them.

Whether I was drunk or drugged or both, these excuses can't justify how stupid and complicit I was, drinking glass after glass of wine, putting on that ridiculous smoking jacket, accepting their suggestion that it was somehow okay for me not to do any actual acting at a motherfucking callback for a network show. And then, to top it all off, somehow going down on the casting director right in front of the showrunner seemed like a great idea to me at the time.

What was I thinking? I wasn't, obviously.

But those two… they knew what they were doing. I should have known better, sure, but I'm still the victim in this situation. They willfully took advantage of me because they knew that they could, given the power dynamic. And that's not okay. Something needs to be done.

But what can I do? Suffice it to say, I've never been in this situation before. And I don't know anyone who has. Plenty of my friends are actors, models, musicians, and the like, but if any of them have ever been sexually abused or taken advantage of like this, they've never told me about it.

It's not exactly something I can ask around about, either. I can just imagine Jared's reaction now. 'Wait, so you're telling me you're upset you got to put your mouth all over this beautiful babe's snatch?'

I can't call my parents. This would only confirm everything they've been saying for years about how toxic and nefarious the entertainment industry is. They'd never shut up again about Los Angeles being a moral cesspool and about how my only real hope for salvation is to move back home and escape California altogether to exorcise myself of all the sin and filth.

Sarah normally occupies the role of sounding board for me when it comes to tough decisions and debates, but she's not exactly an option right now, given the fact I'm most certainly in her doghouse because of last night. Plus, there's the whole I-owe-her-lots-of-money angle, and she's got every reason to come collecting today.

Should I call Brian back, or maybe even Donna herself? Weirdly enough, they might be the best ones to talk to about something like this, given that they're both in the industry. This can't be the first time something like this has happened on their watch. Can it?

Fuck. If only I were rich enough to afford a therapist like Sarah can. Wouldn't that be nice? Now I get why people have those.

I suppose one option I haven't considered is just to let it all go. But I quickly veto that possibility. The idea that I'm just supposed to turn the other cheek and move on with my life after all the hard work I put into this role is both asinine and insulting. There's no chalking this up to being 'just the nature of the business,' admitting 'you win some, you lose some,' or taking comfort in some other meaningless platitude.

Maybe if I'd shown up yesterday and actually read the scene and did some legitimate acting, I'd be able to come to terms with this decision, disappointing and fucked-up as it is. But that's not what happened.

I'm quivering with anger but also with nervousness as I pick up my phone from the floor and call Donna Goodwin's office back. I keep telling myself that this is the right thing to do, as hard as it may be. Someone needs to know what happened yesterday. Even if I can't do anything about it alone, perhaps Donna can. Or maybe she knows somebody who can. There has to be something that can be done. Injustice and abuse cannot be tolerated.

"Donna Goodwin's office, this is Brian speaking."

"Brian, it's Lance."

"Lance… Lonergan?"

Who else would it be? Tell me they don't have another Lance on the roster. That's the last thing I need to hear right now.

"Yes, Lance Lonergan."

"Hi, Lance. How can I help you?"

"Um… I'm wondering if Donna's in, actually."

"She is, but she's with a client right now. Can I take a message?"

Fuck.

"Uh… yeah, can you just have her call me back as soon as she can? It's pretty urgent."

"Lance. Lance-y. This isn't about Legal Eagle, is it? Because I thought we just talked about that."

"It is, but it's different. I just need to talk to her about what happened yesterday… at Martin Schwartzman's house."

"What happened yesterday at Martin Schwartzman's house?"

What do I tell him? I've got nothing personal against the guy; he's always been friendly enough with me, despite the juvenile nickname-calling that I absolutely abhor. He's just an assistant, though, and fair or not, Brian strikes me as the type who has a big mouth.

"I'd rather talk directly to Donna about it if I can."

Right away, I regret the way the words come out of my mouth. Even though it's a perfectly reasonable request, I just know it's the kind of response that's going to offend him.

Sure enough, Brian's tone switches immediately to

become brusquer and more clipped.

"Well. I'll see that she gets the message. She has a very busy day today though, fair warning, so she likely won't get around to this until after the weekend. Of course, if she had more context, that would definitely help speed things up, I'm sure."

If she had more context, or if you had more context? Either way, it's not the answer I was hoping for.

"All right. Well, just as soon as she can, then. Thanks, Brian."

"Sure."

I hear the click as he hangs up. It's the first time that I can recall where Brian hasn't ended a phone conversation with his customary light-hearted 'ciao.' That's not a good omen, and it makes me question whether or not my message will even be delivered at all.

One way or another, though, I need answers. I need accountability. Someone needs to explain to me just what the hell happened yesterday and why it didn't result in me booking the part. I'm not sure if an explanation will be enough, but I need to do something at least so that it doesn't feel like I went through all of that for nothing. Otherwise, what's the point even?

I've run out of options. There's nothing else for me to do now except go straight to the source. If Selene Blackwood thinks that I'm the type of brainless Hollywood meathead she can just exploit for her own sexual satisfaction and then casually discard after I've served my purpose, she's got another thing coming. She has no idea who I am or who she's messing with.

And I'm about to show her.

CHAPTER 10

One way or another, I'm going to turn this thing around. Especially since luck finally appears to be on my side.

First, Sarah must have called in sick this morning, because her bedroom door was still shut and her car was still in the driveway when I snuck out of our apartment. Probably sleeping off the booze from last night. But whatever the reason, I was only too grateful to escape detection and temporarily sidestep any unpleasant conversations about money or my absence from her party.

Second, traffic was surprisingly light on The Four-Oh-Five coming down to Westwood. Though I hit the road during the presumptive lull between most people's morning commute and their early afternoon lunch break, I've certainly been burned plenty of times before while traveling during that same timespan. For whatever reason, it didn't happen today.

And third, because I didn't have a scheduled audition time I needed to arrive by, and thus had no concerns over being late for it, I was free to meander through the surrounding neighborhoods at my leisure until I found free parking.

For the sake of my sanity, it's a blessing that all of these things worked out the way they did. Because every time I mentally replay my first phone call with Brian this morning where he broke the bad news to me, or I replay Marty squeezing my shoulders or drying himself off with a towel, or replay Selene blowing smoke in my face or closing the front door on me, my body starts to tremble all over with emotion. I'm not sure I'd be able to stomach any more inconveniences or injustices.

The first place I check for Selene is that little courtyard inside her office building where I stumbled upon her after my initial audition, but she's not there. Next, I climb the stairs and peek into the room where I had the audition itself, but it's dark inside and the door is locked. Overall, the whole building seems deserted today; I haven't come across another soul yet. If she's hosting auditions, they either already happened or they haven't started yet.

There are other random businesses and offices in the building, but none have any apparent association with Selene's casting studio. A refrigeration company here, an optometrist there. Some offices are dark and vacant, perhaps because their occupants are on early lunch or maybe even off altogether on Fridays.

Just the idea of that—of people setting their own hours or rewarding themselves with flexible time off—makes my blood boil. Why is it that so many individuals can follow their intrinsic passions into stable, supportive career opportunities, while creative types such as myself are forever relegated to hustling and hoofing it, the proverbial 'starving artists' doomed to suffer in perpetuity simply because we have the wrong kind of hopes and dreams?

After zigzagging up and down between the floors and around so many hallway twists and turns, I find myself back on the same level where my audition was held. That room's still dark and empty, but the room across from it now emits a soft light where previously none existed. There's no label beside the doorframe or printed on the glass, but all I need to do is take a quick peek through the window to confirm a familiar face. I'd recognize those half-rim glasses and deep-set frown lines anywhere.

True to form, Selene's assistant appears peeved and impatient—even with her food. She sits hunched over her desk, manically clawing at the knot in a plastic takeout bag that looks like it contains some kind of soup, ramen, or pho. The besieged exasperation on her face switches to surprise and then annoyance in less than a second as she registers the sound of the door opening and realizes she's no longer alone.

"Hi, can I help you?!"

"Hi. Is this Selene Blackwood's office?"

"It is, but we're at lunch right now. And we don't take cold calls without an appointment."

Such warmth and hospitality.

"I don't know if you remember me, but I was actually in here a couple days ago—"

"Any feedback from Selene has already been communicated to representation. And if you left something behind, you'll need to check with security on the first floor, not with me. We don't keep a lost and found up here."

Jesus Christ.

"I'm actually here to see Selene."

The vein in her forehead is thrumming.

"As I just mentioned, we don't do cold calls. You'll need to speak to your representation, or you can go online and register for her next available public workshop. I'm afraid that's all I can do."

There's not much to this room other than the desk and chair she's sitting at and then a small sofa and a couple of chairs against one wall. Across from that vacant seating area is another wall with a single door set in the center of it. This door doesn't have a placard or any identifying writing on it either, but there's an unmistakable orange glow coming from behind the frosted privacy glass.

"I need to talk to her."

Maybe it's just adrenaline, but whatever it is that's coursing through my veins and making my heat beat a mile a minute right now, it convinces me that there's absolutely no point to this 'conversation' anymore. I take matters into my own hands and move rapidly toward that second door without so much as a second thought.

"Excuse me—EXCUSE ME!!!"

I can hear and peripherally see the woman frantically shoving her chair away from the desk as she clambers up to pursue me, but I'm already on my feet and have a head-start, so all I need to do is hope the door isn't locked by the time I reach it. Mercifully, it isn't.

I pull it hard to reveal a larger room that is surprisingly and rather stunningly lit entirely by candles. They line the walls at various heights and quantities, some of them alone and some clumped in small formations, strewn out along floating shelves made of wood, stone, and marble. If there is an overhead light in here, it's not turned on.

Most of the shelf space is occupied by flickering candles, but I also notice an abundance of books. It's dark in here, but at least at first glance, they don't look like the type of mass market paperbacks you'd find in a Barnes & Noble or an airport bookstore. The thick bindings and general lack of legible script along the spines makes me think these must be rare collector's items or antique heirlooms of some kind.

What the room lacks in initial visual clarity it more than makes up for on the olfactory scale. It's not so much that the space stinks as it is there's just an abundance of various smells competing for your immediate attention. There's no mystery as to why, either, since I can both see and smell all different kinds of dried herbs and plants around me. Here and there I spot them in bottles or jars on the shelves, but mostly they're hanging on the walls or even from the ceiling, bound and suspended by what looks like twine.

Bizarrely, the room has no furniture. No chairs, no tables, no couch, no desk. Instead, there are just dozens of pillows, of all different shapes, sizes, and colors, littered along the boundaries of the office.

This office… it's not an office. If I didn't already know that I am actually, physically, in an office building, or if I didn't recognize the casting assistant, it'd be all too easy to assume I'd stepped through a dimensional portal or stumbled into some kind of Narnia or metaverse situation.

There's another reason why I know I'm still rooted in the reality of standing in Selene Blackwood's office, and that reason is Selene Blackwood herself. Right in the very center of the room she sits, barefoot and cross-legged, with her hands resting casually on her knees, but with her spine perfectly erect. She's wearing black fitted jeans and a cream-colored satin blouse that's unbuttoned nearly down to her sternum. A silver pendant necklace rests against the naked skin there and catches the candlelight every now and then… but not like her eyes. Those reflect the fire and bounce it back at me with such a feverish intensity that they themselves appear to glow.

"Selene, I'm so sorry. He just barged in here while I was eating. I'll call security—"

"There's no need for that."

Her voice echoes more than I think it should. The room isn't particularly large or cavernous, but maybe it's because of the sheer lack of stuff in here to properly absorb the sound.

"What?"

I can't see her assistant's face since the woman is standing behind me, but the obvious confusion I hear in her voice is palpable.

Selene doesn't move a muscle other than the tongue in her mouth that she uses to speak. But when she does speak, her tone is calm and full of command.

"Don't call security, Helen. I'll handle him."

I can feel the hesitation, the concern, the all-around bewilderment of the woman standing behind me, who is presumably at a total loss just about now. Truthfully, I can kind of relate.

Selene dips her chin ever so slightly.

"Leave us."

Not a second later, I hear the door close behind me as Helen the assistant promptly takes her leave.

Now that we're alone, it really hits me for the first time just how spooky and odd it is in here. I take another quick inventory of my surroundings, noting the candles, the books, the plants, the pillows, and wonder if maybe this isn't an actual office at all. Maybe it's some kind of New Age-y break room, a place to de-stress and unplug from the hustle and bustle of Hollywood every now and then.

"I had a feeling you would come."

Selene's voice has the uncanny ability to summon my

total attention at will. For that matter, so does her face, her body, and—well, pretty much any and everything about her.

"You're not happy with me, are you?"

She asks the question innocently enough, but I can't ignore the presence of a new sensation bubbling up inside of me, try as I might. I know that she's right: that I have every reason in the world to be furious with her for the way she and Martin took advantage of me yesterday, and for leading me on to believe I had the role in the bag and that I was their guy, only to have the rug ripped out from under me.

Yet, standing here in this weird little candlelit room facing her, seeing her again, and seeing her seeing me, it's impossible not to also think back on the intimacy we shared yesterday.

Because despite all the strangeness, despite the way things ended at Martin's house, and despite the way things started again this morning with the bad news I received via phone call, despite all of that… how can I deny the pure, orgasmic bliss of what it felt like to touch her, to kiss her, to smell her, to taste her?

I can't deny it, because it's the truth.

The more I stand here and look at her, the more I'm reminded of so many sweet sinful details, like the moon-shaped scar about an inch above her right kneecap, or the tiny brown mole on the underside of her left breast right where the skin meets her rib cage. I'm reminded of the way her neck broke out in goosebumps every time I breathed hot air into her ear in between kisses. I remember the way she purred, gasped, and moaned when I moved my fingers in just the right rhythm against her warm inner walls. And I remember the delicious juice and full savory taste of her wetness as she came on my face and in my mouth.

Selene is smiling now. Can she actually read my thoughts?

Speaking of spooky…

I came here for a reason, and it wasn't to reminisce. I'll lose everything if I allow myself to get distracted and succumb to those fertile, fucking fantastic memories. I need to stay focused on the task at hand.

She shifts her weight to lean forward until her elbows are on her knees and her hands meet in a ball of fists that slides out on the ground in front of her. The silver pendant around her neck swings out, as helplessly compelled by gravity to dangle in the air as I am compelled by instinct and lust to gaze down the rich, widening valley of her exposed cleavage.

What was the task at hand again?

Selene reminds me.

"Have you come here to tell me off?"

I did, once upon a time. Or at least, I think that's what my plan was. I know I was angry, that I was furious, and that I was bound and determined to let her know that what she did was wrong. It sort of sounds stupid now, but I feel like there was a time not so very long ago when it made sense to me. That has to be true. Otherwise, why would I have come here?

"Maybe you came here to threaten me? To let me know you'd be reporting me for being a bad, bad girl?"

Christ. I should be doing that. If anything, I shouldn't even be here at all. I should have gone to Donna's office, or the union office, or maybe even the police. What did I hope to accomplish by coming here today?

"Or maybe…"

Selene rocks her body upward until she's perched on her knees.

"…maybe you just came here to punish me."

The breath catches in my throat, and she notices.

"Yes…"

Selene slides one knee forward and then the other, keeping her eyes trained on mine the whole time. Inch by inch, she slowly closes the distance between us.

"…yes, I believe that's it."

There's a lump in my throat that won't go away. I've forgotten not only why I came here and how to speak, but now I've forgotten how to breathe as well.

"You want to punish me."

She finally comes to a stop. Her face is tilted up at mine, and there's less than a foot of space between us now.

"So, punish me."

Selene grasps her wrists behind her waist, arches her back, and licks her tongue out along her lips.

"Punish me, Lance. Whip out that big, fat cock of yours, and punish me with it."

My heart skips a few beats before stuttering and stumbling over itself to get back into proper rhythm. The blood pumping through my body is either so hot that it's cold or so cold that it's hot; I can't remember which is which, and it all feels the same now. Tingling tentacles of nervous anticipation trickle through my muscles and make my bones rattle in their casings.

Can she see my knees shaking in front of her? What about my hands? Can she see my fingers trembling? My palms are sweating again. That never happens to me. My palms never sweat before Selene. Now look at me. I'm a mess. What has this woman done to me?

Selene grins wickedly, her expression conveying the same kind of sadistic pride and pleasure I'd imagine a spider might feel when it discovers a fly ensnared in its web.

"What are you waiting for?"

I can't actually do this, can I? Right here in her office, or whatever the fuck this weird-ass room is? Her assistant is right outside the door, probably with her ear up against the glass, listening to our every word. It's the middle of the day—and a workday, no less. This is a place of business, an office building in the middle of Westwood. There are other companies here, other employees going about their day. Security guards, janitors, receptionists. What if someone hears? Are there cameras in here? Why am I even considering any of this? I'm not actually going to do this, am I?

My body answers for me as my hands start to undo my belt buckle.

Selene looks hungry.

"That's it. Give it to me. Give me what I want."

And I want to. There's nothing I want or need more in this world.

The back of my neck is on fire, like each and every one of the countless candle flames in here suddenly found their way across the room to conflagrate exactly there in that one place on my person. I'm hot but I'm not bothered by it or by anything else, and with my belt undone, I pull open the button on the waist of my pants and unzip my fly.

Selene's eyes grow wider as she takes in the full outline of my rock-hard cock bulging against the confines of my black boxer-briefs. Seeing the way her face changes gives me newfound confidence, and now I want to impress her, to prove to her again that I'm more than she thinks I am, and that I'm not like anyone else she's ever seen or known or been with.

I hook my thumbs into the waistline of my jeans on either side of my hips and push downward until I've dragged both my pants and my underwear down to mid-thigh. My cock rides the pull of the cotton fabric's descent for a while until it finally breaks free and springs back upward in a jerk, and just like that, it's out now, uncovered and proud and fucking inches away from Selene's glistening mouth.

She still hasn't taken her eyes off it this whole time, but now she does that thing again where she wets her lips with a lazy slide of her tongue, and I didn't know it was physically possible to get any harder, but god-damn-it, I do.

"Fuck, Lance. You're huge."

Her voice is a breathless, reverential whisper, and the effect it has on me somehow manages to summon even more blood flow to the one spot on my body I didn't think could possibly handle any more.

"Seriously. You're perfect. Did you know that?"

My mind is a blank slate. I can't think and I can't speak. All I can do is soak and revel in the lush, scintillating majesty of the present moment, of being here and now in my body, completely flush with craving and sensation.

Selene still has her hands pinned behind her back, but she leans forward just a bit, letting her eyes guide her face closer and closer until I can feel her warm breath escaping on my naked skin.

It's too much. What little space there still is separating us is just too much. I can feel the millions of invisible electric particles exchanging between us through the air, swapping charges and cycling information, all of them yearning and thirsting for more, more, always more.

I can't bear it anymore. All it takes is the slightest shift of my hips, and the space closes. The head of my cock finally grazes against her lips, and I can feel instantly how perfectly moist, plump, ready, and waiting they are. All for me. And only for me.

Selene moans, and with the front of her mouth acting as intermediary, the sound vibrates through both of us until I have chills racing up and down my spine.

"Remember what I told you earlier?"

Her lips move at the front of me as she speaks in a hushed trance. I'm a human microphone for her, and I've never felt happier to be so used and objectified.

"I said that I had a feeling you would come."

She moans again softly, then rolls her head back on her neck to look up at me and smile.

"And now, you will."

Before I can even register the full import of what she just said, Selene brings her face back down and opens her mouth, and I feel the tip of her tongue meet the tip of my cock before I can actually see it happen.

My breath catches in my lungs as every remaining outside thought or feeling left in me evaporates in an instant. The whole world outside this room could be engulfed in flame right now, and every living thing on the planet could be screaming my name and begging for help, and I would neither know nor care. All there ever was, all there ever is, all there ever will be… is Selene Blackwood.

That's it. The end.

She runs her tongue down the underside of my full length, then slowly comes back up along one side of it, and then the other. It takes all my concentration not to move, not to tense or flinch. She is so patient, so fucking patient, with how she moves her tongue on me, as if she's savoring every nanosecond of this experience and just exulting in the manifold pleasures it brings her.

They say that anticipation is half the fun, but when it comes to Selene Blackwood at least—Jesus Christ, that's the understatement of the century. She flicks and flies her tongue along, around, and against different sections of my shaft, as well as all the sensitive parts of my body that surround it, stopping here and there to kiss, sometimes light and fast, sometimes deep and slow, but always doing, moving, tasting, enjoying. It doesn't matter that she still has yet to actually take me inside her mouth; not so long as she keeps sending my body into these simmering fits of undulating rapture.

Sometimes she checks in with me, meeting my eyes with her own, as if to let me know she just heard that sigh in my throat or just saw the way my hips buckled for a second under the weight of my ramping pleasure.

At other times, her eyes are closed as she seems to lose herself in the moment and trust her tongue to take the wheel.

And then there are those riveting moments where her gaze is singularly focused in front of her on where exactly she's placing her tongue and her lips, and I swear to God, I can see those tiny sparkly flakes in her irises glowing like electric diamonds.

It's only after she's bathed every last square millimeter of my pelvic area with her attention and adoration that she finally—and rather unexpectedly—slips her lips in a wide 'O' around the end of my cock and slides half of my length into her mouth so smoothly and expertly that I can't help but gasp aloud at the sudden sensorial realization of what has happened.

Now her eyes are fully open and completely zeroed-in on me, and I cannot look away either. Though why would I ever want to? Because seeing is believing, and as unbelievable as this moment in my life actually is, there's no denying that it's actually happening right now, because I can see Selene seeing me, tracking my pleasure and leaning into it as she moves her mouth in accordance to the minute physical cues she detects in my reactions to her.

Selene knows what she's doing. That's another understatement of the century.

More than once, I desperately fling my brain away from what's happening and try to focus on something, anything, other than what she's doing to me. It's a vain, doomed hope that the random, menial, mental diversion I concoct might be just enough to slow me down and delay the inevitable climax I feel building up inside me and threatening to break free at any moment. She's just too good and too intuitive, so it takes all my mental fortitude and powers of self-distraction to keep myself from imploding.

I'm willing myself back from the edge on one of these many crusades just as she decides to up the ante. Because of course she does, because she's Selene. This whole time, she has kept her hands behind her waist, deftly balancing on her knees while relying exclusively on her mouth and her eyes to make contact and communion with me. Apropos of nothing, she now determines the time is right to bring her hands in on the action, and she begins stroking and massaging me in addition to what she's already doing with her lips and her tongue.

As if that all weren't enough, she's humming and moaning now, almost as if she's the one trying to simultaneously savor and establish control over a mounting orgasm. The warm, gentle buzzing of her mouth on my cock makes it impossible to try and distract myself from what she's doing to me, and I can feel the last vestiges of my self-control slipping away like fine grains of sand in an hourglass.

I swear to God that Selene is telepathic, because once again, she seems to read my mind and recognize just how close I am, even without me saying a word or moving a muscle. Her hands wrap around behind me to grip my ass, and with one long, low, satisfied groan, she pulls me all the way into her mouth and then her throat until I'm completely buried there.

That's what does it. My hands instinctually fly up to the back of her head to steady myself, and I bury my fingers in her hair as I fight to maintain my balance and not completely topple over. Wave after crashing wave courses up and through me. Vaguely, my mind flashes and then briefly fixates on a kind of perfect symmetry between this moment and the one at Martin's house yesterday when Selene had her hands on my skull and her fingers in my hair as she came, and I'm overcome by an unexpected pang of tenderness and meaningfulness, even in the midst of my rollicking ecstasy.

Selene rides the waves with me, sucking and swallowing and keeping me upright all at once. She rakes her nails along my lower back, ass cheeks, and upper thighs, willing me further and deeper into her, even as my body convulses and my legs threaten to give out.

Somehow, I never fall. I don't know how she manages to do so much at once and still make it all feel so effortless and easy, but that is Selene. I am powerless in her hands and in her mouth, positively drained of every last drop of my life-force and very essence, and yet I'm still standing, still breathing, still alive. It's all Selene.

I stay there in that sublime moment as long as I possibly can until my heightened sensitivity threatens to actually give me a heart attack. Gently, I extricate myself from her mouth, shivering with the aftershocks of pleasure even as I do.

Selene gazes up at me with an expression so luxuriously decadent and self-satisfied that I'm overcome with the need to lean down and kiss her my passionate gratitude and appreciation. For maybe several whole minutes, we remain in that suspended state of shared bliss and experience, letting our kisses speak for us and speak to one another as we slowly fall back to Earth.

After a while, Selene pulls away from me, gets to her feet, and crosses to the wall. She takes a jar off one of the shelves, opens it, extracts a cigarette, replaces the jar, and lights up on a nearby candle. Her back is to me when she eventually speaks.

"I'd offer you one, but we both know you don't actually smoke."

Was it really that obvious the other day?

She moves with a leonine grace around the perimeter of the room, casually picking two pillows up from the outskirts and tossing them into the center of the space at my feet.

"Sit."

Don't mind if I do; my knees have felt like they were about to buckle for the last who-knows-how-long. I pull my pants back up and get myself all buttoned and zipped together before taking a shaky seat down on one of the pillows.

I'm fully expecting Selene to join me on the other pillow, so I'm somewhat taken aback when I realize she doesn't look like she's going to. Instead, she casually leans with her back against the wall, one ankle crossed in front of the other, smoking and considering me from across the dusky room.

"All right, Lance Lonergan. Now that that's done, tell me why you're really here."

I snort out a little laugh that I quickly suppress when I see that she's not laughing with me or really even smiling. Selene's face actually appears deathly serious and almost sinister in the flickering shadows created by the candlelight.

"Well… I… first of all, thank you—"

"Please don't thank me for that, Lance. Let's be adults about this situation, shall we?"

The end of her cigarette glows and then disappears in a cloud of smoke Selene exhales.

"Um… okay. Sure."

Why does this keep happening? One second, we're sharing a truly special moment, and the next second, she's pushing me away. It doesn't make any sense. And honestly, it's fucking maddening.

Selene is rigid against the wall, smoking in silence, evidently content to wait me out until I speak again.

"Well, to be honest with you, you're right. I did come here because I'm not particularly happy with you or with what you did to me. My agent called me this morning and told me you guys are going with Taylor Lautner for Jason."

I give her a chance to respond, but she doesn't. She just keeps on leaning, staring, smoking.

"And… well, that's fucked, to be real with you. After what we did yesterday? After what you and Martin did to me?"

"What exactly did Martin and I do to you?"

She's kidding, right?

"I mean, come on. You guys plied me with bottles of wine in the middle of the day. You made me put on some musty-ass smoking jacket like I was playing dress-up or in some weird cosplay fantasy or something. We didn't even do any actual acting or read the scene. We just… well, you know what we did."

"I do."

Her cigarette glows orange.

"So, what gives, then? How is that fair? Why do I get a callback and a personal invitation to come read for you and

Martin Schwartzman, and then all of that weird shit happens instead, and the next thing I know, you're giving the role to Taylor fucking Lautner? Like, what the fuck?"

Selene shrugs.

"It wasn't my decision. Marty's the showrunner. He has final say, of course."

"But… but how can he make that kind of call when he didn't even see me do anything? He didn't even hear me read the scene!"

"He can do anything he wants. It's his show."

"But what about all that other stuff, then? The wine, and whatever was in the wine, and the… the oral sex, and him watching? What about all that stuff?"

"What about it?"

"You don't think that's weird at all, or creepy, or inappropriate? That I got subjected to all that during a callback, and then I didn't even get the part?"

"Are you saying you only participated in all that 'stuff' to get the part?"

"No… I mean, yeah. Yes, of course I did. All that Martin stuff? Absolutely. I didn't do that just for shits and giggles, and I didn't do it for me. I did it because I thought that's what you guys wanted from me. Not all of it, though. Everything that happened between you and me, that was different. You know how I feel about you."

"Do I?"

I suddenly feel very foolish and juvenile, sitting here alone on a pillow in the middle of the floor, so I hastily clamber up to my feet to face Selene on a more level playing field.

"I think you know how I feel about you. I think if it wasn't perfectly obvious the night we first met, it sure as shit should be obvious after everything that's happened between us these past forty-eight hours."

"You know what I think, Lance?"

"What?"

She stubs her cigarette out on the wall and slinks across the room until she's completely closed the gap between us.

"I think you're a coward. I think you're too scared to really know what you feel about anything. About me, about what happened yesterday, about what's happening here today. I look at you, and I don't see the fire, the instinct, that killer instinct that separates the haves from the have-nots, the wishers and the wanters from the doers and the takers. You didn't come here to chastise me or to threaten me, and if that—that that that just happened between us—was your idea of punishing me, then you're even more hopeless than I imagined. I served myself up to you on a silver platter, and look at you. You can barely stand up still. Even now, after everything I've just said to you… I can see it in your eyes, Lance. You don't know whether to fight, fuck, freeze, or flee. That's what's missing. Until you have that, you're of no real use to me."

"You don't know me."

She takes my chin in her hand and clucks her tongue.

"Oh, but I do, my sweet, naïve, little boy. I do. I've known hundreds of your kind… thousands, maybe. Every single one of you says the same thing. You all have the same hope and the same dream, and yet so, so very few of you are actually willing to do what it takes, to put in the work, to sacrifice, to kill yourself for your art."

"You have no idea what I'd do to make it."

"Prove it."

Selene crosses to a different shelf, retrieves a small item, and then returns to stand in front of me again. I notice with a start that the item in her hand is a knife. The blade is plain enough, maybe four or five inches long, but the wooden handle is exquisitely carved and detailed with all kinds of strange runes and symbols.

As beautiful as the knife is, it doesn't change the fact that my heart is beating faster now because of it, and not in the good way it was beating before when Selene was down on her knees. I give her a nervous smile.

"What's going on?"

Selene doesn't return the smile.

"Prove it. Prove to me you're not just all bark and no bite."

"What… what do you want me to do?"

Selene raises the knife, and I take a couple rapid steps backward.

"Woah, woah! What are you doing?"

"Prove it. You say you'd do anything to make it. Well, prove it."

Is she crazy? What is she doing? Why is there a knife in her hand?

With her eyes locked on me the whole time, Selene lifts up her other hand, brings the point of the knife to the top of her palm, and drags it down her skin in one long, slow, deliberate stroke.

"Jesus fuck! What—stop! What are you doing?!"

She looks down impassively at her injured hand, squeezes her fingers into a tight, dripping fist, and then holds it out in front of her body toward me.

"So many of you are just words, words, words. You speak of action, you speak of sacrifice, you speak of 'blood, sweat, and tears.' But is that really what you give? Have you ever really given anything? Given up anything?"

Little drops of blood fall from her hand to the carpet below. One edge of the knife is stained so deep a red it appears almost black in the flickering gloom. I can't catch my breath or slow my heartbeat to save my life.

"Jesus Christ. Are you okay?"

"This isn't about me. It's about you and it's about us. There's nothing I won't do to get exactly what I want, but I already know that. Blood is a cheap price to pay when you've already surrendered your soul to doing what you love. Don't you think?"

She holds out her other hand, the one with the knife, to me as an offering.

"Come on, Lance. Show me you're a man of action, a man who knows no fear, a man who isn't afraid to bleed for his craft and his conviction. Pain is weakness leaving the body, right? And what's a bit of blood, anyway? It will come back. I promise you, it almost always does."

This situation has completely veered off the rails. The scene has gone from spooky to sexy to surreal, and I don't know how it happened so fast or what I'm supposed to do about it. Surely, she doesn't actually expect me to cut myself, does she?

But I know the answer to that question just by looking at her. There is absolutely zero chance in hell that this is all some kind of prank, joke, or psychological test she's putting me through. Selene's face is rigid. The knife is already in one hand, and the other hand has already been cut by it. There's already blood on the floor. Nothing about this exchange is empty words, ideas, or conjecture. It's all real. Too real.

Selene steps in closer. My feet are rooted to the ground.

"Don't be a coward, Lance. Don't let a woman show up a man. This is your chance to prove yourself, to prove your mettle, to prove that I was wrong about you. I want you to."

She unfurls the fingers on her maimed hand, and all of it is covered in red now. Before I have a chance to react or shrink away, she reaches down and grabs hold of my crotch. Her voice quiets some.

"Listen. I know you think this is crazy. You think that I'm crazy. And you know what? You're right. This is crazy. I am crazy."

Bloody hand and all, Selene starts rubbing me through my pants… and my body starts reacting to it, whether I want it to or not. She's right: this is crazy and she is crazy. I know I should be screaming out for help or retreating out the door as fast as my legs will carry me.

So why isn't it happening?

Selene keeps rubbing me through my pants, and I keep letting her. The shock and initial revulsion of what she's doing is fading fast. More and more of my body is reacting for me… but it's not alone. She's tapping into something else, something that was buried in my psyche so deep I never knew it existed till now. And I think it wants out.

"But you know who else was crazy? Marlon Brando. Stanley Kubrick. Jim Morrison. Virginia Woolf. Vincent van Gogh."

She picks up her speed and intensity. I fight the urge to close my eyes and succumb to the feeling she's instilling in me. Selene's voice is a fervent whisper that I can feel on my skin. That's exactly where she's going right now: beneath my skin. She's smashing through every red line I may have once held for myself, and I'm letting her because I want to.

"The list goes on and on, across every discipline and across every decade. All the great ones, the truly great ones, the real artists and the visionaries—they were all eccentrics."

Selene leans in to place her face alongside mine. Beads of sweat spring up from my palms, my underarms, my neck, my hairline. I can feel her lips on my ear. Everything is hot and trembling all over. I am soaked through.

"And they were all fearless."

She strokes me faster and faster as my climax builds rapidly. My eyes are on the knife still, but even they are barely open now. With every second that passes, more of my body and brain begins to melt. I can feel my defenses shutting down, my nerves and my reflexes laying down their arms and quietly surrendering to sensation. She is capturing every last part of me with one bold maneuver, showing no mercy and scorching the earth behind her.

Selene puts her tongue in my ear, and that just about does it.

"Lance."

Fuck. The way she says my name will be the death of me.

"Come for me, Lance."

I do. As I do, my eyes close. And as they close, I feel her let go of my cock down there and take hold of my hand up here. Then the next thing I know, I feel a sharp, sudden pain as she slices me open with the knife.

It's unlike anything I've ever experienced before. A perfect balance of pleasure and pain. Even squeezed shut, I can feel my eyes involuntarily watering as a reaction to the cut. I can't help but smile as I'm reminded of what she said earlier. Blood, sweat, and tears. Selene is taking all three from me... along with a fourth fluid while she's at it.

My smile widens as I grit my teeth. Newfound revelation comes suddenly, and I'm profoundly aware that I must surely have passed a significant test in her estimation. I am already giving her more than she bargained for. How about that?

What will she think of me now? I am smiling through the pain and savoring it as much as the pleasure, if not more so. She will see a whole new side of me from this point forward; she has no other choice.

There's a new pressure in the dark now coming from where the pain is, and though I really don't want this beautiful moment to come to an end, curiosity finally gets the better of me and forces me to open my eyes.

When I do, I see that Selene's bloodied hand is grasping my own, and she's looking at me the same way she looked at me earlier—back when it was a matter of passion, not purpose, that flamed back and forth between us.

I realize with a startling sense of clarity that I need her to always see me like this, and I squeeze the feeling of that need as hard and deep into our hands as I can.

"What is it that they say? 'Blood brothers?' I guess that doesn't quite fit us, though, does it?"

Selene's eyes glow and sparkle in the candlelight as blood seeps from our hands.

"Oh, my love. We're so much more than that now."

CHAPTER 11

"ACTION!"

I reach into the open locker and grab hold of a white t-shirt that's intentionally one size too small for me. Sooner or later I think I'm going to rip this thing, especially if Glenn keeps messing up his lines.

But that's not my problem. I shouldn't even be thinking about any of this right now, though I bet it's reading well on camera. Always keep your inner life alive, after all. That's something my high school theatre teacher taught me. He was a bit of a kook, but he was right about that one thing.

Somehow, I manage to finagle my muscles through the tight cotton orifices without tearing the seams. I run my hand through my hair a couple of times and examine my reflection in the small magnetic mirror on the inside of the locker door.

In my imagination, I'm not just seeing my own reflection staring back at me. I'm also seeing my football teammates in the showers, and I'm trying not to stare. But it has to be so hard for me to look away from them when they're in this particular state, completely naked with water running down their rippling muscled bodies and surrounded by steam.

In reality, the only thing I'm seeing other than my own reflection is a middle-aged guy with a ponytail who's wearing cargo shorts, holding a boom mic, and chewing gum. I think his name is Fred or Freddy but I'm also not completely sure, and I keep forgetting to check the call sheet. This makes it especially awkward since he's randomly decided to latch onto me and shoot the shit during breaks. Plus, he always uses my first name and frequently remarks that he thinks Lance is a cool name and that he's never met a Lance before.

But enough about Fred or Freddy or whatever the fuck his name is, and enough about reality. Gotta get back to the scene. Think about the showers, the nudity, and the secret, clandestine thrill of voyeurism…

Right on cue, I hear Glenn clear his throat from the other side of my open locker door.

Fuck—I'm caught. I slam the door shut and see him standing there wearing nothing but a white towel around his waist.

Time to play it cool. Nothing to see here. I wasn't doing anything other than fixing my hair. The thought reminds me to run my hands through it a couple more times, trying to be casual about it, but also knowing that by trying to be casual, I'll read as anything but, which is good. I'm nailing it so far, I think.

"Hey, Ben."

"Hey, Donte."

Keep your eyes up and on his face. Don't look at his shoulders, his arms, his chest, or his chiseled abs. And for God's sake, don't look down at the towel.

"You played well tonight."

"Thanks. So did you."

He flashes me the pearliest whites I've ever seen. There's

no way those are natural. He must have regular teeth whitening appointments with his dentist or something, because that smile is ridiculous. It could blind someone.

Fuck—focus, Lance.

"I'm sorry I overthrew you on that go route in the third quarter. That one was on me. Could've been an easy six with the separation you had on the DB."

"Hey, no sweat. I'm sorry I got called for that push-off in the second. I really thought it was a clean play, but I guess the zebras saw it differently."

Glenn chuckles.

"I don't know what those guys are watching out there half the time. Maybe someone ought to buy 'em glasses."

I chuckle too.

"Yeah. Or gift them LASIK."

He chuckles again.

"Nice one."

I chuckle again too.

Bleh. Who writes this shit, anyway?

Glenn leans one arm up against the lockers and brings his other hand to the fold in the towel. I make the conscious choice to steal a quick glance down there before swiftly looking back up at his face, just in time to hear him start talking again.

"So, listen. I was thinking maybe, I don't know what you're doing or what your plans are this weekend, but I was thinking maybe we could get together at some point. You know, to practice. Nothing fancy, just some pitch-and-catch. Maybe tomorrow night if you're free? Meet up at McClintock Park around seven? Whattaya say?"

"CUT!"

Macy, the first A.D., scurries over. She's trying to hide it,

I'm sure, but I think she looks even more exasperated than the last time this happened.

"Glenn, it's 'McCaskell Park,' not 'McClintock Park,' remember?"

"Fuck. My bad. I really say McClintock again?"

"You did."

Glenn slaps his hand to his forehead and groans.

"Fuuuuuck. Sorry, y'all."

Macy touches her earpiece and listens in silence for a second or two.

"All right, let's take a ten and we'll pick it back up again after."

The set comes alive with activity as crew members move hither and yon. I roll my head around on my neck a couple of times until I can hear the vertebrae crack. Maybe I should try and find a fresh cup of coffee. It's that time of day right around 3:00 pm or so where I always feel like I could go for a nap.

"My bad, bro."

Glenn has taken a seat on the wooden locker room bench. He's still wearing nothing but the towel, and even though I know he's got spandex shorts and briefs on beneath it, I find it a little odd he's sitting there half-naked when he could just as easily go throw a robe on.

"Where I grew up, we had a McClintock Park right down the street from my house. That's why I keep mixing it up."

"No worries."

While I'd certainly prefer to not do a million takes of this one short scene, I'm honestly not too perturbed about it, either. More than anything, I'm just tired. My call time was 6:00 am this morning, and even with a generous lunch break, the long hours are starting to catch up to me. I guess I'm just not used to spending so much time working, even if it is doing what I love. There's an awful lot of standing around, waiting, and killing time, too. More than I expected.

"You from around here?"

"Like, do I live in Burbank?"

"Nah, I mean are you from L.A. originally?"

I shake my head.

"I'm from a small town that I can guarantee you've never heard of unless you've lived in Oklahoma."

Glenn smiles. He really does have a movie star smile. Lucky man.

"Bro, I'm gonna be real with you: I've never even been to Oklahoma."

I laugh and take a seat next to him on the bench.

This is unexpected. Four days of being on set together and the guy's barely said two words to me that weren't typed out on a page. I don't know if he just feels guilty about flubbing his lines and that's why he's suddenly trying to be my best friend or what, but I'll take it. We're supposed to be closeted college football teammates who slowly fall in love with each other over the course of a made-for-streaming movie, so I figure the more we can actually get to know each other and get comfortable in real life, the better.

"You're not missing anything. It's not what anybody would call a vacation destination. What about you? Where are you from?"

"Michigan. I'm from a small town too, though, so we got that in common."

"How long have you been out here for?"

Glenn leans back on the bench and stretches his legs out in front of him.

"Too long, man. You won't believe it, but you know how

old I am?"

"How old?"

"I'm forty-two."

"No way."

Glenn grins.

"I shit you not, bro. I'm forty-two, and I've been out here for over twenty years now. Can you believe that?"

"You look younger than I do."

"I appreciate that. Yoga, basketball, and a good skincare routine."

"And good genes. I mean, come on."

"Black don't crack."

"Wow. Well, damn. Good for you. And here I was thinking I was the big impostor playing a guy ten years younger than me."

"Try half your age. You know what else is crazy? When I was in my thirties, they had me reading for high school kids. It's been that way ever since I got out here. Some people just never look their age, I guess. At least not on camera."

His revelations have rendered me speechless. What a bizarre industry we work in. Here we are, a thirty-year-old and a forty-two-year-old, playing a couple twenty-year-old college kids.

"How long you been out here for?"

"Um… let's see. I moved out here just about five-and-a-half years ago now, I think. Went to New York first to try and do the whole theatre thing, but suffice it to say, that did not go as planned. So, I came out here instead. To be honest with you, man, this is kind of my first big job."

Glenn's brows furrow.

"No shit. Really?"

"Really."

"Good for you, brother. You're doing a great job. I mean that too, by the way. Not gonna lie, I was worried when the guy they originally cast as Ben dropped out, but I'm glad they brought you in. You're a better actor than he was, hands-down."

I blush. Who knew Glenn was such a softie? Apparently, all you have to do is get the guy to loosen up a bit first.

"Well, thanks. I really appreciate that. I owe a casting director my firstborn child now for calling in a favor, but hopefully, this movie will blow up and it'll all be worth it."

"Which casting director?"

"Selene Blackwood. Have you ever read for her before?"

Glenn's eyes go wide as saucers.

"Bro. Selene Blackwood?"

"Yeah. You know her?"

"I know of her. Only read for her once. Once was enough for me."

Glenn sits himself back up straight, and when he does, it's as if his newfound congenial disposition had an expiration date that literally just passed.

"What do you mean? What happened?"

He glances around.

"Man, I don't like to talk shit on set because you never know who might be listening, and everybody knows everybody in this business. You can't afford to say something you might regret."

As if to prove his point, Macy appears out of nowhere and approaches us.

"We're almost ready to start back up. Take it from the same place, okay?"

We both nod and thank her, and she leaves just as quickly as she came.

Glenn stands and begins to move back toward his starting position.

"Wait. What happened? Did something bad happen?"

He truly looks conflicted, like he both wants to talk and he doesn't at the same time. I decide to press him further.

"Was it inappropriate? Did she make a pass at you?"

He glances around again, and I can see the wheels turning in his head. When he finally speaks, his voice is much lower now.

"Just be careful, man. She's fine as hell, I get it. But… just be careful."

Glenn sets his mouth in a grim line, turns on his heel, and walks briskly back to his starting position.

I want to pump him for more information—what am I supposed to do with what little he told me?—but Fred/Freddy/ponytail boom guy, Macy, and all the other production crew members are moving back into their places, so I know I'm out of time. Begrudgingly, I stand up, remove the skintight shirt, replace it in the locker, and try to clear my brain so I can get back in character.

Time to be Ben, not Lance. Anything Glenn said or anything he knows about Selene isn't a Ben problem. I just need to find another moment where it's only the two of us, get him talking, and see if he's comfortable expounding on the subject. Maybe there will be an opportunity to intercept him after we wrap and before he leaves for the day.

While I'm not exactly anxious about his cryptic words of warning, they've definitely got my curiosity piqued. What kind of history does he have with this woman? Is he telling me the full truth? What could have possibly happened in a single casting session?

Enough. Back to Ben. You're not Lance anymore. Selene

doesn't exist to you, and for that matter, neither does Glenn.

All that exists to you is your imaginary football team and the players on it. More specifically, Donte. Think about Donte, and about how you're not supposed to be thinking about Donte.

Feel all of that inside you. Let the inner life bleed through so people will see it crystallizing on camera and then at home on their screens. Experience all of the conflicting emotions, the confusion, the battle brewing inside between fear and lust.

Fear and lust. That's good. Remember that.

CHAPTER 12

It's been thirteen years since I last rode in a limo. I'll never forget the occasion—my senior prom—and it's not because of any fond memories made on the dance floor, at dinner, or while taking photos with friends.

No, the real reason I'll never forget my senior prom or the limo we rented for the special occasion was because that was the fateful night that I became a man.

Bad cliché or not, I lost my virginity that evening to my prom date. It even happened in the back of the limo itself, though not while it was in motion or while the chauffeur was in there with us. Kelsey Cox and I snuck out to the parking lot during one of the slow songs to retrieve the bottle of Southern Comfort we'd stashed behind the limo's rear right tire. I still remember the utter shock and then absolute delight we experienced together when we realized, after several pulls from the bottle, that the chauffeur had inexplicably left the car unlocked and unsupervised.

That was all we needed. In our drunken, delinquent stupor, we took it as a sign that the time was right for us. Mix booze, hormones, and adrenaline together, you'd best lock your doors. Because if you don't, horny teenagers are guaranteed to take advantage of the open invitation.

Kelsey Cox. I haven't thought about her in ages. She was a grade level below me, but man, she was sexy. Maybe it's weird to think that now since she was only seventeen at the time, but technically, so was I.

I wonder whatever happened to her? As far as I know, she was one of the rare breeds (like me) that elected not to waste the rest of her life in Hobart, and she took the first chance she could get to move as far away from there as possible. At least I think that's what happened to Kelsey.

"What are you thinking about?"

Sarah's question snaps me out of it. She's sitting next to me in the back of the limo, sipping on a glass of champagne that coincidentally matches the color of her sparkling evening dress perfectly.

"Honestly? I'm thinking about a girl named Kelsey Cox."

Sarah raises an eyebrow.

"I'm not sure I'm familiar with that one. Can you refresh my memory?"

I laugh and take a sip from my own champagne glass before answering.

"She's not one you'd be familiar with. This is from my childhood—or my adolescence, I guess. She was my date to my senior prom."

"Ahh, I see. Because of the limo?"

"Exactly."

She nods and reaches into her clutch for her compact. I don't know why she keeps checking up on herself since she looks absolutely stunning and elegant in a timeless beauty sort of way. I've already told her as much twice now—once when she first did a big reveal coming out of her bedroom, and again as we were standing on the curb outside our apartment waiting for the limo to arrive.

Sarah and I hooked up once in the early days of our acquaintanceship and then it never happened again. We were both drunk, and neither one of us claims to remember the night very well. What I do remember is that I've never felt more comfortable with someone the morning after than I did with Sarah. Instead of waking up to an empty bed, to snoring, or to snuggling, I woke up to the sound of Raiders of the Lost Ark playing on the TV and the smell of marijuana burning. We became fast friends right there and then.

Maybe once or twice after that we made out a little bit while drinking at a party or a bar, but it quickly became obvious to both of us that our relationship was better suited to being a platonic one. By the time she invited me to move into her guest room, she was basically a sister to me.

"You know I lost my virginity in a limo?"

Sarah snorts.

"Why am I not surprised?"

"I know. What a stereotype, huh?"

"I'm surprised they even had limos in Hobart."

"Pretty sure my parents had to rent one from another county. Must've cost them a fortune."

"Was Kelsey Cox worth it?"

I smile and cycle through the memories.

"You know what? She was. It was actually not bad, given all the factors in play at the time. She told me she was a virgin too, but come to think of it, I'm not sure I believe her. I think I was so caught up in what was happening—and I was pretty drunk, too, of course—that I didn't really put two-and-two together. She was awfully sure of herself and sure of what she was doing."

Sarah shrugs.

"Girls mature faster than boys. Doesn't mean she wasn't a virgin."

"Yeah… I suppose so. I don't know. She seemed really experienced, now that I think about it more. Very in control of the whole situation. Very suave."

Sarah rolls her eyes and laughs.

"So, what are you saying? You want me to feel sorry for you because, thirteen years after the fact, you think Kelsey Cox took advantage of you? I'd say you've probably balanced the scales a bit since then. Wouldn't you?"

There's an edge to her voice that is unmistakable, even though she's laughing and smiling as she says the words. Maybe the champagne's already lowering her inhibitions. By rights, Sarah certainly has more cause to complain about my dating life than anyone else on the planet, given the fact we share walls with each other. Still, if it's a topic that bothers her, she's never intimated as much to me about it before.

I decide to let it go, laugh, and look back out the window. We're almost there now anyway.

I'm just glad that we're cool again, her and I, after all the tension and the fallout from me missing her 'L.A.-versary,' as she referred to it. My apology helped, I'm sure, but probably not nearly as much as me finally paying her my portion of the overdue rent money helped (thank you, Netflix). The cherry on top was me inviting her as my date to this premiere. Once that happened, I knew I was fully in the clear and back in her good graces again.

"So, how are you feeling? Nervous? Excited? Confident?"

"A little bit of all of it, I think. Right now, it sort of feels surreal. I'm not sure it will feel real until we're in the theater and I actually see myself up on the screen. And even then, I'm not sure I'll believe it."

"You better believe it. My roomie's a real-life movie star."

I laugh and reach for the bottle of chilled champagne to refill my glass.

"I don't know about that. Still a long way away from Entourage-Adrian-Grenier-level."

Sarah extends her glass for a top-off.

"You're a hell of a lot closer now than you were before, though. Look at you: dressed in a (rented) tuxedo, riding in a (rented) limo—"

"Accompanied by a (rented) date."

"Wow, you're paying me for the pleasure of my company tonight, too? This really is my lucky day."

We both share a laugh. This is good for us. It's good for both of us, on so many levels.

Sarah lays a hand on my arm.

"But seriously, though. All jokes aside, this is a really big deal, and it's only the beginning. I couldn't be prouder of you. Thank you so much for inviting me to tag along so I can begin my journey of riding your coattails to fame and fortune."

I put one hand on top of hers and raise my glass in the other.

"I couldn't imagine asking anyone else. Thanks for being here for me tonight… and for just always being there for me in general. You're the best, you know that?"

She raises her glass.

"I do know that, but it never hurts to hear it sometimes. Especially from you. Love you."

I clink my champagne flute against hers.

"Love you too."

We drink.

A few moments later, the car slows to a halt. I can see

the modest theater that the production company has rented for this event right outside my window, and my heart races at the sight of the movie title up on the big marquee. For a second, I imagine what it would be like to see my name up there as well, but then I remind myself that such a thing doesn't really happen anymore in the modern cinema-going age, even if you're Tom Cruise or Brad Pitt.

Thankfully, some golden age Hollywood traditions are here to stay, including a red carpet, lights, cameras, and photographers, all of which are on hand tonight. It's not the Oscars or the Emmys of course, and I know it's nowhere near the extravagant affair of a big budget, studio tentpole premiere on Hollywood Boulevard, but it's undeniably progress and an important step forward for a kid who's been dreaming of being a part of this kind of night for decades now.

Sarah squeezes my hand.

"Should we down this and get out there?"

"Absolutely."

We finish our champagne quickly. Sarah takes out her compact to reapply her lipstick and review her overall reflection one last time as I place our empty glasses next to the bottle in the ice bucket. I wait patiently for her to kiss her lips together a couple of times and stow the compact away in her clutch.

"You look absolutely beautiful. Are you ready?"

Her smile is infectious.

"Are you?"

"Let's do it."

I rap my knuckles on the window glass to let the driver know we're ready to exit, and he pulls the door open for us so we can step out and onto the curb.

There's a moment where I expect an excited murmur to rise up amongst the crowd of onlookers as they realize who I am, naturally followed by a barrage of flashing cameras and proffered microphones as the paparazzi and red-carpet reporters descend on me for photographs and interviews.

It doesn't happen, of course, because I'm not a name or even a face yet. I have a supporting role in a glorified Hallmark or Lifetime movie that just so happens to be on Netflix.

But I remind myself of what Sarah said in the limo, and she's right. This is a huge step for me. It may not be my 'big break,' but it's easily the biggest thing I've done yet. And there's certainly something to be said for that.

I turn to check in with Sarah. Her face says it all: this is beyond any of her wildest dreams. For someone like her who's completely outside the industry, this must feel like the Academy Awards. She's certainly dressed the part.

Sarah's eyes drift from the action on the carpet back to me, and she mouths a silent 'wow.' I grin at her and extend my arm like a true gentleman. Together, we step off the curb and walk onto the red carpet.

There's a woman with an earpiece and a walkie-talkie who appears to be in charge of this whole operation, at least based on the way she's politely but firmly directing all the foot traffic outside the theater. She sees us coming and holds up her palm to stop us, then gives a signal to the photographers that they're clear to snap photos of an attractive middle-aged couple posing in front of a step and repeat. I have no idea who they are or what their affiliation is to this movie.

Sarah whispers in my ear and lightly squeezes my arm.

"Do you know either of them?"

I shake my head and whisper back.

"I don't know any of these people."

We stand in silence, smiling and trying to look casual and comfortable, as we wait for the event coordinator woman to wave us ahead.

When she finally does, we shuffle forward and allow her to position us on either side of a small 'X' on the carpet made of neon green tape. She doesn't greet us, introduce herself, or make any pretense of small-talk; she just launches right into giving us the proper marching orders to keep the night running smoothly and on schedule.

When she's satisfied with our positioning, she steps back and gives her signal to the photographers. I have the asinine thought that she didn't tell us 'say cheese,' and that's when the cameras start going off.

She lets us try a couple different poses, and then she gently asks Sarah to step aside so they can get a few solo shots of just me. It's the first moment that I realize at least one person here has recognized me and knows who I am, even if it's just the event coordinator. I give my most winsome smile to the photographers and try to look like how I imagine a movie star should look.

And then, just like that, it's over, and we're done with this portion of the evening. The coordinator herds me over to Sarah and moves us along so she can work with the next person or people of interest arriving on the scene. I offer my arm back to Sarah as we cross what's left of the red carpet in silence and enter the theater through a door that's been propped open with a simple rubber stopper.

Sarah stops suddenly in the middle of the lobby.

"All right, be honest with me. Is it totally inappropriate to get popcorn at a premiere? I don't know what the rules are."

I laugh and shrug.

"Beats me. This is my first time too, you know."

"Tonight's Kelsey Cox all over again for you, huh?"

I playfully give her a light hip check.

"You gotta lay off Kelsey Cox. Don't get me all hot and bothered on my big night."

"Eww. She's a minor, Lance."

"She's at least twenty-nine now! Don't make me feel weird about it. You're the weird one who wants to eat popcorn in an evening gown at a Hollywood premiere."

Sarah taps her index finger on the tip of my nose.

"And you're the pedophile who I know will eat half of it too if I get some, so let's do it."

We're halfway up to the concession counter when a familiar voice stops me dead in my tracks.

"My, don't you look dashing this evening, Lance Lonergan."

It's actually remarkable what just the sound of her voice does to me. Every muscle in my system tenses up and goes perfectly still like a frozen lake in winter.

Except for my heart, of course. True to past precedent, that organ ratchets immediately into a frenzied overdrive, so much so that I swear I can actually hear it smacking against my rib cage all the way up in my ears, which have become so hot so fast that I fully expect steam to come out of them any second now.

Somehow, I manage to will my body into motion. Really, Sarah's more responsible for successfully getting us turned around, since she obviously has no problem spinning to see who this new stranger is that's talking to us.

Am I surprised to see Selene at this event tonight? One-thousand-percent yes.

Am I surprised to find myself profoundly, undeniably,

and hopelessly spellbound by her appearance at said event? One-thousand-percent no.

Selene is far too gorgeous for this quaint, ordinary environment. She's wearing a red sleeveless satin dress that's held up by impossibly skinny straps at her shoulders. The deep neckline of the dress ends just above her navel and leaves precious little to the imagination—not that I need mine to fantasize about what lies beneath the clinging fabric.

Most distracting of all are two perilously high slits in the dress that rise all the way up to her hips, baring both of her long legs in their full breathtaking splendor as she smoothly approaches us from the door.

Some women walk like they've been in heels since childbirth, and Selene is one of those women. Her stride is perfectly sure and natural, even in her tall, rose gold stilettos with their thin, coiling, snake-like straps that wrap and climb past her ankles all the way up to the middle of her calves.

Those rose gold shoes match her shiny, tastefully-understated earrings just as seamlessly as the vibrant red dress matches her lipstick, her fingernails, and her toenails. Selene's sage-colored eyes are accentuated by a heavier amount of eyeshadow and liner than I'm used to seeing on her, and it makes them pop even more than normal. Her hair cascades down to her shoulder blades in perfectly-styled waves that gleam and play hide-and-seek with the lighting in here. How does it do that? For that matter, how does any of her even happen to begin with?

"Hello. I'm Sarah."

Thank God one of us still knows how to function like a human being. Sarah unhooks herself from my arm, reaches out her hand, and gives Selene a friendly smile. Selene returns the smile and shakes her hand.

"And you, Sarah, you look positively ravishing. What a stunner. Now, are you a sister, a friend, or a girlfriend? Or a fiancé? Or a wife?"

Sarah laughs.

"None of the above, actually. Roommate."

"Well, hopefully you're also at least a friend. Otherwise, it doesn't sound like much of a pleasant living situation."

"Yes, whoops, duh, ha ha—we're friends too, of course."

The two women smile at each other.

I still can't wrap my mind around which astounds me more: that Selene Blackwood is here in the first place, or that Selene Blackwood is here and she looks like that. Someone needs to call a paramedic to help me get my jaw up off the floor.

I'm distantly aware that I'm supposed to be doing something right now, but I can't for the life of me remember what it is, and I don't really give a damn.

Sarah clears her throat and combs a few fingers through her hair.

"I'm sorry, and you are?"

Selene covers her heart with her hands, which of course immediately zeroes in my entire focus on her chest. Sorry, not sorry. Jesus Christ, though, that chest...

"No, I'm sorry, how clumsy of me."

Clumsy and Selene are not two words I would ever put together.

"I'm Selene Blackwood. Should we shake hands again?"

They do, and Selene clasps Sarah's hand between both of hers.

"Your skin is so soft. And that scent, what an interesting choice..."

She brings Sarah's hand a bit closer to her face before

releasing it.

"Lemongrass?"

"That's right. You've got a good nose."

"I've got a nose for herbs and an eye for talent. That's how I know your roommate/friend over here. I suppose you could say that I discovered him."

Sarah's demeanor lightens in an instant.

"Oh! Do you work at his agency?"

Selene turns toward me, the faintest pout playing on her face.

"You haven't told her anything about me, have you?"

I swallow hard to force life back into my throat.

"I… Sarah, Selene is a casting director."

"Oh. So, you're the one who cast the film then!"

Selene's lip twitches ever so slightly. She's still staring hard at me, so I try clearing my throat and hitting my fist against my chest a couple quick times to shake off the stupor.

"Excuse me. She didn't cast the film, but she's friends with the man who did. And she's the one who set up the meeting, and the one who put in a good word for me. Basically, if it weren't for her, none of this would have happened."

Selene's red-carpet-worthy smile returns in all its glory and magnificence.

"Now he's being too modest."

Mercifully, she pivots her smoldering radiance back onto Sarah.

"All I did was make a simple phone call. Your roommate/ friend here did the rest. He's really quite talented and motivated when he wants to be. Do you know that?"

"I do. I'm so excited to see him in action tonight."

"As am I."

Is this silence awkward or am I only imagining that it is?

My whole equilibrium is in tatters, so I can't really tell.

Ever reliable in a social situation, Sarah gallops in to the rescue.

"We were just about to get some popcorn before the movie starts. Do you want to join us?"

Again, Selene folds her hands over her chest. And again, my eyes go straight to her chest.

"No, thank you. That's very kind of you, but I should probably go find a good seat."

She extends her hand for Sarah and lets a girlish laugh escape from her lips. Those lips.

"Third time's the charm, as they say. I'm so pleased I had the opportunity to meet you, Sarah. I had no idea Lance kept close company with such a truly beautiful woman."

"Oh, well, thank you. Same to you."

Shakily, I offer up my sweaty hand to her, but Selene ignores it and goes in for a hug instead. I hold my breath as I feel her body press up against mine in all the right and wrong places, and then there's a wisp of hot air tickling my neck and my chin as she moves in to lay a soft, lingering kiss on my cheek. There are firecrackers exploding in my bones and in my blood right now.

"See you on the other side, my love."

She leaves us in her wake, and we both watch her go until the last visions of red have melted into the shadowy darkness of the auditorium hallway.

"Holy shit."

Sarah's still looking after her when she finally speaks to break the spell. I guess it's nice in a way to know that it's not just me. Judging by the mesmerized, almost wistful gaze coming from my roommate and the way that she's absentmindedly combing her fingers through her hair,

Sarah's not immune to the Selene Blackwood effect either.

She finally turns to face me.

"I can't believe she's a casting director. She should be the one starring in the movies."

"I know, right?"

Sarah gives me a look.

"Just be smart, okay?"

"What does that mean?"

"You know exactly what that means. Don't do something stupid and screw up your career."

"What are you talking about?"

"In other words, keep it in your pants, Casanova. Don't shit where you eat."

I close my mouth and try to look appalled by the idea.

"Come on. Give me more credit than that."

"You come on. I know you better than you know yourself."

I roll my eyes and guide her toward the concession counter.

"Okay, all right. Let's get you an extra-large popcorn, extra butter and extra salt, just like you like it. I know you better than you know yourself, too, you know."

Sarah rubs her hands together excitedly.

"Now we're talking. This night just keeps getting better and better."

I couldn't agree more.

CHAPTER 13

Roughly ninety minutes later, I'm alone in the men's restroom on the second floor of the indie cinema house, and all I can keep doing is splashing water over my face and staring at my own reflection in the mirror above the sink.

That… didn't… suck. Far from it, actually. I don't know why I'm so surprised, and I don't know what I fully expected, but I do know it wasn't that.

I'd tried my best to mentally prepare myself for a whole range of potential outcomes, but the most likely ones I kept coming back to were usually the same: disappointment, embarrassment, shame, despair, apathy, indifference. When the lights finally began to dim in the theater, if you'd held a gun to my head and demanded a final prediction of how I thought it would all turn out, I'd have probably guessed the only thing that would suck more than my performance would be the movie itself.

But I would have been wrong. Dead wrong. About all of it.

Against all odds, the movie was actually… good? I don't know how, considering the script I originally read was absolute dogshit. There must have been some significant rewrites along the way. Either that, or the director decided to give her cast more leeway and artistic license to improvise and ad lib at will, because the dialogue was shockingly natural and even pretty jazzy at times. Nowhere near what I first read on the page, that's for sure.

Additionally, the film was shot better than I expected, the editor deserved a fucking medal for the way she spliced it all together, and most of the acting performances—not all, but most—were surprisingly believable for a movie that just as easily could have been broken down and repurposed as a season arc for a daytime soap opera.

I thought Glenn was particularly excellent as Donte, the tortured star college quarterback who decides to finally come out to his family, his coaches, and his fans. Turns out the man can do a whole lot more on screen than just pretend he's half his age.

More than anything—and most importantly to me, of course—I was good. I was very good. The audience was silent during all of my scenes, and I could feel the energy of the theater. People were listening, really listening, to what I had to say as Ben. I could see my inner life happening on screen, and I could practically read the thoughts running behind my eyes in my close-ups.

No one's ever going to be as harsh a critic on you as you will be on yourself, but I routinely found myself both relieved and pleasantly surprised during my early appearances in the film. Later on, as I grew more relaxed in my movie theater seat, certain moments even became riveting for me, all personal bias aside.

I knew I wasn't alone in thinking so, either. Sarah would sit in perfect stillness during each of my scenes until the very end, not even daring to dip her fingers into our popcorn bucket or to crunch anything that had already found its way into her mouth. And then, as soon as the scene was over or the movie cut to something else, she'd turn in her seat and give me a subtle but meaningful look, the likes of which I'd never seen from her before, usually punctuated by a quick, hard squeeze of my knee, and then she'd go right back to being sucked into the story on the screen.

When the movie was over, the crowd applauded vigorously. It wasn't an instantaneous standing ovation, but when the first few people got up to their feet, the rest of the auditorium followed not long after. There's an inherent bias, of course, since most of the crowd was comprised of the people who worked on the picture in some capacity—or their friends or family—but still, a standing O is a standing O.

Even when the director stood up and announced she was going to conduct a brief talkback in five minutes after a quick bathroom break, not a single soul ended up ducking out or missing it. Every person in the theater sat in respectful silence and listened to her speak eloquently about what this film meant to her and her family, and then there was no shortage of questions asked once the floor was opened up to a short Q&A.

The event coordinator for the evening finally had to intercept the microphone in the audience to let everyone know that although we unfortunately needed to wrap things up here at the theater, everyone was welcome to attend the premiere afterparty at a second location, a lounge not far up the street in Hollywood.

I pull out my phone and send Sarah a quick text letting her know I might be a minute because I'm having some stomach problems.

It's not entirely untrue. I was already pretty anxious and revved up on the way here, and then unexpectedly running into Selene in the lobby beforehand turned up the dial even further on both my physiological and psychological states. Throw in half a bottle of champagne and half a bucket of over-buttered, over-salted popcorn, mix in the fact I didn't have any dinner, and then add in the maelstrom of emotions that accompanied seeing myself actually acting on the big screen, and it's really no wonder I feel like I might vomit.

Speaking of vomit, my phone buzzes and reveals Sarah's response to my text: the barfing face emoji. It makes me smile despite myself.

She couldn't stop gushing about how proud she was of me after the credits finished and the lights came up, and she was even more gracious and effusive with her praise every time we found ourselves in conversation with another theater guest on the way out of the auditorium and in the cinema lobby. Sarah is the perfect hype woman. I have to remember to bring her to all my future premieres, assuming I'm not dating Zendaya or someone by that point.

That's another thought that makes me smile. Maybe the reason I've been so jaded and uninterested in dating this past year or so is because I've been subconsciously saving myself for an A-list romance the whole time.

I look up in the mirror's reflection at the sound of the bathroom door opening and freeze.

"You're wasting water… again."

Every time and every place that I least expect to encounter her, that's when and where Selene appears, as if by magic. How does she do it?

I turn the faucet off.

"What are you doing in here?"

She leans against the doorframe. It shouldn't be physically possible to make a movie theater men's bathroom doorway a glamorous or seductive tableau, but somehow, Selene manages to pull all that off and then some. Because of course she does.

"I might ask you the same thing. You've been up here a while now."

My hands and face are still dripping. I can feel moisture on the starchy white collar of my dress shirt, and I hope that it's just sink water and not sweat. The air conditioning suddenly seems to have cut off in here. Or maybe I'm just imagining that it has. Who knows? Maybe the A/C wasn't on to begin with. I honestly have no idea.

Chalk it all up to the Selene Blackwood effect. Everything is probably perfectly normal and perfectly natural. I just need to keep my cool for once in my life around this woman.

"Yeah, I'm not feeling so good, actually."

Selene's face morphs into genuine concern as she steps fully into the room, letting the bathroom door close gently behind her.

"Oh, no. What's wrong?"

I'd sooner actually shit my pants and ruin this tuxedo than tell this perfect specimen that I'm currently suffering gastrointestinal pains.

"Nothing, really. I just needed to take a quick break. Get away from the crowd, you know?"

With every step of a shiny stiletto and every new baring of a long, toned, beautiful leg between the curtained slits of her provocative red dress, she shortens the distance between us and raises the temperature in the room, air conditioning be damned.

"I totally get it. Crowds have never been my scene,

either. I prefer more personal, intimate conversations and connections. Don't you?"

There's something about the added benefit of the dark eyeliner and smoky eyeshadow she's wearing tonight that makes her grey-green eyes even more hypnotic than they usually are… which is really saying something. The closer she gets, the more alluring they become. Even her eyebrows look different tonight. I feel both enticed and challenged by them. And maybe it's the combo of the red lipstick with the red dress, but her smile seems especially mischievous, too. Like she's up to no good.

Honestly, her whole face just radiates sex. I mean, it does that normally without her even trying. But tonight, it sort of feels like she's trying. And I am in no way prepared for that.

She is right behind me now. I can see her in the mirror, and I can literally feel her presence or her aura or whatever the fuck that is right behind me, and it's enveloping. How do you describe suffocating in a good way? That's what this feels like. I could get lost in her forever.

My eyes seem to close of their own volition when I feel Selene's hands on my shoulders.

"I meant what I said earlier. You do look very dashing in your tux."

She starts slowly massaging the muscles there that lead up to my neck. Her fingers are surprisingly strong, but it's far from painful. If anything, it's exactly what I need right now, even if I didn't know I needed it.

"Though I bet you'd look very dashing even without your tux."

Her hands have found their way up to the bare skin above my collar. She kneads away little knots of tension I didn't know existed until this very moment. How is it that she knows her way around my body so well? Everywhere she goes, there is simultaneous relief and pleasure. Even my stomach problems seem to have altogether vanished without a trace.

"Breathe, Lance. You always forget to breathe around me."

Oxygen comes rushing back in through my nostrils as my lungs expand. That's another thing I didn't even realize. How many times have I held my breath around her without even knowing it? She just does things to me.

Selene laughs and keeps massaging away the pain, the tension, the reluctance. Reality itself begins to fade into the background under the intense glaring power of her energy.

"What would you do without me?"

Collapse and die. Wither up into a teeny, tiny ball and roll away into a storm drain like a piece of trash. Fade into nothingness. Fall away from being. Never feel anything, ever, ever again.

She brings her nails into it, scratching and sliding them around my vertebrae and up through my hair. Inevitably, my brain reminisces with a hedonistic indulgence on the memory of her nails all over my skull when my face was buried deep between her thighs.

Christ, it's like Pavlov's dogs now. I'll never not think of Selene Blackwood's vagina when someone scratches my head. I'm actually really okay with that association, though.

Her fingers find their way around to my face, and she begins rubbing my temples. Now I'm viscerally experiencing the warmth and pressure of her body behind mine as well. I can feel her arms resting on the outside of my arms. Even more excitingly, I can feel the fullness of her breasts pressed up flat against my back.

"Can I tell you a secret?"

You can tell me anything. I won't ever tell a soul. You can trust me. I would do anything for you.

"Lance."

"Yes?"

"Can I tell you a secret?"

"You can tell me anything."

There's a soft, moist, hotness at my right ear, and I know even with my eyes closed that Selene is leaning in there with her perfect fucking lips. I remind myself to keep breathing, even as I want to quiet every muscle and organ in my body so that I can be completely still, silent, and ready to receive in absolute totality whatever miracle of a message she deigns to bestow on me.

Her voice is a whisper that licks my ear like a lollipop.

"You were incredible tonight."

If my heart was racing before, it's flying now.

"Seriously. From the moment I first met you, I knew that you were special."

She thinks I'm special. Selene Blackwood, the great casting director, thinks I'm special. I've proven myself to her. At last, she realizes what I'm capable of. She underestimated me, like everyone else has always underestimated and misunderstood me, but now she knows. Who cares what my parents, my relatives, or my friends think. They don't get it. I'm special. She gets it. Selene understands. I'm going places. I have what it takes.

"But tonight, seeing you in your element, watching you work…"

She moves her fingers in tighter circles on the hinges of my jaw. Her voice is warm honey oozing down and dripping into the belly of my soul.

"…I realized just how special you truly are. Lance…"

I shiver at the way she says my name. Every. Damn. Time.

"…you are a luminescent talent. That flaky, indescribable thing we call acting—real acting—that 'it factor,' that powerful, sheer, raw magnetism that cannot be denied… you have it."

Selene runs her fingernails down my throat to the knot of my necktie as my ego does backflips and my soul sings out to the heavens.

"Let me cultivate it. Every artist needs a patron saint. Let me be yours."

She loosens the knot, and suddenly, I can breathe like I've never breathed before. It's easy now. Her fingers dip between the buttons of my shirt, and I get goosebumps as I feel Selene on the bare skin of my chest.

"You don't wear a necklace or a chain?"

The question is just unexpected enough that my eyelids flicker open. I see myself in the mirror and I can feel Selene pressed up against me from behind. There's still a wet heat at my ear, some lingering phantom sensation from when her lips were last there, even though they're gone in the reflection because her face is nowhere to be seen. Her hands are still on my chest though, I can feel them there, with her fingers slid under the fabric and her nails on my skin. But I can't see them in the reflection. In the mirror, I don't see her hands or her arms or any part of her at all.

Wait, what?

"It doesn't matter."

She's right. It doesn't matter. My eyelids flutter shut again, and I'm aware that she has her hand over my heart, and it's slowing down finally, and there's an instinctual sense of knowing that Selene is the person responsible for this reaction. Whether consciously or unconsciously, she controls the speed and direction of my every blood flow. She holds my heart in the palm of her hand.

"Lance."

"Yes?"

"I do need something from you, though."

"Anything."

"How about this?"

She still has one hand on my heart, but I can feel her other hand has taken hold of my own hand. I open my eyes, and Selene is there in the reflection, because of course she is because that's only natural, just behind me and to the side, one arm wrapped around my torso with that hand tucked between the buttons of my shirt, all exactly as expected.

Her other arm and hand shadow my own arm and hand, except all the fingers of her hand are now touching a small silver band that I wear around my finger.

"My ring?"

"Does it mean something to you?"

Yes and no.

Yes, my grandfather willed it to me upon his death. And yes, he was and remains to this day the only member of my whole family who ever really supported my interest in the arts and expressed any modicum of confidence in my ability to make it as an actor in Los Angeles.

But also, no, it's just a stupid Claddagh ring. It's about as trivial and hackneyed as those dumb half-heart necklaces that couples or best friends purchase because they're supposed to symbolize that their hearts are only truly complete when they're both together and can join their pieces as one. I'm also not even sure if the ring is real silver, anyway.

"Do you want it?"

"Are you giving it to me?"

It's just a ring, a thing, an object. Material possessions don't matter. Fame, legacy, immortality… those are all forever. If my grandfather was still alive today and in my shoes, he'd give it to her in a heartbeat. The man was married three times and divorced three times. If anyone had a weakness for the opposite sex, it was him. He'd have willed his entire estate to Selene if he met her.

"If you want it, it's yours."

Selene's fingers tighten on the ring and on my chest as her body sinks deeper into mine.

"I want it."

Given the situation, it's a remarkably easy action for me to take, removing the ring from my finger and placing it in her waiting open palm. I don't think twice about it. Seeing the way her molten eyes ignite and the smile that spreads across her face in the mirror is all reward enough for such a minor sacrifice.

"Lance."

I shiver.

"Yes?"

"Thank you."

I should be thanking her for the way she makes me feel all over.

Besides, what I said before to Sarah was true. None of this would have been remotely possible without Selene. Without her, I never would have received an invitation to audition for this film's casting director. She's the one who put in a good word for me. Who knows how much she fought just so I could have this opportunity to begin with? She's the one who made the greater sacrifice. And she did it all for me.

She slides the ring onto her finger in the mirror.

"You have no idea what's still to come. Your future—our future—is infinite. Every wish and every dream you've ever had…"

Selene brings her delicious mouth closer to my neck again and purrs into my ear.

"…we will make them all come true. Together."

She plants the softest, slowest kiss imaginable behind my earlobe. It takes all my willpower just to keep my eyes open, but I have to. I want to see her—I want to behold this magical, mysterious goddess of a woman in all her glory and power. Because I worry that if I close my eyes again, even if only for a second, she will disappear again, she will leave me here with a broken heart, a broken body, a broken soul. I am addicted to her. Without Selene, I forget to breathe, to swallow, to think, to act.

Selene trails kisses down the back of my neck, and now both of her hands are working on the outside of my shirt, unbuttoning and undoing every last pretense of defense I ever had against her charms. I reach my hands back behind me in the mirror and find her body, and when I do, I dig my fingers into her hips, and she moans in response.

Fuck, I love to hear her make that sound. If I had to pick only one sound to hear for the rest of my life, it might be Selene's moan. That, or the sound her voice makes when she says my name. Either one of those could last me a lifetime.

I reach my hands even further back so I can take a firm hold of her ass, and I pull her forward so that her whole body is against me now. Not just her chest, spectacular even as that is alone. Feeling her beneath the sheer silk fabric of the dress, I'm overcome by the need to be as close as possible to what I have in my fingers. Touching is not enough. Nothing is ever enough with Selene.

I want to sink my teeth into her ass cheeks and bite the supple muscles beneath the skin there like I'm eating a fucking peach or an apple. In my mind, I can hear Selene whisper 'harder,' so that's what I do in my mental fantasy… and it's also what my cock gets here and now in reality. I want to squeeze and caress and spank and bite and lick and kiss and suck and tongue her ass all over. It will never look the same again after I'm done with it, which I never will be, because now it's mine forever.

Selene has made devastatingly quick work of my formal attire this evening. At this rate, I'll be lucky if I can still return this tuxedo rental in one piece, but that's the last thing I care about right now. She keeps teasing me, walking her fingers along my waist, dipping a nail below the pants line here, toying with the belt buckle there.

Meanwhile, my shirt is open, my tie is undone, and my jacket is rumpled. Christ, my whole being is rumpled. Selene has run roughshod over me, and I don't know how I ever possibly thought it was fun or fulfilling to fuck any other girl. I am born anew every time we are together. Every wish and every dream, she is going to make them all come true. And I believe her with all my soul.

As unbelievable as it always is to have her magnificent ass right there and right here in my hands, I know that I can do more for her. I want to do it for her and I want to give her more, but if I'm honest with myself, I also want it for me.

So, without another second's hesitation, I slide my hands forward around the silken arches of her wide, sloping, luscious hips, savoring every piece and parcel of the journey as I go along.

Thanks to those soaring high slits in her dress, it's not hard to find the way to my final destination, even with her pressed up flush against my body, even with her behind me, and even with her only barely visible now in the mirror's reflection. I can feel the heat emanating from beneath her dress, and that is more than enough to guide me. Like moths to the flame, my fingers move with a thirsting fervor toward their greatest desire and their highest purpose.

Selene is already wet for me, because of course she is. This is what we do to each other. It's been this way with us since the very beginning, and now I know that it will always be this way as well. Our future is infinite, that's what she said. And it is. Until the end of time, I will make her wet.

I keep my left thumb and the heel of that hand active on her clit while I hook two fingers of my right hand into her pussy and find her G-spot. When I do, Selene starts to quiver in my hands, and all of the activity she'd previously been orchestrating on me comes to a sudden, satisfying halt.

That's good—that's what I wanted to have happen. I can't stop thinking about everything I want to give her. She has already given me so much more than anyone else ever has, and on every level: professionally, personally, sexually. All I ever needed was the right opportunity, and she delivered for me, just as she said she would. Now it's my turn to deliver for her.

Abruptly, I decide to switch positions so I can get better leverage—and a better view. Some part of my brain lights up and remembers what she said back in her office that day. She almost seemed to goad me—she's done that a few times now, actually—like she wanted me to take charge and be more assertive, aggressive, and dominant with her. 'Punish me,' she said that day. And while I'll never forget what it felt like to have her take me in her mouth for the very first time, I certainly did not 'punish' her. I was anything but a dominant in that situation as it enfolded in real-time.

Now's my chance to change that. It's never too late to rewrite the narrative. In the eyes of my family and all those other fools I grew up with, I was just another living, breathing stereotype: the starving artist. By profession, I was more banquet server than working actor, at least in the eyes of them.

But not anymore. I'm not who they thought I was or who they thought I'd become. Because of her, I'm so much more than that now. I'm becoming my highest self, the kind of winner who takes what he wants and brooks no resistance.

So, fuck them, all the haters and the doubters. Fuck them all. Look who's getting the last laugh now.

I take what I want, moving quickly and forcefully so I can catch Selene by surprise, which I do. She actually gasps as I roll out from in front of her, spin her around, grab her midsection, and lift her up onto the bathroom countertop in one smooth stroke.

Her knees bend and poke out from between the dress slits. As much as I'd love to go slow and taste every last centimeter of her freshly-exposed legs, I need to uncover far more precious terrain than that right this very moment. Without another second's hesitation, I wrap the center fold of the fabric in a tight fist and part it to the side so I can fully view her there in front of me, glistening and inviting.

I've seen, touched, tasted, and fucked more than my fair share of pussies over the past thirty years, but nothing compares to Selene's. Hers is the queen mother of the universe, the gold standard by which all others should be gaged, the kind of vagina you want to immortalize for the rest of time and human existence in a sculpture or a song. It never ceases to both amaze and astound, to make me feel unworthy but simultaneously oh so very special, oh so very lucky, and oh so very blessed that at least in this particular time and in this particular place, it can be mine.

Here and now, I devour her. Every squeal and stuttering breath she makes from up above is just another signpost to guide me along the way and egg me on further. As is fast becoming habitual, her hands are all over my head, gripping me firmly and pressing me further and deeper into her as I feel her nails drag along my scalp and her fingers squeeze my skull between them.

Meanwhile, here in front of me, Selene is so fucking wet, so fucking juicy, and getting more so by the second.

"I—I can't take it anymore…"

I'm only vaguely aware of her soft, panting voice coming from somewhere high and distant in the ether. It's not important to me now. In this very instant, the only thing that matters to me in my whole entire life is to make her come. I want her to explode like a geyser, to douse and drench me until her voice goes from a gasping tremble to a shrill scream and her legs won't stop shaking for another thirty minutes minimum.

"Fuck… FUCK… I'm coming!"

She doesn't need to tell me because I already know. Not only do I have a front-row seat, but I am also in the driver's seat, the catalyst of her conversion.

Selene is gasping for air. When she's finally able to speak again, she sounds desperate.

"Lance… Lance, I need you to fuck me."

This isn't about her, though; this is about me now. I'm delivering for her, but I'm also taking charge and controlling the situation. She's not calling the shots this time. That day in her office, she didn't just suck my cock—she sucked my whole soul away from me, it felt like, but in the best way possible.

Now it's my turn to repay the favor. I'm far from finished with her. I am going to drink up her essence until it flows through my veins. Until she has nothing left to give and it feels so good for her that she has to beg me to stop before her heart explodes into a million sharp, sparkling pieces.

"Come here."

She tries to pull me up, but I resist and double down because I'm not done yet.

"Fuuuuuuuck…"

Selene releases me as I begin to sense the faint early stages of another orgasm building up inside of her. When my hands aren't being used on her pussy, they're roaming all up and down her legs and along her stomach beneath her dress, and I can feel her muscles twitching once again as her breathing intensifies and speeds up.

"I want you inside me."

"I am inside you."

Somehow, I manage to get the words out as my lips buzz against her lower lips.

Selene moans and wraps her legs around me in a tight knot. I can feel their tremors growing ever more pronounced and violent against my body. She's getting close again.

"More… Lance… I want more…"

I move two fingers into her and rub right where I know she needs me, my thumb doing the same but on her clit. For a second, Selene's legs shoot out on either side of me like lightning bolts, and then they're back again, wrapping around my shoulder blades and hooking at the ankles. If I know her body—and I'm beginning to think I really do— she will come a second time any moment now, and when she does, it will be so much greater and more rewarding than the first time, and for the both of us.

Her legs squeeze me even tighter, and now her fingers slide down my jaw and grasp me beneath the chin, pulling upward.

"I need you to fuck me."

"Not until you come first."

I pause just long enough to gaze up at her mischievously.

"You want my cock, you need to earn it."

Selene meets my eyes. But when she does, her face catches me off-guard. The expression there isn't one of pleasure, lust, or excitement—it actually looks a bit like anger.

"I said: I need you to fuck me. Now."

Something happens. There's a sudden tingling feeling in my joints and muscles, almost like an itch or a spasm.

My first thought is that this is a terrible time for my body to cramp up, especially with Selene so close to a second climax. I fight the sensation mentally for a few seconds, and then I decide to try and ignore it altogether in the hopes that it will just fade away into the background.

It doesn't, though. The more I try to block it out, the stronger it grows. Wrestling with it head-on doesn't seem to be working, either. The tingling reaches a higher frequency that borders on outright pain.

It's no longer just a physical sensation, whether phantom or not. There's a psychological component to it now that wasn't there before. My brain is telling me—no, it's ordering me, actually—to stand up, pull my cock out, and fuck her as she told me to do. I'm actually hurting myself now even more, simply by resisting these forces.

Who knew that I'd end up being the one shaking all over?

Inch by inch, my spine straightens as bones, muscles,

ligaments, and tendons grind and grab ahold of one another to bring me back upright, with or without my consent. My hands drift away from Selene's body on the counter until they are finally drawn to the fly of my tuxedo pants. I can feel my fingers trembling as they slide the zipper down, down, down…

And all the while, Selene's aura seems to glow triumphantly and grow stronger, until it becomes my aura too, and I'm aware of this somehow and on some level, that she has brought me both to her and into her, metaphysically first, and soon to be physically in the literal sense, as well. Stranger still, I'm aware that she wants me to be aware—she wants me to know what is happening and who is making it happen—before she gives me to herself.

The door opens behind me in the mirror's reflection, and I can only watch helplessly as a procession of emotional reactions play out over Sarah's face: first, timid curiosity; then, shocked realization; and finally, instant outrage. Her skin turns a completely different color, though I'm at a loss to say whether that's more a manifestation of her embarrassment or her fury. She could be shaking her head or she could just be trembling so violently it only appears like she is. Before I can say or do anything though, she spins on her heel and disappears as the door closes behind her.

"Sarah…"

It's only now—now that she's gone—that I can speak again. I turn back to Selene accusingly, and I'm surprised to find her wearing a similar expression to how I'm feeling right now.

"Just a roommate/friend, huh?"

She can't be serious. Is she actually jealous? That's what she wants to talk about? How about we talk about the fact that she just somehow voodooed me into moving against my will?

No—that can wait. I'm not even sure what just happened. All I know for sure is what Sarah thinks she saw, and I know that she's hurting right now.

It has nothing to do with what Selene is implying. I told Sarah I wasn't feeling well, and that was true at the time. But she won't believe me now, of course.

And after everything she's said and done tonight, after the way she's been the perfect premiere date and best friend I could possibly ask for, I can't let the night end like this. I need to go to her, explain what happened, and make this right. She needs to know that Selene ambushed me, and that what happened wasn't what she thought it was. I wasn't even in physical control of my own body when she walked in.

It takes more effort than it should to pull away from Selene, and I try not to notice.

"Where are you going?"

I can't look at her. Somehow, I know that if I make eye contact with her, it might happen again. She'll find a way to make me stay, and that's not an option.

"She's waiting for me."

Selene hisses.

"You lied to me! Who is she really to you?"

It's like trying to push my way through quicksand just walking across the bathroom tile toward the door. Try as I might, it's impossible to ignore the resistance I'm encountering.

What is it, exactly? Is it some kind of weird mental or psychological thing I'm doing to myself, or is Selene actually responsible? And if it's the latter… how?

"She's exactly what we both said she was: a friend and a

roommate. That's it. But that doesn't excuse the fact that she came here with me tonight as my date, and that we took a limo together, and that she's waiting for me still to ride home with her—she's been waiting for me for too long, and I have to go now—"

"I don't believe you. Your heart's racing too fast."

"My heart? If my heart's racing too fast, it's because I'm freaked out right now."

I want to confront her. But to do so, it would mean turning myself around and facing her head-on. And I don't think I can do that right now. I'm too close to the door finally. Plus, if I stay any longer, it will just make matters worse with Sarah.

"Don't walk away from me, Lance."

"Or what?"

I stop, ever so briefly, with my hand already pressed flat against the door. Do I dare? I can't. Now is not the time. If she really can… do things to me… I am not prepared to find that out fully. Not tonight. Maybe not ever.

Summoning up all my inner and outer strength, I resist the devastating urge to look back at her. Unbidden, the recent memory of her perfect body in that perfect dress makes its way front and center to the spotlight of my brain.

I know she's there still, up on the counter, waiting and ready for me. It'd be so easy to go back to her. She'd be so willing to take me back, to wrap her arms around my neck, to guide me into her for the very first time.

And I can't deny how much I want that… how much I want her. In many ways, it's all I want and all I think about. And she's there—right there—and I can have her finally. Have her the way I've wanted her from the moment I first saw her.

All the air in my body floods out in a fluttering breath as I throw myself into the wooden door and practically topple out into the hallway beyond.

The second I do, it's better. The want is still there, that desire coursing through my every vein and artery. But I feel like I can move again now that I'm out here, walking with increasing confidence down the carpeted movie theater hallway. There's a newfound lightness out here, and I'm surprised and a bit disturbed to remember that this isn't actually a new or unusual feeling; it's just freedom. This is what it normally feels like, what it's always felt like, to be in complete control of my own body and my own decisions.

Thankfully, the premiere crowd has completely cleared out, so it's not as if anyone familiar is around to accost or interrogate me about where I've been for who knows how long now. I remember there's an after-party down the street at a Hollywood lounge; that's where everyone must be by now, assuming they didn't call it a night already. Sarah and I hadn't had the chance yet to discuss whether we planned to attend. I can't imagine she'll want to now, which is fine, since I don't think I have the inclination to go anymore, either.

My phone goes straight to voicemail when I try to call her. A bad sign, if ever there was one. I doubt her phone is dead. No, she's either ignoring me intentionally, she's turned it off, or she's put it on 'do not disturb.' I send her a couple texts asking where she is. Unsurprisingly, she does not respond.

Worse still, the limo is gone, and I know it's not as if the driver just up and abandoned me here during the film. Knowing Sarah, she came right out after walking in on Selene and I, clambered into the car, and told the driver I wouldn't be coming back with us. And honestly, I don't blame either of them if that is indeed what happened. I deserve nothing less.

That said, I'm not about to walk home to Reseda all the way from Hollywood, so I pull out my phone and begrudgingly fire up a rideshare app. Much to my dismay, it's evidently prime-time for pickups in the area, so what normally would cost about $30 now is going to cost me $70. Thank you, Los Angeles. This is just what I needed on top of everything else.

"Lance? Lance Lonergan?"

My heart skips a beat, because for a second, I think it's Selene, and I'm confused by the immediate swath of accompanying emotions. There's adrenaline, panic, curiosity, and—perhaps most inexplicable of all the feelings—relief. I can't deny that there's a part of me that wants it to be Selene, just as there's a part of me that really wants to go back into that movie theater bathroom and pick up where we left off.

But it's not Selene, of course, because that's not Selene's voice. I know Selene's voice, just like I know every other part of her. Or at least, I thought I did…

This voice is huskier, and it belongs to a thin woman clad in a smart black pantsuit. She looks like she's maybe in her late fifties or early sixties, and she's standing against the brick wall of the movie theater smoking a cigarette and wearing sunglasses—at night. As soon as I take her in though, she promptly removes the shades and tucks them into a small purse she has strung over her shoulder.

"I thought that might be you. I'm Gilda Fontenoy."

Gilda stubs out her cigarette on the pavement beneath her shoe and steps forward.

"I'm a friend of Selene's."

That figures, given the slightly-vampiric vibes I'm picking up from this woman. I shake her hand.

"Nice to meet you."

Her narrow, bluish lips twist up into a weathered smile.

"Selene said you'd be good in the film tonight, and you certainly didn't disappoint. How long have you been out here now?"

I can't suppress a bitter laugh.

"Too long, sometimes, it feels like."

She nods all-knowingly.

"I get that. It's a brutal industry that will chew you up and shit you out before breakfast, isn't it?"

Gilda actually spits on the ground to the side of us when she says this. I'm not sure if I'm more amused or disgusted, but there's no denying she has my full attention. I laugh again just to cover some of my surprise.

"Yeah, it can definitely wear on you. Are you a casting director, too?"

"No, I'm a director director. Selene and I have worked together, though, dozens of times over the years. She's certainly one of the best—if not the best—in the business. You're very lucky to have her in your corner. But I'm sure you know that by now."

It almost—almost—comes across like a warning. There's something about the way Gilda doesn't even blink when she says it, and I think it's also the tone that she uses, too.

Of course, I've only just met her, so maybe I'm being ridiculous and imagining things. I'm certainly still a bit on edge. Plus, she's got a gravelly smoker's voice, so everything she says sounds a bit harsh and foreboding.

Gilda's still waiting for me to respond.

"I do. I'm very appreciative for all that she's done for me."

"Good boy. That's the right attitude to have: confidence, modesty, and gratitude, all rolled up in one. Maintain that kind of demeanor, and you might just have what it takes to survive in this rotten town. And on that note…"

She reaches into her purse and digs out her cigarette box along with a thick paper card, which she passes over to me.

"That's all my information. I'm actually in the midst of shooting a feature right now. It's an arthouse project, but it also has major studio backing, plus a contract clause that prohibits a direct-to-streaming release. Goddess willing, it'll find its way to a real-live-movie-theater-near-you when all is said and done."

Gilda lights up another cigarette and then puts the carton away.

"I'd offer you one, but I know you don't smoke. Anyway, one of our leads just had a major relapse and drove his car into a pedestrian and killed her. I'm sure you heard all about it in the news—if you haven't, just Google it or check TMZ. Terrible tragedy, but it also now leaves me in the pickle of needing to stay on schedule, recast our man here, and reshoot all his scenes."

Yet again, I find my heart racing. Even though it's a chilly night in Hollywood, there's a growing warmth inside me radiating outward with every word I'm hearing.

"Selene recommended you for the part and suggested I attend tonight's premiere to get a feel for what you might bring to the role. And as I've already mentioned, your performance more than proved her correct. I've never known that woman to be wrong about anything."

Gilda chuckles, coughs, and takes another long drag, her eyes shining yellow and black with the reflection of the lit cigarette glowing in her pupils.

"So, what do you think, huh? You game to take that next step up in your career?"

It's not even a serious question.

"Absolutely. Thank you so much. I'd be honored. When is the audition?"

Gilda wheezes out a rasping laugh.

"Tonight was the audition. The part is yours if you want it. Shoot me an email tonight with your height, weight, and all your other body measurements for wardrobe, and I'll make sure to send you back the script and a contract you can forward over to Donna's office for her to take a look at. I think they'll find everything to be more than fair. And also… I don't mean to rush you, but assuming you're interested, I'll need an answer by tomorrow. We'd want you on set first-thing Monday."

Christ. What a whirlwind. Is this really happening? Has this woman been standing out here chain-smoking this whole time just waiting for me to come outside?

Or maybe she's waiting on Selene? For a second, my imagination runs wild and conjures up a scenario where Gilda is very much aware of exactly where I just came from and what I was just doing there, either from her own intuition somehow, or because Selene told her or tipped her off.

The thought makes me all the more self-conscious of my rumpled, half-unbuttoned appearance. I clear my throat and try to make myself look a bit more presentable, even though I know it's too late. We're already far too deep in this conversation for me to successfully run damage control. It is what it is at this point.

"So, I'll hear from you then? One way or another?"

"Absolutely. I'll send you that email tonight. And thank you again, so much, for this opportunity. I can't wait to dive into the script and the character."

Her eyes glint.

"Good. I have a feeling it's going to be right up your alley. You're perfect for the role. Like I said earlier: terrible tragedy, what happened to such a promising talent, the man you'd be replacing. And to the woman, of course. But where one door closes, another one opens…"

A black town car knifes out of nowhere down the street and then comes to a gliding stop in front of the theater. Gilda tracks it all the way before stubbing out her cigarette beneath her heel and putting her sunglasses back on.

"That's me. Need a ride? Maybe you want to come with?"

Again, I can't get a solid read on this woman. She poses both questions innocently enough, but there's also an undercurrent of suggestion brought on by the way her eyebrows arch above the dark lenses. It has to be all in my head, though. There's no way, given her age, my age, the situation at hand. I'm being ridiculous. This is what happens when you start mixing business with pleasure, just like Sarah warned earlier tonight.

Sarah…

I need to get back home. And just to be on the safe side of things, I need to do it my way, which means I need to go alone. Best not to take any unnecessary chances or risks, even if it's all in my head.

"Thanks, but I think I'm all right. I was just about to call an Uber actually."

"You sure? It's no trouble."

"I am. Thank you, though."

She nods and starts walking toward the back of the car.

"Suit yourself. Good work again tonight. Very impressive."

"Thanks."

"All right. I'll look forward to your email."

"Absolutely. Me too."

Gilda steps into the backseat, and the second her door closes, the car veers off into the night, tires squealing and all.

Mercifully, the surge pricing has grown substantially more reasonable since the last time I checked my rideshare app. I call a car to pick me up and spend the few minutes that I have before it arrives looking up Gilda Fontenoy on IMDB.

She appears every bit as legit as I could have hoped her to be. Her television credits are a mile long, and she's also been at the helm of several low-budget films over the years. My relief and excitement both intensify as I realize that I even recognize a couple of the movie titles she's directed—one of which I've seen, and it was good. Damn good.

'The next step up in my career.' That's what she said, and if her credits online are any indication, I think she's not bluffing. The lead in a Gilda Fontenoy movie that's slated to be released in theaters—actual movie theaters around the country, where people will pay admission to come in and see me up on the big screen. Wow. It's so much to take in.

Tonight was certainly a landmark moment for me. But Netflix also rented this theater, and the audience was comprised of people who worked on the film as well as their friends, their family, their representation.

What Gilda's talking about—that's the big time.

My car pulls up and I hop in the backseat. The driver asks if I want to charge my phone using his cable, which I gratefully accept. I'm plugging it in as he shifts the gear into drive, and just as we start to move off from the curb into the street, I happen to catch a flash of shining red out of my periphery. I turn in my seat to check it out.

Sure enough, there she is—right outside the theater, as if she's been there the whole time. She looks every bit as riveting, enticing, and utterly un-rumpled as ever, like she wasn't just perched up on a bathroom counter with my head between her legs. She's smiling and staring right at me even as her figure diminishes behind us, and I swear it's as if she just wanted to make extra sure I never forget who it is that makes the world go round for me.

CHAPTER 14

For as long as I can remember, my parents have been 'happy for me.' Whenever they greeted me after a high school theater performance, it was never 'we're so proud of you' or 'we really enjoyed that' or 'wow, you did such a great job.'

No, it was always just my dad, unnecessarily sporting his old high school varsity football letterman jacket, stiffly leaning in to shake my hand, slap me on the back, and mutter that he's 'happy for me.' Maybe if I was lucky once or twice, he threw in a couple bonus words that he was happy for me that I 'found something' for myself.

After that awkward exchange, my mom would pull me in for a quick hug and regurgitate whatever my dad had just said, perhaps rearranging the words, shortening them, or pretty much just saying 'ditto' without actually saying 'ditto.' Then she'd go back to nervously scanning the faces of the other parents around her. I never understood what she was so worried about, but unfortunately, my teenage brain tended to think the worst, so usually I just assumed she was painfully ashamed of my choice to be a drama club dork.

Looking back now, I'm sure they must have thought I was gay. It's an unfortunate stereotype to buy into, but in rural

Oklahoma, there are plenty of those to go around, even amongst those who are meant to love you unconditionally.

For all I know, maybe they still think I'm gay. After all, I'm unmarried at thirty, and I've never brought anyone home to meet them. If only they knew my true nature. Boy, would they be surprised at some of the stories I could share.

All of this historical context is why it's frankly a bit startling for me to take in their reactions now on this FaceTime call. Time and time again, I find myself wondering if these two individuals on the screen are actually my parents. They're practically unrecognizable to me.

It feels like it's been years since my dad even made an appearance on one of these calls. I've always just assumed there was some college football game or Fox News story on the television that, in his mind, trumped the idea of a virtual catch-up with his California-dwelling black sheep of a son.

And yet here he is now, crowding into view in the narrow rectangle of my phone screen, hovering over my mother's shoulder as she holds up her phone at the kind of nauseatingly impractical angle only a Baby Boomer would ever think to use.

Nevertheless, unless I'm really not seeing things straight, it seems to me that there is a genuine level of curiosity and even, dare I say it, excitement in the coal-black eyes of my father.

"So, does it have your name on the door?"

I move with my phone across the wood-paneled floor of the trailer, open the door to step outside, and pivot the camera around so they can fully take in the paper sign that reads 'LANCE LONERGAN' in thick all-cap letters.

"Huh. I thought it'd be a star."

Now, that's more like the Ted Lonergan I know.

"No, I think you're thinking of the Hollywood Walk of Fame. That's where they have the names in the stars."

"Does it have running water?"

I resist the urge to respond 'who cares?' to the woman who bore me into this world, instead electing to show rather than tell her that the faucet does indeed operate as a normal faucet should.

"Oh, that's wonderful!"

Is it? It's just water coming out of a tap. My 10th grade performance as Puck in A Midsummer Night's Dream, now that was wonderful.

"And you've got a flushing toilet, too?"

Want me to go take a shit and show you?

"I do. Everything in here works. It's basically like a little, miniature house."

I half-expect this to be the moment where one of them asks me when I'm going to start saving up for the down payment on an actual, full-sized, real-life house, but it doesn't happen. Either my parents truly are a bit star struck seeing their son in a 'movie star trailer' with the family name plastered out front on it, or maybe aliens abducted my real parents and these are just carbon replicas they left behind.

"So, it's the real deal, huh?"

We've probably spent at least fifteen full minutes now playing show-and-tell around this air-conditioned makeshift mobile home. I appreciate their interest and enthusiasm— given I don't know when or if I'll ever receive it again—but there's a part of me that wants to curtly remind my father that there are plenty of trailer park homes in Hobart if he's really that fascinated by this one.

"Yep. It's a real trailer."

"The movie, I mean. There's someone with a clipboard

who does the snap thing, someone says action, the whole shebang, huh?"

"Yeah. They did all that for the Netflix movie, too, you know."

I don't need to ask again if they've seen it. Despite the fact that it's about football, it's also about homosexuality, and that means it's on the permanent entertainment blacklist for the Lonergan family. Never mind the fact their son is in it, or the fact they could watch him live out his lifelong dream from the comfort and convenience of their living room right on their own television set.

"Yeah, but this one's gonna be released in theaters, right?"

I suppose it's hard to entirely fault the man for his preferences, given my parents didn't even have a Netflix subscription until about a year ago.

"That's right."

My mother's smile looks genuine to me. She, too, seems legitimately excited.

"Well, we're really happy for you. We just wanted you to know that."

It's impossible not to smile back, even if the familiar refrain isn't lost on me.

"I appreciate that. Thanks for picking up my call."

"Oh, sure. We were just about to run out to Walgreens."

A couple seconds pass as I wait to see if there's going to be any more to that story, but apparently, that's the end. Not that I really care about why they're running out to Walgreens, anyway.

"Sounds good. You guys take care."

"You too."

My dad maybe starts to give me a nod or say something more, but then the camera on their end abruptly drops down to a shot of their beige carpet before cutting out entirely.

All things considered, that really couldn't have gone any better. I need to try and remember their reactions today in the future. It would be nice to keep that memory handy for the next time I get asked when I plan to give them a grandchild or settle down with a nice, young Southern girl.

There's a knock at the door. I glance at the clock on my phone, surprised that time has flown by so quickly and that my break's already over.

It's not over, though—I should still have another half-hour before we're scheduled to pick back up where we left off with shooting. I was hoping to use this time to review my lines and do some additional imaginative character work to better drop in before returning to set.

The knock sounds again, firm but not aggressive. Maybe it's someone from hair and makeup coming to do a touch-up or something? I have to admit there are still so many aspects of this job that I'm learning as I go. It's a daily game I play just trying to find the balance between pretending like I'm a seasoned pro at all this and then asking for help or an explanation when I really need it.

"Coming."

I open the door and find a tired-looking elderly man standing at the base of the trailer steps with a stack of white pages in his hands.

The first thing I notice is that he's not looking at me—he's actually not looking at much of anything. I follow his gaze up to a spot somewhere above the corner of my trailer, thinking maybe there's an interesting bird there or a plane overhead or something, but there's nothing except sky. The man's eyes are glazed over and his lips are moving ever so slightly, even though there's no audible sound coming out from them.

Maybe he's got the wrong place or the wrong person. He clearly looks lost.

"Hi there. Can I help you?"

Nothing. He just keeps staring into space and working his lips without purpose.

Is that a practical joke? Who is this guy? I hope he's not someone's grandfather or great-grandfather they brought with them to set. If he's having an episode or suffering from dementia, I'm not sure I'm equipped to handle this situation adequately.

I lean forward to touch him on the shoulder lightly.

"Sir? Are you all right?"

That seems to finally do the trick, as he tilts his head in my direction. His brows are furrowed, and now he looks like he's trying hard to focus and having a difficult time concentrating, but at least he's giving me a modicum of attention at last. I watch with growing pity and concern as he struggles to form words from his quivering lips.

"G… g… g'day, Mr. Lonergan. I have some rewrites for you."

He passes the pages over to me slowly.

"Thanks."

His job is complete, but the man doesn't look like he's in any great hurry to leave. I start to step back inside the trailer and close the door a bit behind me.

"Have a good one."

No response. He just keeps looking at me with those dead eyes. Standing. Staring. Motionless.

Do I know this guy from somewhere? Is that why he's lingering here on my trailer steps? I'm almost positive I haven't seen him on set. Though given the high volume of people working on this production, I obviously can't be sure.

Still… there's something distinctly familiar about his pale blue eyes and the makeup of his face. That accent, too—I'm almost positive that it's Australian, and that's just not something you hear every day on the street.

"Do I know you from somewhere?"

The old man scratches his thinning hair and screws his eyebrows together as he thinks, summoning forth a whole field of wrinkles along his forehead and under his temples. It's almost enough to make me want to retract the question, as it looks like he's under serious strain and duress just racking his brain for what should be a simple yes or no answer.

I'm about to tell him not worry about it when there's a faint glimmer of a spark. It catches just enough of a hold on his mind that his features show a bit more animation and his speech improves somewhat.

"M… maybe. Ever watch the SyFy channel? I was a series regular on 'Starforce Prime' for a season until they killed me off…"

"No, it's not that."

I've never even heard of that show, nor have I watched that channel, but I keep those thoughts to myself so as not to insult him. I also don't want to get him so worked up on a meaningless subject that he ends up hurting himself. Crazy as it sounds, that might be a legitimate concern with this particular character, whoever he is.

But who is he… actually? I feel like I do know him from somewhere, I just can't place it right now for the life of me.

The old man gets another glimmer, and his lips sputter as he tries again to form a connection with me.

"What about commercials? B… Barbells and B… Bros. I did a spot for them once."

I shake my head no. Not to be insulting or condescending, but I find it extraordinarily difficult to believe the emaciated skeleton standing before me ever got cast in a gym advertisement. Unless he was the 'before' in a 'before and after' segment.

"No, I don't think that's it, either."

And then it hits me like a ton of bricks, and I suddenly realize I know exactly where I recognize him from: Royalties. This is the guy from the bar, the guy who came out of the bathroom after having sex with Selene. We had a brief verbal exchange at the sink before he disappeared after her into the night.

But… what happened?

This man looks absolutely awful compared to how I remember him. Sure, it's been a couple months or so since that night. And granted, we didn't talk for very long. But still…

The man I met that evening was handsome and rugged, a sleek silver fox with a chiseled body who was dressed to the nines. It was impossible not to feel jealous of him—and not only because he'd just fucked an absolute goddess, either.

Now, all I feel is confusion and sympathy when I take this man in. Inexplicably, he seems to have grown shorter, gaunter, and paler at an unnaturally fast rate. This man has lost an impossible amount of hair, to the degree that I wonder if more is falling out even now as he scratches again at his scalp absentmindedly. His clothes are shabby and oversized for his frame, almost like they're hand-me-downs from an older, bigger brother.

That night we met, I remember being dazzled by his gleaming white teeth and his sparkling eggshell blue eyes. Neither seem all that bright anymore. Everything about this person has been dulled and decayed. We all have our good days and bad days, but this—this isn't normal. This man doesn't just look tired or sick or sad. It looks like the life has all but gone out of him entirely.

"I—I think I know what it is now, actually. I met you at a bar a couple months back. At Royalties Tavern in Studio City."

His gaze remains vacant, his eyes milky and inactive. He may as well be playing an extra in a zombie film that's shooting nearby, just with less blood, guts, and gore.

"In the bathroom area. You—you know Selene Blackwood, right?"

Finally, there's another glimmer of recognition and mental activity in his expression. His focus seems to narrow on me—really narrow on me for the first time, actually—and I watch a procession of thoughts move slowly across his face, as if the cobwebs are getting blown off and his brain is creaking back into function after eons of inactivity.

"What?"

Is he about to have a stroke? His lips are twitching again in a funny way, and the jugular vein in his neck throbs like a quickening drumbeat.

"Selene? Selene Blackwood? Do you know who that is?"

Should I not have even asked? I'm really beginning to wish I'd just accepted the papers, thanked him, and closed the door. This poor guy looks like he's short-circuiting right before my eyes, and I guess it's all because of me, though I have no idea what I really did or why he'd act this way.

"Forget it. My mistake."

I take a step inward and start to close the trailer door, but he throws his hand up against it to stop me. The movement doesn't startle me so much as the sudden concern that I may have shut the door on his hand or even just shut it against his hand—the guy's so brittle-looking, I'd hate to find myself on the other end of a workplace injury lawsuit.

"Wait!"

Christ. What the fuck is going on here? Aussie is having a conniption fit. His eyes are bloodshot now. He really might actually be having a seizure. Is there someone I should call? Maybe 9-1-1 at this point…

"How do you know Selene?"

It occurs to me then that maybe I'm the one who's overreacting and misreading this altercation.

Yes, this man has inexplicably transformed from Hugh Jackman to the Crypt-Keeper seemingly overnight. But once upon a time, he did sleep with the same woman as me—at least on one occasion that I know of.

Did I just inadvertently open my door to discover a jealous ex-boyfriend or ex-husband? Could this be one of those melodramatic scenes you see in the movies, on TV, or particularly in a soap opera? He's the jilted ex-lover, and now he's seething with uncontrollable jealousy at the idea that I'm the new guy who's bedding 'the one who got away.'

I have neither the time nor the interest in playing this particular cliché out. Best to keep my answer short and innocuous. Plus, it's the honest truth.

"She helped me get this job."

Now the vein in the old man's forehead is thrumming along with the one in his neck, and his mouth convulses and convenes into a manic sort of smile thing that makes my stomach lurch. I'm all too aware that he still has his arm lodged up against the door to keep it open.

"How, though?"

"What do you mean?"

Deranged Aussie licks his chapped lips, still smiling, still unhinging.

"What'd it take? Come on, now. You can tell me. What did she make you do to get it?"

That sets off even more alarm bells. Now, I'm not just worried about this guy keeling over at the foot of my trailer; I'm concerned about the implication in what he's saying. What does he know about us? And how does he know anything to begin with?

"Look, man, I'm sorry, but I don't know what you're talking about. I auditioned for her a while back and she recommended me for this part to Gilda. That's it; that's why I'm here. Now, I really need to get back to work—"

"You fucked her, didn't you?"

Here we go. It's life imitating art, all right. Little does he know I actually have not fucked her, not technically. But I doubt that nugget of truth would help any. Do I need to call security? How does one even do that?

At least he's a wasted, diminutive shell of the man I encountered back at Royalties. If he tries to take a swing at me or charge inside, I doubt I'd have much of a problem holding my own and protecting myself. He's working himself up into a fairly good lather for somebody who appeared dead-on-arrival at first, but the mania in his face lets me know he's still far from laser-focused… and probably far from sane, as well.

"Dude, I don't know who you are or what your deal is, but you need to go. Right now."

I push against my side of the door and drop the pages from my other hand in case I need to use it for self-defense.

"What did you give her? Sex? Blood? Or more?"

The muscles in my arm go slack against the door.

"A vow? A talisman?"

I find it momentarily impossible to speak or really even think much of anything. All I can do is stare at him in bewilderment.

The man's eyes start to water. And then, just like that, he's full-on crying at my doorstep.

"Did she take you yet? To the house? Did she bring you with her?"

His chest heaves as he struggles to breathe. More tears fall. I have no idea what to do.

"She... she... she never took me."

The man's weeping eyes bore into me with a despair that knows no depths. It's horrifying.

"She... she promised. She promised me. And... and I never got there. To the unity. To communion. To become something... greater... in the end..."

I keep repeating his words over and over again in my head, trying in vain to make sense of them, trying to make sense of this whole exchange.

"The end? The end of what? Whose house? What are you talking about?"

He drags the back of his hand across snot from his nose and continues blubbering.

"You... you took her from me. I gave her everything. Everything I had. And still... it wasn't enough. She said... she said I wasn't worthy..."

"Worthy of what? What are you saying? Who are you?"

And then, out of nowhere, there's a kind of wave that washes over him from head to toe.

His face and his body—all of it grows so suddenly calm and flaccid. It's as gravity itself just vacuumed all the nervous, quaking hysteria right out from under him until it soaked up into the earth. And just as he was when I first saw him on the other side of this trailer door, the man looks lost again.

Actually, worse than lost. He looks empty. It's just the same utterly dry, drained, and dead remnants of a human being as before.

His arm falls limply to his side as the static glazed state returns in totality. The man grows so still he could be mistaken for a statue, until he finally moves, taking a full, lumbering circle in place, the way someone might act if they were lost in the woods at night with no semblance of direction or instinct on where they need to go to find shelter.

After a moment or two of confused spinning and aimless staring, he shambles off to my right for a few steps, stops, pauses, turns, and changes his course, walking to my left without a backward glance, until he finally disappears from my vision altogether behind the corner of another trailer.

I hear the sound of someone clearing their throat nearby to my right, and it makes me jump.

A young woman with a radio headset has materialized completely unbeknownst to me. I have no idea how long she's been standing there for. Come to think of it, I have no idea how long I've been staring off at where the old man went, either. Time could have jumped or have frozen, and I'd have no real awareness either way.

"Sorry if I scared you. Just wanted to say that we're ready for you now, Mr. Lonergan."

Alicia. This girl's name is Alicia. I know who she is. She came here to tell me we're starting back up again on set. The break is over.

"Mr. Lonergan? Lance? Did you hear me?"

The best I can do is nod.

"Okay, then. Great. Do you need anything?"

I shake my head, because I have no idea what it is that I need. Even if I did know, it's not as if Alicia is going to be able to help me. I'm only just now remembering where I am and what I'm supposed to be doing.

Try as I might, I'm finding it exceptionally difficult to get the strange encounter with the man out of my head. My brain wants to keep replaying our conversation and focusing in on the tidbits—especially the comments he made toward the end—instead of on the task at hand.

"Okay, then. I guess… I guess I'll just let them know you're on your way?"

In a daze, I nod again. She must be looking at me the way I looked at the man when he first appeared outside my trailer. I'm sure I appear to her every bit as foggy or stoned as he did to me. But that was just my initial impression of the man. What do I think now? Now that I heard him say everything he did?

Alicia seems unsure but also understandably uneasy, so she just gives me an awkward little smile before departing at a brisk clip and escaping the situation. It's hard for me to blame her. I would probably run for the hills too.

What… the… fuck… just happened?

CHAPTER 15

I wake up to the phone ringing on my nightstand.

"Hello?"

"Lance! Good morning. I hope I didn't wake you."

Donna says it with a playful chuckle. I clear my throat and check the time on the screen. It's 10:52 a.m.

"Not at all. Just, uh—got a frog in my throat."

"Oh, no! You're not sick, are you?"

I clear my throat a second time. It's just a Hollywood cold, the kind of 'illness' that usually accompanies a late night out with Jared. But I don't need my agent knowing any of this.

"No, I'm good. How are you, Donna?"

"To be honest with you, Lance, I am fantastic. And you, my talented friend, are the primary reason why."

Well, that's nice to hear. This is quickly shaping up to be an interesting morning. My head and body ache all over from the partying done last night, but I've never heard Donna sound so jolly and upbeat on the phone before. Frankly, I'm still getting used to hearing her on the other end of the line to begin with. Every time the agency gives me a ring nowadays, it's her, rather than her assistant Brian, who's making the call.

"What's going on?"

"I've got great news and great news. Which one do you want first?"

She sounds so giddy, her voice is practically sing-song.

"Whichever you want first. I'm all ears."

"Well, I just got off the phone with the studio about an hour ago. The first cut is in, and Lance, they could not stop raving about your performance. Molly Ramirez even went so far as to say that Gabe's little relapse and accident were probably the best possible things that could have happened for the picture. She was gushing about you. I think it's safe to say you'll be at the top of their list for the foreseeable future when it comes to any new projects they might have coming down the pipeline."

"That's awesome news. I can't wait to see how it turns out."

"That makes two of us. I'll keep you in the loop if I get any more updates. This is big, Lance. Trust me, when there's this kind of buzz this early on and from these types of people, it can only mean good things for us. I'm very excited, and I'm very proud of you as well for sticking through it. All your hard work is really beginning to pay off."

What a remarkable turnaround. I wonder if she even remembers that around this exact same time last year, she had Brian call me and gently suggest I consider opening myself up to 'other representation opportunities that might better be able to advocate' for me. Thankfully, I never got dropped, but I'll also probably never know how close I may have come to the chopping block, especially not now—though thank God for that.

"I appreciate it, Donna. Thanks for sticking with me, too,

this whole time."

"Of course. Never had a doubt."

That's not true, but whatever. I'm not going to let myself get hung up on the trivialities. This is a good day, after all.

No, this is a great day. That's the word she used.

"What's the other piece of great news?"

"Ah, yes. Guess who I just got off the phone with?"

As much as I'm relishing this conversation so far, I'm still too hungover to be in the mood for guessing games.

"Who?"

"Selene Blackwood."

My heart does a somersault just at the sound of her name. I haven't seen Selene since the Netflix show premiere, though I've missed a few calls from her since then. I'm not intentionally trying to dodge her, but I suppose I also don't know why exactly she keeps calling… and for some reason, that fact alone makes me uncomfortable. She hasn't left any voicemails and she hasn't texted. If it were a business call, I'm sure she'd do one of those things. Besides, she's always calling from her personal number; it's never her office line.

"Okay. What was she calling about?"

For a second, I imagine a ludicrous, nonsensical scenario where Donna informs me that Selene has revealed everything to her about the true nature of our relationship.

Wouldn't that be something? Not that it would ever happen. Still, the thought makes me nervous: this notion that somehow, someone might find out the full, lurid extent to which we've violated all manner of professional boundaries and decorum.

"When it rains, it pours. Remember what I said to you in our very first meeting?"

I don't. And to be honest, I don't think Donna herself

remembers anything she said to me in our very first meeting, either. That was a couple years ago now, and I'm skeptical that I've even truly been on her radar until I actually started booking paying gigs recently.

"I told you that work will beget more work. And that's exactly what's happening now. Selene is casting a new film adaptation of 'Pride and Prejudice' that's set entirely in modern-day New York City, and she's already suggested you for the role of Mr. Darcy. Are you familiar with the story?"

"Not really. Maybe I read the book in high school, but I don't remember it."

"Well, here's everything you need to know: he's the lead, and more importantly, women all over the world go gaga for him. This is your fast-track ticket to not just fame and fortune, but also to status as a true-blue Hollywood sex symbol. And we're not talking another indie release here, either; this is a major studio picture with an A-list cast and an A-list director. Get this: Kathryn Bigelow is already attached to direct, and Emma Stone is currently in talks for Elizabeth Bennet, the other lead."

If my heart was somersaulting before, it's been performing a complex Olympic gymnastics routine for the past sixty seconds. I'm just glad that I'm already lying down, because I think otherwise, I would have fainted by now.

"This is… this is just… wow. I'm speechless."

Donna lets out a full-throated laugh into the phone.

"I don't blame you! This is huge, Lance. I know I said I had great news and great news before, but that doesn't really do any of this justice. I'm always cautious with my clients when it comes to getting ahead of ourselves or counting the proverbial chickens before they hatch, but truth be told, you've got some real momentum here on your side. This is how you make it to the big-time. Again, I don't want to jinx it, but these are potentially star-making developments."

Fuck me. If I would have known this call was coming today, I never would have agreed to go out last night with Jared. My oatmeal brain isn't going to be able to remember all this, but man oh man, I wish I could have recorded this conversation. What I wouldn't give to be able to play it back again and again in the future, particularly at my lowest moments.

"Wow. I'm still at a loss for words. I guess… well, what's next? Do I need to audition or send in a tape, or how does this work?"

"I've already asked Molly's assistant to send some footage over to Kathryn and the studio. She's seen the Netflix film, too, and she's fully on-board. I'd imagine the next step is having you come in to screen test with Emma. But assuming that goes well, I think it's a done deal. Sound good to you?"

Um, yes. Duh. Sounds fucking unbelievable to me.

"Absolutely. You just tell me where I need to be and when, and I'll be there. Whatever they need, you know I'm ready."

"I do. And I love to hear it. All right, I'll keep you in the loop. Take care of yourself now. This is not the time to come down with the flu, okay?"

She's laughing as she says it, but there's also the faintest wisp of a warning in her voice. I'm very quickly becoming a sort of cash cow for her agency, and she knows it. I don't blame her for wanting me at my very best, and I read the message loud and clear.

It's time to cut back on the late nights, the drinking, and the general acting like I'm still just another would-be actor/part-time waiter who can get away with showing up to work hungover. I'm oh-so-close to realizing a lifelong dream. The last thing I need to do right now is screw it up.

"Totally agree. I'll take care of myself. You do, too."

"I always do. Talk soon. Bye now."

"Bye."

What a way to wake up. A solid thirty seconds or so go by where all I do is stare at my dulled reflection in the blank black mirror of the phone screen and mentally replay everything that just happened.

Donna Goodwin. Kathryn Bigelow. Emma Stone. Pride and Prejudice. Holy. Fuck.

I soak it all in, breathing in the prosperity and breathing out the acrid remains of my hangover. How can anyone stay disheveled in the face of so much positivity?

Great news, indeed. Sensational news. Life-changing news. 'These are potentially star-making developments.' Christ.

Sarah is going to lose her mind. She loves 'Bridgerton,' 'Outlander,' and all those other period-piece romances that are so wildly popular with the female demographic these days. Pride and Prejudice has to be like the O.G. of that whole genre, so she's going to freak. Besides, I know she thinks Emma Stone practically walks on water. I may never hear the end of all this.

A quick peek out the blinds of my window reveals a muted landscape bathed in a grey haze. It's almost misty out there, which is unusual for this side of town at this time of day. Normally, the sun would be out in full force, omnipresent and merciless.

I'll take it all, though. This weather looks much more sympathetic to those still experiencing lingering headaches and acute light sensitivity.

Venturing out into the common area of our apartment,

I'm surprised to find Sarah standing up and working from the kitchen counter, her laptop nestled in between a coffee mug and a nearly-empty French press. She's wearing jeans and a sweater, and her hair's still damp, like she just took a shower. It's all extremely unusual, since if anyone's the type to embrace a cool, gloomy day by staying in their PJs and working from bed under a big pile of blankets, it's Sarah.

"Wow. Look at you, Miss Go-Getter."

There's a brief gleam of surprise on her face as she registers my presence before she glances back down at her computer screen.

"Hey. You're up early."

I wonder which one's stronger: the sarcasm she's dealing or the coffee she's drinking.

"Ha, ha. Yeah, it was a bit of a late night."

"You think? I heard you rustling around in here at four."

Try as I might, it's impossible to spot even a whiff of playfulness in her tone or facial expression. This feels more like a pure, genuine rebuke, and I'm quickly starting to sense that I could be in store for a full-blown lecture if I'm not careful. Needless to say, that's the last thing I need right now on top of a stubborn hangover that won't go away.

"Sorry. I tried to be quiet, but there's only so much you can do with potato chips and popcorn."

Stony silence is all I get by way of response. I guess that beats getting chewed out, though.

Oh, well. So, she's mad at me this morning because I made a little too much noise last night coming home. It's not the first time and it won't be the last. I'm not about to let her sour mood ruin my day—especially not after the morning I'm having so far.

"Guess who I just got off the phone with?"

"Can it wait, Lance? I'm in the middle of something."

Wow. I must have been much louder last night than I thought.

"Yeah. Sure."

Seemingly, it's best to save my news for later, even if I'm sure it's the type of information that could lift her spirits in an instant. Everything I'm getting from Sarah by way of vibes is warning me that it's best to tiptoe around her until the storm clouds completely pass, so that's what I guess I'll do.

I'm literally tiptoeing as I inch around my grumpy dragon of a roommate to retrieve a mug from the kitchen cabinets. Let me just get in, get a cup of coffee, and get out of here before she really lets me have it.

My hand is halfway to the French press when she wheels on me, and I realize I'm already too late.

"Are you serious right now?!"

"What?"

"You just have no consideration for anyone but yourself, huh?"

"Jesus Christ, Sarah. Do you want me to make more?"

"I want you to just think about someone other than yourself for a change. Why is that so hard for you?"

"It's coffee. I didn't know it was so important to you. It's fine, I'll brew another pot."

"It's my coffee. I'm the one who bought it, who shopped for it, who brought it home and made it. I'm always the one who does all of those things—you never offer—and I share it with you because I'm a good person and because I don't want to be a bitch. But then you crawl out of bed at noon and you come out here and try to take the last cup without even asking me? Like, does any of that even remotely register for you as being inconsiderate behavior? Can you see even a tiny bit why I might be upset?"

"Listen, I didn't know any of this was such a big deal for you. I'm sorry. I'll go to Starbucks or something and buy a bag of beans on the way home. It's just coffee, okay? Relax."

Sarah folds her arms across her chest. She's actually quivering, like it's taking all of her self-control not to physically attack me. I'm not sure I've ever seen her like this before.

"It's not just coffee, though. It's everything. I'm not just talking about groceries or money, either. You constantly disrespect me by acting as if somehow my time isn't as important as yours, or my feelings, my wants, my choices, my opinions, my anything."

Did I wake up in an alternate universe where Sarah and I are in a romantic relationship? Since when did I sign up for a girlfriend or a wife in addition to a best friend?

And to think: all of this over the dregs left at the bottom of a French press. Come on, now. This is absurd.

"Look, I really don't know where all this is coming from, but I'm sorry if I've upset you. I don't think my time is more important than yours, or my opinions, or any of those things you just said. Truly. Is this... I guess I thought we already talked about the premiere, and you said you were good now. No?"

Sarah presses her thumbs into the socket spaces above her eyes, but she doesn't immediately say anything, just letting out an exasperated sigh instead, so I continue. I need to find a way to fully defuse this bomb.

"Was I wrong? If you're still salty about that night, you know you can just tell me. I'd rather hash it out with you and be done with it once and for all than have you keep holding it over my head forever."

She glowers at me.

"Salty? Let me be perfectly clear with you: I'm not still salty about it. I've never forgiven you for it. There's a major difference."

This argument is going nowhere. We've talked ad nauseam in the past about what really happened in the movie theater bathroom with Selene. Despite a limitless litany of explanations and apologies, Sarah has either treated me with thinly-veiled hostility or she's outright ignored me ever since that night.

So, I guess I'm not really surprised to hear it straight from her mouth that she still hasn't forgiven me. I just don't know what it's going to take from me to finally get her there.

"What more can I say? We've been over this a million times now. There are only so many ways a person can say sorry for something that really isn't even their fault to begin with."

Her eyes grow wide.

"Right… because Selene forced you to have sex with her. I forgot."

If only I could explain to her how accurate that statement actually almost is.

"We didn't have sex."

"No, don't start with that again. I know what I saw."

"When are you going to let this go? I've explained what happened, I've apologized for it, I've promised to never let it happen again, I've tried to make it up to you I don't know how many times now… I don't know why you can't just accept my apology and move on. It's like… I don't know. It's like you're weirdly jealous or something. And I just don't get it."

Sarah's chest rises and falls with her labored breathing. It's officially official now: I have never seen her this angry. And while I wish I wasn't the cause of such consternation, she's driven me to defending myself here. Clearly, she's been itching for a fight for hours now. Maybe days.

She steeples her palms together in front of her lips and closes her eyes. Without the proper context, you'd be tempted to assume she was praying, but I'm going to hope it's just her way of regaining calm and composure. It's not like Sarah to let her emotions bubble over and run unchecked for this long. After all, she's the one who devotes good money each week toward seeing a therapist.

After an uncomfortably lengthy, pregnant pause, Sarah finally opens her eyes again and drills them into me.

"I think it's time you move into your own place."

More seconds pass between us. I'm not convinced I heard her correctly. Even if I did, I'm not comprehending. Is this a joke, or a threat, or is she just being rash and saying things she'll inevitably regret and apologize for later?

"Come again?"

Sarah doesn't flinch.

"I said I think it's time you find your own place."

"To live?"

"Yes."

She can't be serious. We've had our ups and downs over the years like any pair of roommates or friends, but this is asinine. Over a cup of coffee?

"You're joking."

"I'm not. I've given it a lot of thought, and I think it'd be best for both of us to get a fresh start."

She looks like she's being earnest, but I still can't believe it. This is completely out of left field.

"Where is this coming from? Is this something your therapist suggested?"

Her jaw muscles tighten.

"Not that it's any of your business, but no. Like I said, I've been thinking about this for a while now—even before your premiere, so don't think it's just because of that. I'd like you out by the end of the month."

Now, I'm the one whose breathing is beginning to intensify.

"That's in less than two weeks. Where do you expect me to find an apartment that quickly?"

"That's not my problem. Go stay with Jared or one of your other cronies. Find a hotel or an Airbnb. I don't care what you do."

Who is this vindictive monster and what has she done with my sweet, supportive best friend?

"You're honestly doing this right now? Throwing me out on the street?"

Sarah shrugs, gives me her back, and returns to her laptop screen.

"Don't be so dramatic. You're a big boy. Plus, you've got your movie star money now—assuming you haven't spent it all already. You'll figure something out."

"I can't believe you're doing this. Can't we at least talk? Tell me what I need to do to make this right."

She pulls her headphones up around her neck, and it doesn't take a rocket scientist to understand that any second now, I'm going to be completely shut out.

"This is how you make things right: by moving out. Maybe after enough time and space apart, we can re-evaluate one day. I don't know. But I do know that this is the right decision for the time being—and not just for me, for both of us. So, do whatever you need to do to be out by the end of the month."

"Sarah—"

"I need to get back to work."

With that, she slides the headphones up over her ears and resumes typing.

How in the world can one person experience such high highs and low lows in such rapid succession? It's a wonder my heart hasn't exploded after so much turbulence and seesawing between emotional states.

Even though I'm still staring at Sarah and I'm barely a yard or so away from her, it's as if I'm suddenly the Invisible Man. I'm half-tempted to yank the headphones down and insist we're not finished with this conversation, but I also have no idea how she'd react to such an intervention. This isn't the woman I thought I knew inside and out. The Sarah I know would never turn her back on a friend—literally or figuratively—and she certainly wouldn't do it to me, of all people.

And yet, that's exactly what she's done. I don't believe for a second that she acted alone, either; this decision has the fingerprints of her shrink all over it. Sarah is far too patient, too understanding, and too non-confrontational for this kind of rash behavior. I'd bet money on the fact her therapist put her up to this.

Sarah just needs some time to cool down. She said it herself about needing time and space apart so she could get a clearer head and re-evaluate. I'm sure I can crash at Jared's for a couple of days until she realizes just how far she's gone in this overreaction. Maybe by then, she'll finally be ready to actually move past this whole episode and focus instead on all the good things that are happening for me.

For us, actually. Anything good for me is good for us—as long as she's still my roommate.

She thinks I'm not paying my share or covering enough costs when it comes to shared goods? No problem. I can buy a whole fleet of fucking espresso machines with the paycheck I'll get for this next movie. I'll put a coffee mini-bar in her bedroom, and then we'll see just how selfish and self-centered a roommate she really thinks I am.

Christ. A part of me needs a drink, but another part of me knows that I'll never hear the end of it if I go rooting around in the liquor cabinet or grab a beer from the fridge right now. No, if I'm going to de-stress, I'm better off taking an edible or two.

It's hard not to feel like a dog with its tail tucked between its legs as I skulk back to my bedroom to dig out the bag of gummies from my closet. Nobody wants to feel unwelcome in their own home, but that's exactly what it feels like right now.

What I need is a breath of fresh air. As much as I don't want to give Sarah the satisfaction of witnessing me flee the premises, nothing can be gained from forcing a second round in the ring with her, either. Not while she's in this state. It would only make her resent me more for trying.

I pop one chewy, strawberry-flavored THC square into my mouth, and then another. Where do I have to be today, anyway? I'm in a holding pattern until Donna calls me back with next steps on Pride and Prejudice. Until then, my time is my own.

"Fuck it."

I pocket the bag just in case, flip the closet light off, and move as quickly and as quietly as I can out through the living room toward the front door. Sarah's still standing there like a stone column at the kitchen counter, but I'm careful not to even glance in her direction as I pass her by. If she wants to be left alone, I will leave her alone. It looks like a perfect day to go chill up on the rooftop of our apartment building anyway.

My phone buzzes against my thigh as I scale the staircase. Selene is calling me yet again from her personal line. True to form, I find myself conflicted as to whether or not I want to pick up. There's no denying that no one gets my heart racing like Selene Blackwood, but I don't know if that's a good thing or a bad thing anymore. She excites me, but frankly, she also terrifies me.

I let the call go to voicemail, knowing full well she won't leave a message and she won't send a text. Until I know exactly how I feel about her, about what she's done for me, and about what she's done to me, I think it's best to keep my distance.

Still, there's a pang of guilt in my stomach as I twist the doorknob and step out onto the roof, knowing she has once again paved the way for another level-up in my exhilarating ascent to potential stardom. Sooner or later, I will need to pick up the phone. If nothing else, to thank her. Even though I know in my heart of hearts that thanking her verbally over the phone will never be enough.

As I drag a heavy cinder block over to wedge open the door, I realize for the first time that perhaps I'm much closer than I thought to no longer needing Selene after all. Of course, there's no denying I wouldn't be where I am today without her, and I'll forever be grateful for that. But after the call with Donna this morning, it's perfectly evident that my career is finally beginning to take off on its own accord.

Work begets work, and I've been working plenty of late.

Maybe I'm finally at a point where I don't need to rely on anyone else but myself.

Wouldn't that be nice. I've certainly struggled and worked my ass off long enough to get to this crossroads. Provided I don't do anything to screw it up, this is my moment. This is everything I've dreamed of and everything I've worked for my whole entire life.

Someone at some point in time found a way to get some of the pool area furniture all the way up here: a couple of chairs that fully recline out and a small metal end table. Rarely have I ever encountered anyone else up on the roof, and even when I have, it's always been at night.

Today, I have the whole space to myself, which suits my fancy just fine.

I fold one chair all the way flat and luxuriously stretch my body out atop it. Any second now, the edibles will start to kick in and wash away all the bad stored-up energy from my tense encounter with Sarah. In the meantime, it's best to just focus on the Donna phone call and enjoy the cool, misty weather up here on this early afternoon.

'Star-making developments.'

Fuck. Yes.

CHAPTER 16

Who knows how long I've been asleep for when the gentle raindrops finally do enough to rouse me back to consciousness. The sky above is just how I remember it being before I slipped into sleep: more silver-blue than grey-black and still nothing to be afraid of. I can't remember the last time I heard real thunder or saw lightning that wasn't on a digital screen.

It takes me longer than it probably should to recall that I'm on edibles, given the drowsiness and disorientation humans so often experience while transitioning between states of consciousness. When I do remember the gummies, though, I'm aware of their tangible effect on my overall state of being. It's hard not to feel relaxed and refreshed after taking a nap outdoors and then awakening organically to a light mid-day sprinkle, but the drugs add an additional filter, subtle but not insignificant, to the way my body senses itself laid out along the pool chair and the way my brain processes the world around me.

This is nice. This is really nice.

Mentally, I pat myself on the back for my earlier decision-making. Nothing makes quick work of a hangover like the proper dosage of THC. Add in the perfect mix of cool, cloudy weather with just a hint of moisture, and it's no wonder I feel like a million bucks again. This is all not even mentioning the life-changing news I got on the phone this morning.

Of course, remembering my conversation with Donna naturally leads me to remembering the conversation with Sarah that followed soon after. I try not to replay what happened, but the reality of what transpired is hard to escape, even with the added layer of chemically-induced peace and tranquility.

I just can't believe it. After everything we've been through—not just as roommates, but more importantly, as best friends—to have her kick me to the curb with absolutely no warning and no preamble, it just doesn't make sense. Sarah has bad days and mood swings just like the rest of us, but not like this morning. That was completely out of character.

Hopefully, she's already had a chance to calm down and reflect on the ramifications of everything she said and asked of me. Cooler heads have to prevail when push comes to shove.

There's no way she already has someone lined up to take my spot in the apartment. It'd presumably be just as hard for her to find a new roommate in less than two weeks as it would be for me to find a new place. Sarah can be emotional at times, but she's the furthest thing from an idiot. The best course of action for both parties here is to mend the fences and avoid doing anything rash, dumb, and financially impractical while in the heat of the moment. She has to come to recognize that fact eventually, and I'm confident she will.

Emitting a sleepy groan, I slowly push myself up to my elbows, blink a raindrop from my eye, and realize with a start that I'm not alone anymore.

Somehow, someway, and against all rhyme, reason, logic, and sense, Selene is here. Even with her back to me, I'd recognize her figure anywhere.

She's leaning against the edge of the rooftop with her forearms flat along the railing, one leg straight beneath her and the other at an angle behind her, the heel of that leg bouncing aimlessly up and down on the ball of her foot, in and out of a black stiletto. Fishnet stockings hug the delicious soft fullness of her calves and thighs. They climb higher and higher until finally vanishing about six inches above the back of her knees below the hem of a midnight blue dress that knows how to perfectly adorn her curves in all the right places.

Am I still dreaming? Selene is a vision I can't trust, and it's not just the sleepiness or the drugs, either. There's no earthly explanation for what she's doing here on the roof of my apartment building. I have half a mind to close my eyes, lie back down, and wait for the slumber mist to claim me once again and carry me off to true unconsciousness, since I have to be experiencing some kind of lucid dreaming episode. There's just no way. This can't be real.

Hallucination or not, I cannot tear my eyes away from her. Like a siren, she calls to me, begging me with her body to get nearer. Her mere presence alone in this grey haze is the wet beam from a lighthouse tower, simultaneously drawing me in from the blank swirling eternity of the sea and promising certain calamity if I get too close to the shore. I never had a chance and I never had a choice, but it doesn't matter, because from the depths of my soul, I know there's nowhere else I'd rather be.

Getting to my feet and closing the short distance between us, I wonder vaguely just how long she's been here for. It's one of thousands of potential questions I could ask if I really cared more, which I'm surprised to find I don't. All that matters to me is that she's here, here in my home practically, the place I live—or lived. She's come here for me, and now, I'll come to her.

Selene doesn't say a word as I silently approach, but I know she doesn't need to, just like I know that she's acutely aware I'm here behind her without needing to turn or see me.

Every time, every single time, I've ever been anywhere even remotely near her, there's been this sort of electric charge in the air between us. I know she feels it in her bones and in her blood just as I do. It's always highly pleasurable yet borderline painful at the same time, like immersing yourself after a long, weary day into a scalding hot bathtub.

There's a heavy stillness in the air, a cool carpet of humidity that coats my pores like a translucent oil. I stand for a couple seconds behind her, breathing shallowly and admiring how tiny drops of moisture from the air collect in her hair, which she's done in a long French braid I haven't seen her wear before. As expected, it's impossible to ascertain with any degree of clarity what the dominant shade of her hair is, even in this new style. It's just one of the many countless mysteries that accompany a woman the likes of which I've never known before.

"You've been avoiding me."

Profound, unbearable guilt washes over me, and I feel my cheeks burn red-hot with shame. I do my best to clear my throat so my voice won't crack and betray me further when

I answer her.

"I'm sorry. It wasn't my intention. I've just been busy."

Selene tilts her head back to gaze up at the clouds above us.

"Don't you think I know that better than anyone?"

If my cheeks were hot before, they're on fire now, along with whole swaths of skin across and around my neck.

"Of course, you do."

"You remember what I told you the night of your premiere, don't you? Or have you already forgotten?"

I swallow hard and stare at the ground. I'll never forget that night for the rest of my life.

"You told me that my future was infinite, and you said that every wish and every dream I'd ever had would come true."

"No."

The unexpectedly harsh flatness of her tone slices into me and forces me to look back up. When I do, I see that she's turned her head over her shoulder just far enough to lock eyes with me. There they are, too, those mesmerizing orbs with the dancing metallic flakes of gold. I'd swear her irises stole the exact color of the sky today.

"I told you that our future is infinite, and that we would make every wish and every dream you've ever had come true together."

She dares me to contradict her, even though only a fool would. Plus, I know she's right and that I've misspoken.

"That's what I meant to say. I remember what you said, believe me. I'll never forget what you said and what happened that night—what we shared, I mean."

Selene turns her attention back to the urban jungle splayed out in front of her. I'm possessed by a sudden fantasy that she's an ancient Egyptian queen, Amazon warrior, or Mayan goddess, unchallenged and unshakable, who has made a simple daily habit of surveying her fiefdom from high up above on her mountaintop. It's an imaginative notion, to be sure, but one made all the more believable thanks to the potency of these edibles.

"Lance…"

Christ. It's been too long—far too long—since I heard her lips speak my name out loud. I make up my mind in this very moment to never again let so much time go by between spells.

"If I ask something of you, will you do it for me?"

Anything. Everything. Name it.

"Of course."

"Think about your life. Your whole, entire life. Do it for me. Do it for me now."

It's an overwhelming directive, but I try my best, scanning at random through blips and flashes of my childhood, adolescence, early adulthood, and other assorted memories formed throughout the years.

She waits a few moments before continuing.

"Now tell me the truth. When you think about your life, was it better or worse before you met me?"

That's not even a question.

"Worse. Undeniably worse."

"I thought so. Since the day you met me, your life has exponentially improved, has it not?"

"Without question."

"Then tell me: why have you been avoiding me?"

I sigh and wipe a thin gleam of water from my eyebrows.

How can I put into words what happened between us at the end of our last meeting? I've thought about it daily—

actually, more like nightly, to be exact, and usually while lying in bed and staring at the ceiling—and still, I don't have an explanation for how she seemed to take command over my body and brain the way she did in that bathroom.

Of all the people in the world I could discuss such a phenomenon with, the perpetrator herself seems like the worst possible candidate—even if she might be the only one who could truly explain it. I'll be honest with her because I doubt my ability to lie to Selene, but as bewitched as I always am in her presence, I'm still unwilling to fully plumb the depths of what I don't understand about her.

"Honestly, Selene…"

I take a deep breath.

"…I'm afraid of you."

She does exactly what I feared she would do and turns all the way around so that now she's facing me again. Except this time, she's really facing me, full-on. But it's too late now. There's no going back.

"I don't fully understand you. What your aim is. What you want from me. Yes, my life has undeniably gotten better— of course, it's gotten better—since I met you. And I think about you… all the time. But I don't know what you want from me. Or what's in it for you, I guess. And it makes me nervous. Because the truth is, I've never met someone like you before. And again, if I'm being honest, I've never felt this way about anybody else before, either."

Selene's expression is unreadable, but she seems to be listening intently, so I go on.

"That's why it scares me, and that's what I mean when I say that I'm afraid of you. I suppose it's also why I guess I've been avoiding you. Even though I don't want to, and even though I owe you everything I have."

The drizzle starts to pick up around us as Selene stares into me for a long, long time. I'm not sure what she's searching for, if anything, but I can't deny there's a newfound sense of lightness and ease in the cavity of my chest. Every inhalation comes a bit freer now that I've spoken my piece and confessed a sizable portion of the thoughts and feelings I've been wrestling with for weeks now.

Only when she's good and ready do her moist lips begin to slowly curl at the corners and stretch up toward those picture-perfect cheekbones, until finally there's no mistaking it as one of those sinfully classic fuck-me-or-fight-me-or-hell-maybe-do-both-at-the-same-time Selene Blackwood smiles that I know I'll never be able to resist.

"You know what I want from you, Lance Lonergan."

And I do. She made it crystal-clear to me the last time we saw each other. Why bother trying to resist any longer when I know that it's a hopeless endeavor? I still want this every bit as much as she does.

So without another word, I reach forward to clasp the back of her head with one hand and the small of her back with my other hand, pull her body flush against mine, and meet that smile with a kiss.

Selene responds in kind, pressing herself further into me and into the kiss, and it's like we both know we need to make up for so much lost time and opportunity that has been escaping us.

I kiss her with a ferocity and a thirst I haven't felt since the night I met her. It's like I've never kissed her before at all, and like this is the very first time I've ever held her in my arms. And though it's far from the first time for both of those acts, I silently vow to myself that I'll also make it far from the last time, even if it's the last thing I do in this lifetime.

Expertly, Selene's fingers undo my belt buckle, the top button of my jeans, and the zipper at my crotch, working with the same deftness her tongue displays in my mouth. I'm never hard as fast or as frequently as I am with Selene, and today is no exception. She doesn't have to tell me how much she wants this, and she doesn't have to ask my permission. Because I need it myself right now like a drowning man needs oxygen.

She moans against my lips as I feel the flat of her hand rub smoothly, slowly, luxuriously against the long, hard outline of my cock. I'm half-expecting the thin fabric of my boxer-briefs to rip a seam and reveal my full naked length due to all the delicious pressure she's creating for me down there. I never feel as massive as I feel with Selene.

Thanks to the rapid engorgement, the tip of my cock drives upward and strains against the cotton confinement surrounding it. It's crafted a narrow gap between the elastic of my underwear and the bare skin beneath it, and Selene wastes no time exploiting this new space she alone is responsible for creating. She trails her index finger along my waistline between the fabric and the flesh, teasing me and undoubtedly savoring the way I keep tilting my hips toward her with a groan, begging her gutturally to finally make skin-to-skin contact between my cock and her hand.

When it happens, it's fucking sensational, as always and as expected. Selene slides her whole hand around the head of my cock, squeezes it several times, then smooths her fingers and her palm up and down my shaft, working her way lower and deeper into my pants until she's massaging my balls too. She repeats this process several times over, touching and stroking every part of my privates with varying levels of intensity and duration. It's keeping me on my toes—literally—as I rock forward into her grip to give more and more of myself over to this woman.

And all the while, she lays into me up above as well, kissing me like no one else ever has and like I know no one else ever will. She just gets me. Selene uses just the right amount of tongue, takes a breath when I need to take a breath too, and chooses to suck on or bite my lower lip at all the most ideal intervals. It's almost as if she's in my head and can read my very thoughts. Every time I feel like this is as good as it can possibly get, she one-ups herself, and then it's improbably even better somehow.

Two can play this game. My hand drifts up from her lower back and between her shoulder blades until my fingers find a small zipper just below the vertebrae in her neck. It doesn't take much effort at all to glide the zipper down, down, down all the way to the bottom, where it finally comes to rest at the end of the track… just above her perfect ass.

That. Ass.

I can resist no longer, so I dip my hand back there and grab hold of as much of her cheek as I can fit between my fingers and thumb, squeezing like my life depends on it, because maybe it does. One hand is not enough. Nothing is ever enough with this goddess. I need more. So much more.

I've had my other hand in her hair and on the back of her head this whole time we've been kissing, but I have a much better use for it now. There's a slight pause where Selene pulls her face back to meet my gaze, and I take advantage of the opening, letting my fingers fall with gravity along the smooth, bare skin of her back until they find their way underneath her dress, take hold of her other ass cheek, and squeeze.

Selene's eyes light up like lanterns.

"Find something you like?"

She makes me ravenous talking like that, all flirty and fuckable.

"I can't get enough of you."

Selene bites her lower lip and raises one eyebrow.

"Then don't."

Yes, ma'am.

Selene starts to move in for another kiss, but I twist her by the hips to spin her around away from me instead. She lets out a surprised little cry of delight, and impossibly, I might be even harder now than before. My balls feel like they're about to explode, but the ache is as pleasurable as it is painful, so I'm not complaining. Every millisecond I spend with this woman in my arms is my own private preview of heaven, only right here on Earth.

If it weren't for her perfect teardrop tits, this dress would have been on the ground long, long ago. But I'm not mad at them for it. Quite the opposite. Eager to show my everlasting gratitude for God's exquisite craftsmanship, I reach around her waist, move up past her toned stomach, and cup the pair in my hands, grinding my pelvis against her from behind as I do this. Her nipples are perky and hard between my fingers, and I lean forward so I can suck on the back of her neck and relish yet another point of contact between our bodies.

Every time I grind my crotch up, into, and against her from behind, it happens with a bit more force and intensity, though I swear I'm not doing it intentionally. My libido has completely taken over and relegated all other faculties— mental, physical, spiritual—to obscure backburners in the distance. Mind, body, and soul are united in needing one thing and one thing only right now: to fuck Selene like she's never been fucked before.

Her whole neck is moist from the misting rain, and that just makes this moment so much hotter for me. My lips and tongue slide like butter across her slick skin, and the thought strikes me that even Mother Nature is wet right now watching us get it on from our perch above the City of Angels.

I tug one corner of the dress down her shoulder with my teeth, but it's not going anywhere on its own. Gravity is as helplessly ineffective with claiming this garment as it is with claiming Selene's chest. I'm not convinced this woman knows how to age, because I truly wouldn't be surprised to see her breasts utterly unchanged even fifty years from now.

Some people just aren't people—they're not plagued by the same types of predestined genetic traps and troubles the rest of us mere mortals have to contend with in a normal human lifespan. Maybe Selene is immortal. Hell, maybe she's a vampire. I think I'd probably be okay with that, actually. It certainly wouldn't come as a surprise.

As much as I'd love to take her dress off completely with my teeth—and as much as I really don't want to tear my hands away from caressing her chest—the clothing's clearly not going anywhere unless I pull it off myself, so I do. When it's finally free of both her shoulders and breasts, the dress flutters to the ground in a heap around her ankles.

Selene doesn't skip a beat, stepping out of it with one foot and using the other to kick it off to the side like she's okay if she never needs it again. And perhaps she doesn't. If her mind is anything like mine right now, maybe she's also desperately hoping she never has to do anything other than this for the rest of existence.

She wasn't wearing a bra and she sure as shit isn't wearing any underwear, either.

Christ. How does this woman go about normal life every day? Did she actually go into her casting office today wearing a skintight dress with nothing on beneath it except a pair of black stilettos? Who does that? And even if she didn't go to work, was she out running errands like this? Who goes to the grocery store, the post office, or the gas station looking like Selene?

No one does. Nobody dresses like Selene, nobody talks like Selene, nobody kisses like Selene… and I'd venture to guess that nobody fucks like Selene, either. I'm about to find out for myself.

As if her gloriously curvaceous figure alone wasn't enough to make my knees knock, Selene decides she'd like to be even more sadistic, so she spreads her legs out wide in an upside-down 'V,' bends forward at the hip, and grips the edge of the roof. Without exaggeration, I'm not sure I've ever seen anything so fucking beautiful and so fucking exciting at the same time as what I'm bearing witness to.

I'm suddenly aware of how ridiculously overdressed I still am compared to this magnificent naked angel standing in her high heels and nothing else. The need to get on her level fast becomes all-consuming. Trembling with excitement and anticipation, I pull my shirt up over my head, rip off my shoes and socks, and peel my unzipped pants and boxer-briefs down my legs before finally tossing the whole lot to the side. All the while, my eyes never leave Selene's body.

Are we really about to do this? The full gravitas of what's going on is only now beginning to truly sink in. Selene and I have had several passionate, intimate encounters to date, but we've never actually had sex. It's happened on numerous instances in my dreams and daydreams since the night I first met her—and it almost happened in the movie theater, whether I wanted it to or not—but this time feels different. She doesn't need to coerce me, and there's nobody else nearby watching or waiting on me. It's finally just us and us alone.

That is, assuming you don't count the hundreds (thousands?) of people going about their lives down below us. Each and every one of them is blissfully ignorant and unaware of what kind of hedonistic debauchery is about to take place between them and their God.

The idea that maybe one or two lucky souls might happen to look up at just the right time and catch a glimpse of Selene's perfect breasts bouncing as I fuck her from behind is enough to get my blood boiling at a fever pitch. Despite a long and storied history of amorous exchanges, I'm pretty positive I've never had sex in public before, and the concept—specifically, the possibility of being seen or getting caught in the act—adds a whole new layer of hotness to this moment.

I can't wait any longer, not with all these thoughts racing through my brain, and especially not with Selene still bent over the railing and her legs spread wide. She hasn't moved a muscle since assuming that pose, nor has she said a word to me.

Of course, she doesn't need to do anything more, either. Even if she did, I'm not sure my heart would be able to take it.

Selene's whole body is wet from the weather, which by now has intensified beyond a mere drizzle into a steady rain. Her skin glistens and gleams as little beads of water trickle down her arms, shoulders, back, ass, and legs. I reach two fingers down between her inner thighs to check if she's as wet inside as she is outside, and she is. Selene clenches around them and shifts her plump, juicy ass even closer to me with a soft moan.

"Give it to me, Lance. I need it. Give it to me now."

CHAPTER 17

There it is again: that feeling.

It's the same sensation I experienced the night of my premiere while we were in the bathroom together. First, it's a light tingling all over my body, like someone's tickling every pore with a microscopic feather, or like there's an extremely low-voltage current of electricity flowing across the surface of my skin. Gradually, that feeling sinks lower and intensifies until it's an itch I can't scratch, and then my muscles start twitching and spasming of their own accord.

I know better than to try and fight it this time. Doing so would only cause me pain, both physical and psychological, since there's no resisting her will when she does this thing to me. I want to tell her that she doesn't need to do it—whatever it is—because I'm a willing participant, and I want this as much as she does. But it's too late anyway since she's already initiated the convergence between us, so I just surrender to it fully with my whole body and soul.

The second I do that, my hips float forward until the tip of my cock presses between her ass and her thighs. I want to enjoy every second of what it feels like to be inside her for the first time, and she lets me.

With a mouthwatering slowness, our bodies melt into one another, and I finally get to experience what has to be the absolute best sensation known to mankind. I still don't know how I ever got to be so lucky, but thank all the stars in the universe that I'm the man who's here and now, and the man who gets to know what it feels like to put himself inside this woman.

Inch by inch, I slide into her, and each individual fragment of a moment is more satisfying than the last. I want to do this forever. Words cannot describe the immeasurable pleasure that accompanies such a simple yet incredibly profound physical action. All the way up to the very end, Selene feels like she's tightening around me, pulling me in and guiding me further, deeper, longer, until I'm completely buried in her body.

"About time."

She whispers the words back to me, and I'll be damned if the fucking sky doesn't flash all around us as lightning streaks across the clouds at that exact same moment.

Here? In L.A.? I guess anything is possible when you're making love to a celestial goddess.

Thunder follows a few seconds later, but it's already an afterthought that's relegated to little more than background noise in my consciousness. Even if it were a full-blown hurricane, I doubt it'd be able to stop us. Selene is both eye of the storm and lightning rod. She is the center-point of my focus, and everything else around us is just set dressing and extra flavor thrown in to enhance the main attraction, which is her. It's always been her, and it always will be her.

And so, we fuck in a rainstorm.

My strokes are measured and drawn-out at first: lengthy, gliding explorations of her inner space. She lets me savor it independently for a while, remaining mostly motionless and only responding with a low, luxurious moan each time I slide myself all the way back inside of her. But then she starts to meet me halfway, driving her hips backward as I thrust forward, until there's a sweet new sound of skin-on-skin slapping every time her cheeks swallow up my cock.

Is it better to see, hear, or feel? All three senses could make a compelling argument right now. Fucking Selene is a sensory overload in every way possible and in the best way possible. It dawns on me that this might already be the greatest day of my life, and something tells me we're just getting started.

I've got a hand on either side of her waist, and my grip tightens as our speed intensifies. Rainwater splashes up between us as my groin smacks rhythmically against her ass. She pushes herself back onto me over and over again in perfect timing with my pumps, using the railing of the roof for balance and for leverage as we seek in concert an ever-deepening connection.

Selene whips her wet braid back over the top of her head, and it just screams out an invitation. I coil it around my right fist and dig the fingers of my left hand even deeper into that scrumptious wet softness around her hip. When I pull her hair, she whimpers but she doesn't stop fucking me back. On the contrary, she's even more forceful now, ramming herself harder along me in a never-ending quest to achieve even deeper, more toe-tingling penetration.

I move my left hand around her so that my fingers can find her clit from the front as I fuck her from behind. Selene immediately responds, tilting her head on her neck toward me and arching her back. The angle she's at now is almost enough to make me lose myself inside of her; that's how sexy she is when she's bent like that and I'm pulling her hair.

In true Selene Blackwood mind-reader fashion, she tips her head back even further so that she's now staring right at me, albeit upside-down, and holy shit I don't know if I'm capable of restraint much longer when she looks at me like that and I get to witness up close and personal just how much she relishes getting fucked by me. Her eyes are aflame with carnal bliss, and yet even still, there's a thirst there and a desperation that tells me her desires might never be fully slaked. She's simply too ravenous, too lustful, and too sexual of a being to ever grow dormant or satisfied.

I wouldn't have it any other way.

But those eyes… I can't have them on me now. Not with her body at this angle, not with her hair wrapped around my fist, and not with all the sounds coming from her throat and from where the rain keeps splattering upward every time we thrust into each other. It's all too much when it's combined, and I don't want this moment to end yet. To be clear, I also don't want it to end ever. But first things first, I need to regain a level of composure before I completely rupture.

I unwind her hair from my hand and slow my strokes, until finally, I pull out entirely. This need to preserve is a selfish one, though, and Selene shouldn't suffer because of it, so I keep my left hand active on her clit all the while. Now that my other hand's free, I put that one to good use as well, reaching down between her soaked upper thighs until I find her glistening pussy. Sliding two fingers in from behind has to be the easiest thing I've ever done in my life, given not only how wet we both are from head to toe, but more importantly, how wet she is inside.

Selene is like putty in my hands as I finger her. My whole body is pressed against hers from behind as I lean forward to kiss along her shoulder blade and up her neck.

When I reach her ear, I breathe hot air there in between the kisses, and she shivers against me and sighs her approval. Little goosebumps break out along her skin, and the texture of it all, merged with the raindrops, brings to mind the most beautiful artistic canvas imaginable.

Whether you're a creationist or an evolutionist, you have to agree that Selene Blackwood broke the mold. God, Mother Nature, someone or something… whatever it was, it deserves not just my eternal gratitude, but the thanks and praise of every other living creature that's ever been so fortunate as to lay eyes on this woman as well.

"I'm gonna come."

Good. I want to feel her squirt all over my hands until it's impossible to differentiate what came from the heavens above us and what came from the heavens inside her. I want to feel her contract and then pulse around my fingers as convulsions rip and ripple through her body like hot sugar waves. I want her orgasm to be so full and so powerful that her legs give out beneath her, and I have to completely support her in my arms.

"Not… yet…"

Her words are as surprising as they are discernible somehow, even above the din of the storm. I'm momentarily disheartened she won't give me the satisfaction of letting go and releasing herself onto me.

But that disappointment is short-lived, since now she's extricating herself from my grasp and turning around to face me head-on. Selene is every bit as mouth-watering from the front as she is from the back. And with rain pouring down her every curve and crevice? Christ.

Her lips curl into that crooked, seductive, challenging

smile that I love so much.

"I want us to come together."

She leans back against the railing on her elbows and spreads her legs out wide again beneath her.

I stand in awe of her. Always.

"How about I make you come now, and then you can come a second time with me? That sounds like a better plan."

Selene shakes her head.

"No. This is our first time. We come together. Now get over here and fuck me again."

I need no further invitation, so I'm moving in on her before she has a chance to coerce me into action with her power. I'm about to flip her around again when she presses a hand up against my chest and over my heart. Without another word, she bends herself backward all the way until her torso is flat atop the rail ledge. The roof barrier is wide enough to semi-support her, but not so wide that her position doesn't instill a sense of vertigo and alarm just by looking at her and observing the way a good portion of her upper body is hanging loosely out in space.

"Lance. I trust you."

Always the mind-reader. How does she do it?

Then again, it's a reminder that nothing is normal with this woman. If ever there was a person capable of living a life without fear or inhibition, it has to be Selene. I'm not entirely convinced it's even possible for her to fall. I think I'd be less surprised if she flew instead.

Gravity and danger both be damned, if she wants me, she can have me. All of me.

I put her face between my palms and give her a deep, hungry kiss that hopefully lets her know just how much her faith in me actually means to me. When I finally do break away, it's only so that I can guide myself back into her. Back where I belong. It really does feel like the most natural thing in the world to be inside her. She just feels right. She feels like home.

Once I'm completely encased in her, I hook my hands beneath her thighs and lift her pelvis up to meet me. She's lighter than I expected, given all her womanly curves and the soft spots she has in all the right places. It helps of course that some of her weight is supported by the balcony railing, but now that her feet are up off the ground, it seems like the majority of her body truly is floating in the air.

If Selene does have any fears or phobias, heights is certainly not one of them. I can feel the way she surrenders herself to me; it's evident in how relaxed she is in her body, and in how utterly non-tense she feels all over as I hold her aloft. Her arms are stretched out on either side of her along the ledge, but she's quite literally put her welfare in my hands, and it's obvious by her closed eyes that she wasn't just paying me empty lip service earlier when she said that she trusted me.

I'm sure I've done some risqué and unconventional things over the years when it comes to sex, but fucking someone who has their head and a decent amount of their body stretched out over a rooftop six stories off the ground has got to take the cake.

For all intents and purposes, it seems my personal scenario couldn't be further from the truth on Selene's end of the equation. She seems so absolutely at ease with our position—and more specifically, with her position—that it makes a guy wonder just how many times she may have done some version of this specific interplay before. People have all sorts of kinks, after all. Maybe one of Selene's is risking her life during intimate acts.

If that's true, I'm beginning to see the appeal, even from my perspective as the person with two feet planted firmly on the ground and the whole of my body on the safe side of the ledge. There's just something about this scene that gets my blood racing. I love getting to actually see myself move in and out of her, and I love watching the indulgent rapture take hold of her expression every time I do. Add in the inherent risk elements involved in our positioning, and you've got yourself a tantalizing recipe that I'm confident would appease even the most cynical veteran sex addicts.

Stunningly, but yet again unsurprisingly, Selene has decided to up the ante even further by going 'no-hands.' Mere seconds earlier, she had her arms out on either side of her, presumably to help her balance and enjoy some modicum of foundational support besides what my muscles could provide. Since then, however, one hand has moved down to play with her clit, and the other has moved all the way up to her head, where she combs her dripping hair and the rainwater back from her face. Her eyes are still closed as she continues unabashedly reveling in what we've created here today between us.

More lightning. More thunder. More rain.

Everything about this situation feels unnatural but also sublime. It's like one of those moments where you feel like your life is a movie, like reality has somehow transcended into something far greater than normalcy and expectation, to the degree where it doesn't even feel like it's actually happening to you, even though you know full-well that it is. There's a second awareness there, a knowing on a deeper level that what you're experiencing has far greater ramifications and means so much more to your soul than you could possibly comprehend in the moment. That kind of intrinsic, bone-deep knowing is pervasive and omnipresent here with Selene.

"I'm close."

Her fucking voice is enough to make me come. Just the way she speaks, the sound that comes out from her vocal cords, it's the most breathtaking music I've ever heard. How on Earth am I ever going to survive this woman?

Selene's chest is moving quicker now as her breathing picks up, and I can tell from experience that she's right: her orgasm isn't that far away at all. I'm under express orders that we climax simultaneously, and while normally such an edict might strike me as overly optimistic or even foolishly naïve, I know better than to doubt Selene Blackwood at this point.

Besides, I've been ready to orgasm for who knows how long now. I've been keeping it at bay since the very beginning of this encounter. If she wants, all Selene probably has to do is say my name out loud while she comes, and that will be the end of me. I'll follow her right over the edge of the world into that quaking peaceful eternity.

It occurs to me how fitting it is that there's an entire city spread out before me—a teeming tapestry of distractions, scenic views, and blinking diversions—and yet the only thing in the whole wide world I have eyes for is the woman I have here in my arms, right smack dab in front of me. What more do I need? Honestly, though? What more could any man need?

"Are you there?"

Her eyes flicker open for the first time in ages, and it's like I've never seen them before. Those little gold flakes I've grown to adore and obsess over in my dreams at night are absolutely radiant, despite there not being a sliver of sunlight in the sky above us. Selene has all the light and all the warmth this world could ever need right there inside her. Fuck, it feels good to be inside her.

"I'm there."

"Come with me."

"Should I pull—"

"Don't you fucking dare."

I'll do anything she says, and this instruction is all too easy to comply with. With a soul-splitting shudder, I give myself over to what is immediately known to me as the greatest orgasm I've ever experienced. My body contracts and expands at the same time in a million different places—some of which I didn't even know existed until this very moment—as I lose my soul in Selene. I might actually be going in and out of consciousness altogether.

Best of all is that I'm not alone. We come together, just like how she wanted… or planned… or manifested… or foretold. It doesn't matter how it happened, just that it happened. And, of course, that it's fucking spectacular.

Selene and I ride the current of our shared climax together for as long as it will carry us, which also turns out to be much longer than any orgasm I can remember. I always lose track of time when I'm with her, but I wouldn't bat an eye if I learned later that minutes had passed us by now, because here we still are, quivering all over and folding ourselves further and further into one another.

It's honestly like I've never truly orgasmed before until now. This is insane.

After what feels like forever in the best sense possible, Selene finally lets out a long ooze of a sigh and allows her body to slide forward off of the railing as her heels move slowly but steadily toward the ground again. I'm there the whole way to guide her down from the edge, but I'd be lying if I said my intentions were completely benign and altruistic. Even fresh off an orgasm, there's no denying the fact that feeling the way her thighs slip along past my fingers until I have her full ass there in my hands again is enough to make me hard and ready to go for round two.

What a power she has over me. Normally, I'd need a bit of time to regroup, but not with Selene. I just can't ever get enough of her.

The thunder tolls again, but it's further off now, a signal that perhaps the meat of the storm has passed. It's still raining pretty substantially, at least by Southern California standards, but it's far from a downpour now.

Selene combs a few strands of her slick hair back from her face and smiles at me like she's about to share a dirty secret.

"I think I like fucking you."

"I fucking love fucking you."

Her eyes twinkle at my response, and she rests a hand on my cheek. Despite her being naked and soaking wet, her fingers and palm actually feel hot against my skin somehow. This woman really does have all the warmth in the world right inside of her, I guess. It's also a reminder that I, too, am completely naked and drenched. The thought makes me shiver, which Selene notices.

"What do you say we go back downstairs to your place and take a hot bath together?"

I didn't think it was physiologically possible to get this hard, this fast, this shortly after sex… but goddamn. Selene Blackwood. Sheesh. I take her hand off my cheek so I can bring it to my mouth and kiss each of her fingers, one by one.

"You have no idea how good that sounds to me…"

She raises an eyebrow.

"… but?"

"… but… Sarah and I… we're having some issues."

She recoils from me as if I'm the one with the furnace glowing beneath my skin.

"I don't share, Lance. Don't lie to me again: who is she to you?"

Some women look hot when they're angry. Selene looks hot all the time, but she actually looks terrifying when she's angry. Like I'd-be-nervous-if-I-was-the-one-standing-with-my-back-to-the-roof-edge terrifying.

"I wasn't lying then and I'm not lying now. She really is just a friend."

Selene appears unconvinced.

"I'm not lying to you. Of course I care about her. She's my best friend and she's my roommate. Or she was my roommate. But that's it. I promise. You don't have to share me with anyone. I'm yours."

Those last two words surprise me when they come out of my mouth.

But what surprises me more is that I don't instantly want to recant them. I've spent a lifetime saying things to women in the heat of the moment and the throes of passion that I've later gone on to regret. Blame it on the alcohol, blame it on intimacy or emotional issues, blame it on whatever you want, the bottom line is I'm at least somewhat self-aware that I have a recurring tendency to put my foot in my mouth when it comes to these types of situations usually.

This one seems different, though. I genuinely want Selene to know the truth of how I feel about her. Yes, she scares the living shit out of me sometimes—like right now—and

I still don't understand the full extent of why she has this profound power over me. Nor do I fully comprehend her uncanny ability to manipulate not just my own thoughts, actions, and feelings, but also major aspects of the world around me and the outside forces I come into daily contact with.

I'm also not entirely convinced that I want to know any of that or learn the full extent of her abilities. Some mysteries are better left unsolved and unexamined.

Despite all of that though, I can't help finding myself increasingly drawn to her. From the moment I first laid eyes on her—even earlier actually, when I first heard her having sex at Royalties with another guy—I was hooked. She has had me spellbound from the jump like I never dreamed possible, and the more time that I spend with her, the more helplessly addicted I become.

So, yes, there is no fear or hesitation hearing those words in my brain or on my tongue, because they're true. I am hers.

What a magical, life-changing discovery that is to realize on such a profound level. I am hers. So, this is what… it… feels like. This is what… love… feels like.

Selene studies me intently, and I let her. I have nothing to hide. I'm realizing just how smart she is, how razor-sharp and intuitive and insightful, as she scrutinizes my expression and the things I've told her. There are no nerves on my end as the receiver now. I'm just in awe that someone so strikingly attractive can also possess such a powerful, critical mind.

And what's more, this person—this goddess—is for some inexplicable reason jealous of me and Sarah. She does not share; she said that much herself. The first person on the planet who has ever made me truly want to give myself over to them—heart, body, and soul—actually feels the same exact way about me. What a fucking world this is. What a fucking miracle.

Whatever she needed to locate, she finds it at last in me. When she does, Selene the inquisitor becomes Selene the temptress once again. Her whole demeanor changes as her face softens and her muscles relax.

The rain has finally stopped completely, and there's even a faint hint of sunlight threatening to break out from behind the grey clouds high above. I can feel it on my skin. How fitting. Can she control the very elements? I wouldn't be surprised.

"What do you mean, 'was' your roommate?"

I'm still bound and determined not to focus on this particular development. So much has already been so unbelievably amazing for me today, and that was even well before Selene showed up on this rooftop to gift me the best sex of my life and make me realize just how crazy I am about her. My tiff with Sarah is a drop in the bucket compared to everything else that's happened since I woke up.

"I don't know. Sarah's still upset with me about the premiere night. About what happened between you and me."

"She's jealous."

"I… I don't think so. It was my fault for not communicating with her better that night, but she also blew the whole situation way out of proportion. I've apologized a million times, but nothing seems to be getting through. It's like everything I say just makes the problem worse somehow."

Selene leans back against the railing. I try hard not to look at her chest.

"And I'm the problem."

"I wouldn't say you're the problem. But I will say she doesn't like you or trust you. I don't know why, though, since it's not like she knows anything about you."

Selene lifts her eyebrows, tilts her head back, and gazes up at the spot where the sun is cautiously contemplating peeking down upon us.

"Women never like me. I'm not the least bit surprised."

I don't know what to say to that, so I just stand in silence and in awe of this heavenly creature. She closes her eyelids, and I swear to God, the second she does that, a thin, gentle ray of sunlight finagles its way through the clouds and falls just perfectly across her face, neck, and upper torso. Selene soaks in it for a few long seconds before speaking again.

"What do you say you come stay with me for a while? Sometimes, a woman just needs her alone time and a little space. You know, to properly sort out her thoughts and emotions. It can be... tricky sometimes when two platonic friends share a living space, especially if they're not on the same page. Sometimes, the best thing to do is to walk away before it's too late, before the relationship can't be salvaged."

There's a lot of sense in what she's saying, but I'm also stuck on the very first part. Did I misunderstand her, or did Selene just invite me to come live with her for a while?

"Are you serious?"

She lowers her chin and focuses back on me.

"About which part?"

"About me coming to stay with you for a while."

"Oh, yes. I would never just casually suggest something like that unless I was deathly serious."

I'm again at a loss for words. Selene has a habit of shocking me like no one else I've ever encountered. To say she keeps me on my toes would be a gargantuan understatement.

She takes her hair between her hands and wrings out some of the water onto the ground. Stunned as I might be,

Selene couldn't appear more at ease if she tried.

"It's your call, obviously. I don't know the full extent of your conversation with Sarah or where you two left things. But if you need a place to stay while you figure out your next move, it would be my pleasure to offer you some hospitality in the meantime."

Am I going crazy, or did she just put a little extra added emphasis on the words 'pleasure' and 'hospitality?' Whether intentional or not, it has my imagination running wild with all sorts of thrilling images and fantasies.

Selene crosses to where our clothes are puddled in a sodden heap and slowly bends over to retrieve her dress. She has to know what kind of view she's giving me, especially since she seems to be in no great hurry moving all my soggy attire out of the way.

Enough is enough. I can't take it anymore. What kind of sweet, sick torture is this, anyway? No one on Earth could just stand here and resist this kind of temptation. Honestly, I deserve a medal for lasting even as long as I have, which isn't long at all. It's inhumane to ask somebody to look but not touch… or taste.

I come up behind her and start to squat down so I can put my face where I desperately need it to be right now, but she turns around and stops me mid-motion.

"As much as I want that too, I unfortunately have somewhere I need to be. But I'll make you a deal: meet me at my place once I'm done, and we can pick back up where we left off."

She glances down, licks her lips, wraps her fingers around my stiff cock, and strokes it.

"Sound good? No pressure, no expectations. This isn't me asking you to move in with me permanently. I'm not a crazy person. Let me just take care of you for a while. Kiss it all better, you know what I mean?"

Before I can even contemplate a proper response, she squats down in front of me and plants a soft, slow kiss on the tip of my cock. My hips drift forward as a shiver runs down my spine, and then Selene breaks the kiss to gaze up at me with a questioning look and an unspoken longing in those magnetic, magical eyes of hers.

How could anyone in my position ever say no? They'd have to be clinically insane to even think the word. An aching moan escapes me, and when she smiles in response, I swear I can feel her lips grazing against me, that's how close she is and how badly I want her.

"Is that a yes?"

"Yes. A million times yes."

"Good."

Selene gives me another kiss down there—this one much faster and lighter, but no less blood-stirring—and then she grabs her dress from out of the pile, stands, and wrings it out. I know I should be following her lead and getting my clothes together too, but I don't want this moment to end.

And that's when a voice in my head chimes in that it doesn't have to. So long as I'm with Selene, the dream never has to die. It can go on and on forever. Our future together is infinite. Every wish and every dream I've ever had, it's all possible—it's only possible—with and through the magic of this woman.

"Um… where do you live?"

She laughs and starts to step back into the dress.

"I'll send you my address when I'm ready for you to come over."

"Do you want to borrow some dry clothes? That doesn't

look very comfortable."

She laughs again. I'm slightly stunned at just how easy and free this exchange has been. So many of my post-coital conversations have historically been littered with awkward silences and stomach-turning small talk. Selene makes every moment we spend together feel simultaneously transcendent and routine. It's a seemingly paradoxical combination, but it's true.

"I'll be fine, but thank you. I need to stop at home anyway before my little errand."

Selene gives me her backside again as she slides the dress further up.

"Give a girl a hand?"

She winks at me over her shoulder.

At this point, I'd give her just about anything she asked of me. Zipping up her dress for her is the absolute least I can do. When I'm finished, she turns back around and runs her thumb across my lips.

"Pack light if you pack anything at all. I have everything you need, trust me."

Oh, I don't doubt it. Right now, I'm not sure I even need oxygen to survive. All I need to stay alive is for this woman to keep looking at me like that, like I'm the only man she ever wants to know her, hold her, love her.

Selene wraps her arms around my neck and pulls me in for a kiss, and there I go again, dropping in and out of consciousness. You can kill me now because I've experienced the very best that life can possibly offer.

But also, don't. Because: my God. I don't ever want this to stop.

It does stop eventually, like all good things do. Selene's eyes sparkle in the dim misty daylight, and in them, there lies a promise of an eternity like this. An eternity spent making love and moving mountains. Fulfilling dreams and creating new ones. Always together. Always forever.

"I'll let you get dressed."

I don't want her to go.

"Do you have to?"

Her smile is devilish.

"I don't want to, but I have to. See you soon, okay?"

I try to go in for another kiss, but she laughs and playfully spins out of my grasp.

How does she already look so put-together again? I'm sure I look like a sloppy, horny, waterlogged stoner, standing here naked with a hard-on and with all my clothes and belongings crumpled in a damp mound beside me. But even wet and fresh from getting fucked in the sky off the side of a roof, Selene has an unmistakable air of elegance and composure about her as she makes her way back toward the stairwell door in her stilettos and skintight dress. How does she do it?

"Selene!"

She has her hand on the doorknob when she turns to me. Truth be told, I really just wanted to see her face again. I don't have anything else I need to say, so I end up waving at her like the lovesick idiot I've become.

Selene waves back though, and my heart somersaults. We share a knowing smile together, and then she opens the door and disappears through it.

I'm left with a strange, unfamiliar sensation in the pit of my stomach as I stand here on the roof and stare at the area she's only just vacated. Absurd as it sounds, especially to me, I realize with a sudden, stark clarity that I miss her. I actually, truly feel a sense of loss, like a part of me just left and walked down the stairs with Selene.

It's not lost on me how insane this revelation is, given how many times I've rolled my eyes when similar sentiments have been expressed by other people in my life, or particularly when I've heard such lines spoken by characters in romcoms and on TV.

But now I'm the one experiencing firsthand that jarring, abrupt emotional impact, and it's no longer a laughing matter or a tired cliché. I get it now. This is what happens when curiosity and enchantment merge and then mature into a full-blown, enraptured obsession.

I am so totally fucked, and I couldn't be any happier about it.

CHAPTER 18

My inner life needs a cold shower about as bad as my outer life needs a hot one. The steam I'm generating in the bathroom is substantial, but it's still nothing compared to the steam Selene and I generated together up on the roof.

Originally, I just wanted to warm up a bit after I had to put back on all my wet clothes and slosh down the steps to our apartment. Or to Sarah's apartment, I guess. Whatever.

At least she wasn't there when I got back down—which was good, since she probably would have yelled at me for dripping on the floor or disrupting the humidity level or breathing too loud or something. Whatever her reason was for stepping out, it certainly didn't break my heart to not find her there glowering at me or giving me more of her patented cold shoulder technique when I walked through the door.

I wasn't planning on taking this long of a shower, but I also wasn't planning on finding myself this hot and bothered well after the fact, either. The more I kept thinking about my rooftop encounter with Selene in the rain and replaying all the individual moments we shared together, the harder it became to resist the urge to rub one out.

So finally, I surrendered and complied with my baser

instincts. Maybe that makes me some kind of degenerate, considering I literally just got done having sex within the past hour, but it is what it is. I swear there's really nothing I could do to resist the drive—it was that overpowering.

It doesn't matter though, anyway, because I'm still wound up. Even after giving myself yet another release, I can't get the images out of my mind: Selene's legs spread apart in her high heels, water running down her lower back, strands of wet hair sticking to her neck and shoulders, veins popping on top of her hands as she gripped the railing for support, her eyelids pressed shut against the world as she surrendered herself to me when I fucked her missionary-style on top of the ledge with half her body hanging out over Los Angeles...

Jesus. I have to stop. This is a vicious cycle with no end. I need to give both my brain and my cock a break. Besides, if I stay in this shower much longer, Sarah's bound to come home and somehow find out I've been in here running up the water bill, just because I know that's what will happen. Begrudgingly, I twist the knob and cut the stream.

I've barely toweled off before I reach for my cell phone to see if I've missed any calls from Selene. It really is like an addiction. I am addicted to Selene Blackwood. Like a junkie, I went from saying goodbye to her on the roof to masturbating over her memory less than thirty minutes later, and now here I am, frantically checking my phone to see if she's been trying to contact me in the interim that I've been in the shower. How did this happen so fast?

The answer, I know, is that it didn't. This whole seismic shift wasn't seismic at all, even if it may feel that way to me now.

As much as I wanted to believe I'd put myself in a position where I didn't need Selene in a professional sense any longer, that had nothing to do with my feelings for her on a personal level. She's still been dominating my subconscious on a near-nightly basis, the same way it was in all the days that followed our first introduction. Did I really believe I could just walk away from all that and that these feelings and emotions would just die off on their own?

Maybe I did. This is uncharted territory for me, that's for sure. I've never had problems walking away from relationships in the past that no longer served me. But I've also never met a woman like Selene before, just like I've never cared about a woman the way I care about Selene.

I shouldn't be thinking about her this much. It's not good for me. This is already an unhealthy obsession. It was an unhealthy obsession long before anything even went down between us physically, and then once those lines were crossed, the fixation truly ventured into perilous terrain.

But my God, is it amazing. It's fucked and it's dangerous, and I'm playing with fire and I know it. But man, it feels good getting burned.

The phone rings in my hand and my heart skips a beat. I recognize the digits displayed on the screen even though they're not the ones I was expecting, because this is her work number, not her personal line. She didn't say she was going into her office, but then again, I guess she didn't say she wasn't going there, either. All she said was that she was swinging by her house to change before running an errand, and then she'd meet me back at her place once she was done.

I answer the call.

"About time. I'm actually low-key going crazy over here just thinking about you."

There's a second or two of silence before I hear the person on the other end of the line clear their throat. As soon as they do, I realize with a mortified pang of panic that it's not Selene who called.

"I take it this is Lance Lonergan?"

Fuck. Fuck, fuck, fuck, fuck, fuck.

"Hi. Sorry, yes, this is Lance. I'm sorry, who's calling?"

"This is Helen Mortimer calling from Selene Blackwood's office."

Of course it is. I should have known right away it was Selene's assistant calling. I'd recognize that acerbic, hostile voice anywhere.

"Sorry about that, Helen, I thought you were someone else."

"I'm sure."

She has got to be one of the most unlikeable individuals I've ever crossed paths with in this industry—which is really saying something.

All the same, I remind myself to be on good behavior. For one, it is a well-known Hollywood best practice to be syrupy sweet and polite to assistants at all times for the sake of your career and reputation. More importantly, this particular assistant is the right-hand woman to the major power broker who's responsible for planting, watering, and harvesting both my professional and my personal interests these days.

"What can I do for you, Helen?"

"I'm calling with a message from Selene. She wanted me to let you know that she got tied up unexpectedly."

It's as if the whole world just came crashing down in meteoric flames around me. Not only am I devastated to hear this news, but frankly, I'm also hurt that it's coming to me secondhand from Selene's assistant and not from Selene herself. She's been calling me non-stop for days now from her cell phone, and now that she finally tracked me down and got what she wanted, she can't be bothered to cancel on me herself? Did I do something wrong or say something wrong that scared her away?

Impossible. She's the one who came up with this idea in the first place of me staying with her for a while. That was her suggestion, not mine, and it was totally unprompted.

Unless it was just something she said in the heat of the moment? Christ, wouldn't that be an ironic twist of fate after everything I've said and done in the past...

"I'm sorry to hear that."

"But she wanted me to give you her address and let you know to go over there now. She'll be there shortly."

Wait... what?

"I'm sorry, can you repeat that, Helen?"

She sighs out her frustration over the phone.

"Selene said you can go over now and she'll meet you there. Do you have a pen and paper for the address?"

This is bonkers. Why would she want me to go there now without her? I mean... at least she still wants to meet up, I guess. And at least this means I still have a place to stay for a while, assuming she's not just having me come over to tell me she made a mistake and got carried away.

"Can't you just text it to me?"

"I can't. This is an office line."

Does she talk to everyone like this? There's no way.

"All right, just a second. Let me find something really quick."

I pin the phone between my ear and my shoulder and then scamper out of the bathroom down the hallway to my bedroom, wrapping a bath towel around my waist along the way. Good thing Sarah's still not home, as I'm sure she'd take umbrage with how I didn't completely finish drying myself off or making myself decent before walking around my own place of residence.

Enough. I can't let women like Sarah or Helen get me to stoop to their level of being bitter and cranky about everything. All that matters right now is that I quickly find myself back in the company of the one woman in the world who I really want to spend time with anyway.

"Okay, I'm ready for—"

"8-6-5-7…"

I guess I wasn't as ready as I thought I was, considering I didn't know she'd just dive into the full address like that without any word of warning or preamble, but I still manage somehow to get all the information written down in ink on a sticky note. Helen even does me the great courtesy of emitting a grunt after I read the address back to her for confirmation.

"And you're sure she said I could just go over there now, right? I'm not supposed to wait for her to call or anything?"

"I'm sure."

"Okay. Is there like a gate code or a number I need to buzz—"

"No."

It's like pulling teeth. I've had more than enough of her, and I'm confident that the feeling is decidedly mutual.

"All right, well, thanks."

"Yeah."

Click.

Good riddance.

As I put on some clean, warm clothes and get myself ready, the word that keeps coming up in my brain is 'giddy.' That's how I'm feeling about everything that's happened to me today. Never mind this minor blip on the radar generated by a jealous roommate who maybe does wish she was just a little bit more. Between the early buzz over the first cut of the film, the star-making Pride and Prejudice news, and then my rooftop encounter with Selene, there's just too much good stuff happening to me these days that it's impossible not to feel giddy.

You know what? Fuck this place. Fuck this teeny two-bedroom apartment in the fucking Valley. Fuck being someone else's roommate and their sub-renter. I don't need any of this shit anymore. Star-making developments, baby. This is the beginning of the end of the life I knew. From here on out, life can only get better and better. Starting now.

I take Selene's advice and pack light. Honestly, there's not a whole lot I even have to begin with. It's really just a matter of packing enough clothes and toiletries. I'm sure she has a fully-stocked kitchen in terms of appliances and equipment, and it's not like I have any large pieces of furniture that I own besides my bed, really, since most of the furnishings in the apartment belong to Sarah. I'll figure out what to do with the bed and anything else later. I certainly won't be lacking a place to sleep, I know that for sure.

Giddy… and exhilarating. I'm almost laughing to myself like a deranged lunatic, that's how exhilarating this is. The last time I felt this kind of buoyant excitement and optimism, I was moving across the country to New York, and then later, to Los Angeles. I remember what that felt like and how it was simultaneously electrifying and terrifying, leaving behind a safe yet tired past life for a sparkling future in the great, vast unknown as an aspiring actor. There's nothing like the thrill of adventure to spike your pulse and get your organs whirring.

I have half a mind to leave a note for Sarah, only because I know how much it would aggravate her to learn I'd gotten kicked out of her Reseda apartment only to fall upwards into the welcoming arms of a gorgeous woman—one who also just so happens to own a house on Mulholland Drive, of all places.

Satisfying as it would be, I resist the urge to twist the knife and have the last laugh, so to speak. Better to be the bigger man and give her the time and space she might actually need right now. Plus, I don't want to burn this bridge. Who knows if she'll change her mind, and if so, how long it might take her to do so.

Though if these jobs keep coming and these paychecks keep clearing, I might be in a position to consider getting my own place much sooner than I ever could have imagined. And I could buy it, too. How about that? Buying a place in Los Angeles. Utter insanity.

After making a couple trips back and forth between my room and my car, I feel satisfied with what I'm bringing. This is anything but final. I have to come back anyway to figure out what I'm doing with my bed, so if I forget something, it's not the end of the world. Even if things go sideways for some reason with Selene—not that I think they would or will—there are always other options available to me. I could hit up Jared or one of my other friends, temporarily sublease a place online, or even find a hotel if all other options get exhausted.

It's still a grey, cloudy day outside, but at least it's not raining anymore. As fun and unique as the rain made that experience up on the roof, I've never been a big fan of driving in it, so this is perfect just the way it is. This whole day, this whole situation, it's all perfect just the way it is.

The traffic also appears to have gotten the message not to do anything that might disrupt my mood today, as the streets and freeways are wet but uncongested. It's smooth sailing all the way down The One-Oh-One and Laurel Canyon until I hit Mulholland.

Even then, it's not backed up, though drivers seem to be a bit more cautious taking the twists and turns due to the slick road conditions. Between all the leftover precipitation and the fresh mud that's slid off the surrounding countryside down onto the pavement, it's hard not to blame any of these motorists for taking it slower than normal.

I'm right there with them, too. About the only thing that could bring me down at this point would be to suddenly veer off the side of a cliff and die in a gruesome car crash. That would certainly put a damper on the kind of day I'm having.

A gentle drizzle is picking up again as I close in on the address given to me by Helen. Every thirty seconds or so, my GPS likes to freeze up, even though I know I'm still moving obviously because the car is still in motion. These little pockets where phone service drops out unexpectedly aren't entirely surprising, given the remote nature of this particular stretch of road that cuts through the Hollywood Hills. Still, you'd think we as a society would have figured this out by now, especially considering it's the second-largest city in the country—not to mention the sheer number of rich and famous people who live up here.

Whether it's because my phone is wigging out or it's because I'm distracted paying too much attention to it, I realize too late that I've driven right past the place I was supposed to turn off at. The side streets and driveways are few and far between up here, but Mulholland is still a major road, so it's not like I can just idle along at five or ten miles an hour and count the numerals on the homes or curbsides. Most of these houses I can't even see from the street, and if they have mailboxes at all, I feel sorry for the postal workers who have to find them each day.

I keep driving a bit further until I find a portion of the road with a wider shoulder. It allows me to pull over to the side, bide my time for a lull in traffic, and then flip around in a U-turn. Even if it means I have a car riding my tail around the curves, I'm committed to taking it even slower this time around, just because I don't want to miss her turn. It's finally starting to get dark outside, and between that, the return of the rain, and the spotty phone service, I'm realizing it's in my own best interests to get to Selene's house both quickly and safely.

The GPS on my phone stalls again just as I'm supposed to be within a minute of making my turn. I know it will be on my left this time around, but I've resisted switching my blinker on because I don't want to be 'that guy.' There's a pick-up truck following me pretty closely, and I definitely have no clue when exactly I'm supposed to get off Mulholland.

All of a sudden, the app unfreezes, and the icon that represents me and my car is now much further along the road than I was a minute ago. As it turns out, the turn I'm supposed to make is here and now, so I slam the brake pedal and turn on my left blinker. An unfamiliar warning light illuminates on the dash, but judging by the way the car responds, I think it's some kind of automatic braking or traction control system kicking into gear, because I can feel it in the steering wheel as the tires skid a bit on the slippery road.

The truck behind me blares its horn and swoops around me on the right. I can actually feel the force and speed of the larger vehicle as it whips past me, and I can certainly hear and see the male driver shout an obscenity in my direction and flip me the bird from his open window.

My cheeks flush, but at the end of the day, all that matters is that he didn't hit me and he didn't stop for a confrontation. His truck disappears out of sight around a bend just ahead, and when the car coming in the opposite direction passes me completely, I carefully take the left turn that I'm supposed to make across oncoming traffic and coast to a stop at where my phone claims is my final destination.

My first thought is that this can't be right. I've pulled into a little dirt patch off the side of Mulholland, and all I can see beyond the front of the car is an impenetrable wall of forest. Perhaps I'd be more trusting if my phone had shown any degree of reliability over the past fifteen minutes of driving, but this reeks of yet another technical difficulty.

I close out of the app, reload it, and type in the address once again, fully expecting the map to show that I'm in an entirely different place than I'm supposed to be. But surprisingly, that's not the case. It shows I've arrived at my target location already. How can that be though? There's nothing out here.

The thought occurs to me that maybe Helen, Selene's assistant, is the evil mastermind behind this whole exercise. It's been obvious since the moment I first met her that she does not care for me in the slightest. Could it be possible she intentionally gave me a bogus address just to send me on a fool's errand?

Possible… but highly unlikely. The Hollywood code goes both ways. Even though she's a nasty bitch, I have to be nice to her because she's Selene's assistant. Similarly, she might think I'm a tool-bag, but she'd certainly never risk her professional reputation, her relationship with Selene, or her job overall just so she could fuck with a person she doesn't care for.

It dawns on me that I've neglected an obvious solution: I can just contact Selene herself. I give her a ring on her personal line, but it goes straight to voicemail.

Odd. It's not like a busy Hollywood casting director to have their cell phone switched completely off. Unless she ignored my call?

No, it's best not to even go there mentally. There's no point stressing over something that may not exist to begin with. I'll just send her a text to confirm I'm at the right place and wait till she gets back to me.

Of course, there's not much I can really send. I can have her confirm that the address Helen gave me is correct, and I guess I can send her my location and have her verify that I'm at the right spot. Maybe there's another entrance. Helen certainly didn't give me much info to go off of other than the exact street address. I send Selene a quick text just letting her know that I think I'm at the right place but that I'm not completely sure.

Time passes without a response. The rain picks up quite a bit on my windshield, to the point where I finally decide to turn the wipers on. It's also dark enough outside that I figure the car's headlights are now warranted, particularly considering that I don't really know where I am, so I flick those on, too.

Something reflects back at me the second I put the lights on. It's hard to make out just what it is, but it's definitely coming from the midst of this strange thicket just up ahead. I know I didn't see it before either. There's almost like a dull, metallic glow coming from a specific spot right in the middle of the leaves, but it's heavily obscured. It's there, though. I can see it still.

Leaning forward in the car seat, I blink and try to better ascertain what it is exactly. But between the rain, the wipers, the trees, and the darkening sky, it's an impossible task to achieve. Whatever it is, I think the only way I'm going to be able to find out for sure is to get out of the car and move up closer.

Easier said than done, of course. Once upon a time, I may have owned an umbrella, but that time is long, long gone. The same could be said for a rain jacket, a poncho, or any kind of waterproof apparel or paraphernalia. These just aren't staples of daily life in a city like Los Angeles.

What I do have, however, is a suitcase in the backseat that is crammed full of clothes, so I twist around, open that up, and start rummaging through to inspect all my options. Somewhere in here is a black nylon windbreaker with a hood that might just do the trick. I find the jacket I'm looking for, zip it on, and pull the hood up over my head.

Well, here goes nothing. Selene still hasn't gotten back to me, and I've committed to coming all the way out here. I may as well do a little exploring, so I take a deep breath, open the door, and step outside into the elements.

Shockingly, it's not nearly as bad as I expected it to be from inside the car. This rain almost feels warm. Granted, I've got a hooded windbreaker on that's shielding me from most of it, but there's a softness to it, kind of similar to what I imagine a light summer rain in a more humid place might feel like. It's certainly not unpleasant.

The mysterious, shiny object calls out for my attention once again. Is it silver? Even without the windshield wipers and the rain-covered glass between us, it's difficult to make out at this distance.

I approach the tree wall to get a closer look, taking pains to ensure my body doesn't get in the way of the headlights. There are no streetlights up here, and if there are any visible stars out tonight over the city, they're currently hidden behind rainclouds, along with the moon. The only real illumination I have at my disposal is either my car or my phone, and I'd rather not risk getting the latter wet.

It's a mailbox. How anticlimactic. The way the foliage has grown in around the rusty metallic cylinder, I'd guess it's been here for quite some time now. This mailbox looks like it belongs in Hobart, not Hollywood.

Discovering 'S. Blackwood' or 'Blackwood' written somewhere would be all too easy, of course. I don't mean to snoop, but I also wouldn't mind having a bit more confirmation that I'm actually in the right place, so I open the front of the mailbox and take a peek inside.

Nothing. No letters, no bills, no magazines, no junk mail. There's literally a cobweb all the way back in there, and unless my eyes are deceiving me, the spider hanging out on it is a black widow.

Yikes. Let's close this latch back up again quick.

I'm about to move away from the mailbox when I notice something else I didn't see originally. It's sort of smeared and rusted over, but I think what I'm looking at is a number written in Sharpie on the top of the mailbox itself, further back and on the side. Stumbling upon that black widow spider has me a bit on edge, though, so I pull one of my jacket sleeves up to cover all the exposed skin on my fist before sticking that appendage into the bramble and pushing it further back off the point in question.

It's faint but it's legible, and I sigh out my relief when I read the same numbers that Helen gave me earlier and that I plugged into my phone. At least I'm in the right place—or better said, at least I'm in the place that Helen told me to go to. Assuming she gave me the correct information, this is where Selene lives and where I'm supposed to meet her.

But… where? The question still remains. Because there's nothing out here.

Well, nothing, that is, except trees. Man, there are a lot of trees… and bushes, and hedges, and ferns, and all sorts of leafy vegetation. This particular spot on Mulholland seems unnaturally fecund and overgrown compared to what is largely a semi-arid, low-scrub area. There's plenty of nature and open land around here, but most of it is brown with only the occasional patch of green.

What I've got my face up against is the exact opposite. This teeming flora seems as impossible here as it seems impenetrable. In every direction and dimension—width, height, depth—there's no getting around, over, or through. Any rational person would walk away confidently knowing that there couldn't possibly be human civilization right here in this particular place. Maybe elsewhere on this road, but not here.

But then how do you explain the mailbox? And how do you explain the addresses lining up?

My phone vibrates in my pocket. I glance at the screen and smile when I recognize Selene's cell phone number before quickly tucking the phone up to my ear inside the hoodie.

"Perfect timing. I was just about to give you another call."

"Are you at home yet?"

Hearing her phrase it that way so casually is equal parts exciting and surprising.

"Um… I'm not sure, actually. That's what I was gonna call for. I think I'm in the right place based off what my phone is telling me, but I'm not seeing a house."

"You can't see it from the street. Did Helen give you directions to the garage in the back?"

As I speak to Selene, I'm pacing along the greenery, scanning for anything that looks like it could be a garage or even a hint of a driveway to a garage, but it's just more of the same.

"She just gave me the address. I asked if there was a code or anything, but she didn't really say."

Selene swears on the other end of the line, and that makes me smile again. I wouldn't mind her assistant receiving a thorough tongue-lashing at the end of this whole ordeal.

"So, you're not at the garage, then?"

"I mean, I might be, but I'm not seeing it if I am. All I'm seeing are a bunch of trees and bushes. And a rusty mailbox."

"You're in front. Keep hugging the tree line and head north from the mailbox. In thirty yards or so, you should come across a wooden gate. Go through it and follow the path down to the house."

I'm not completely sure which direction north is, but I take a stab at it and start jogging as she's still talking to me. At this point, it's nearly pitch-black out, and now that I've abandoned the narrow area lit up by my headlights, I'm truly searching in the dark for this mysterious wooden gate she's describing.

"Is it—"

I stop mid-sentence, because just like magic, there it is. Based off color and material alone, it would be very easy to miss. The wood of the gate looks identical to the surrounding bark, trunks, and branches of all the plants grown in around it. Plus, it's significantly smaller than I thought it would be, especially given the sprawling nature of many of these estates up here. It's shorter than I am, meaning I'll have to duck a bit under the overhanging vines and branches above it just to get through.

But what the gate lacks in visual contrast and size, it more than makes up for in craftsmanship and detail. Even in the dark, I can tell that it's both unusual and exquisite. This gate looks like a set piece straight out of The Lord of the Rings. It's not just any old ordinary front gate; it's a real work of art. I trace a finger of my free hand along the carvings.

"Did you find it?"

"I—I did."

Why am I so entranced all of a sudden? I've never been one for woodworking, and I certainly wouldn't consider myself even a casual admirer of art or the ornate.

"Wonderful. Go through it and follow the path all the way to the house. The door should be unlocked, so let yourself in and make yourself comfortable. I'll be there shortly."

"Oh… okay."

The line goes dead, but I keep the phone pressed up against my ear for several seconds afterward, still running my finger along the various patterns. I realize well after the fact that some time ago the rain must have stopped, though the atmosphere still feels warm, thick, and sticky. There's a weird energy in the air now—not unpleasant, just sort of surreal. It almost feels like I'm in a movie again, or like time has slowed down to allow for a special added emphasis on this moment.

Curiosity gets the better of me. I hit the flashlight button on my phone and shine it on the gate to reveal what appears to be a forest tableau. There are several different types of animals featured throughout, as well as plenty of trees, bushes, and flowers. I recognize a wolf, an owl, a dog, a cat, a snake, a beetle, a rat, a toad, and what looks like a fly or a bee. Lining the top of the gate above all these creatures and plants are several moons, each represented in a different phase.

Everything I'm looking at is quite literally interconnected. Whoever carved this wood intentionally allowed the lines and curves of one object to flow into the next. It's an interesting choice, and one that lends a sense of the dreamlike and the abstract to the whole picture. My eyes effortlessly follow the movement from one area of the gate to the next, until I'm sure I've visually traced every detail several times over without really meaning to.

For whatever reason, I think I could be out here forever doing this if I don't start moving forward, so I decide to double back to my car quickly, kill the ignition, and turn the headlights off to save the battery. I debate grabbing some of my things, but I ultimately elect to just come back for them once I know for sure where this house is—and that it's even open to begin with and available to me.

After locking the car, I jog back along the foliage until I find the gate again. There's a sound behind me that makes me jump, but I realize it's just another car speeding past. Once it's gone—and once my heart rate has leveled out again—I place my hand on a gnarled wooden knob at the side of the gate, twist it, and push the whole door open to walk through, bending beneath low-hanging bramble as I do so.

It's a good thing it's not raining anymore, which allows me to keep my phone out with the flashlight on, because it is dark as fuck out here. Does Selene entertain at all? If she does, she must use the back entrance exclusively, since I can't imagine anyone coming this way on a regular basis. It's becoming increasingly apparent that her assistant Helen must have done all this on purpose just to waylay me and make my life more difficult than it had to be.

For starters, there's no path. I mean, I guess this narrow grassy walkway cut through the trees is the path, but it's definitely not paved. There are no lamp posts or even little solar lights stuck in the ground to show me the way forward, either. I may as well be walking along a hiking trail in the wilderness—which is ridiculous, since this is supposedly the 'front entrance' to a residential plot on Mulholland Drive.

At least there is a somewhat-clear walkway, though. It could be worse. And while the moon and stars are all still buried beneath heavy clouds above, my phone's battery life is solid, and the flashlight is serving me well enough as I follow the narrow grass strip deeper and deeper into the unknown.

It's a surprisingly long walk through the woods before I come upon the house, but when I do, it stops me dead in my tracks.

CHAPTER 19

Where before there was only dark, now, there is light. Like a beacon or a mirage, the house strikes me as being almost out of place after spending so much time traipsing through dark green and black.

What I'm looking at is actually more cottage or cabin than house. Again, this surprises me, given what I thought I knew about all the homes up here. It's a modest structure in size and scope, though it's anything but run-down. Based off the mailbox out front alone, you'd be tempted to assume the corresponding house was a shit-hole, but this definitely isn't, even just from my immediate observation on the outside and at a distance. Instead, the building gives off woodsy, cozy vibes, like it's the kind of place you'd want to retreat to during a winter snowstorm or on a camping trip in the forest.

It's mostly made of wood, but there's a decent amount of stone as well, especially around what is clearly a fireplace and chimney. The cottage has several small, square windows inset amongst the walls, each with the curtains drawn. I think normally there'd be no way of knowing or seeing those curtains at this time of night, at least not from this distance and not in this degree of inky darkness. But for whatever reason, the lights are on inside.

More than anything else, I think that's what made me freeze mid-stride. It's just so unexpected. After encountering no streetlights on Mulholland, no outdoor illumination on the tree line, the mailbox, or the wooden gate at the front, and no lights whatsoever along the path between the gate and this point, it's frankly a shock to finally come upon the house and find it so well lit up from within.

Selene said she'd be home shortly, but did she really beat me here? I turn off the flashlight and check the time she called on my phone log. Sure enough, it was just a few minutes ago. There's a chance she really was that close, but at least it didn't sound like it when she was talking to me. She made it clear that the door was unlocked and that I was free to let myself in, which made me think she still might be a while getting here.

I have half a mind to call her back or even just shoot her a quick text, but I also wonder if maybe I'm overreacting. Just because Sarah has me trained not to leave any lights on when I leave the apartment doesn't mean the rest of the world operates the same way. I'm sure someone who lives on Mulholland Drive isn't particularly concerned about their energy bill. And besides, the lights could be on a timer or an automatic system of some kind to give the illusion the house is occupied. It's not like she has the best security—or really any security at all—here on the property if you're entering from where I came from.

The front door is just up ahead, and I'm an invited guest, so I don't know why I'm hesitating. Is it weird that the lights are on? Maybe, maybe not. It's also weird that someone who lives up here doesn't lock their front door or their front gate.

Then again, Selene Blackwood is nothing if not eccentric, so I don't know why I should be surprised by any of this.

She's right about the door: it's unlocked. I open it cautiously, but there's no stopping the immediate and total bombardment of smells I fall under. The closest thing I can equate it to is touring a candle shop, but even that analogy doesn't really do justice to how overwhelming and overstimulating of a sensory experience this is. Whereas a candle shop features a diverse array of artificial scents meant to simulate seasons or feelings, the smells I'm encountering are all so much less filtered, less manufactured, less processed and pared down.

Though my eyes are watering, it's not unpleasant. It's just strong and unexpected. While it's impossible to pick out anything specific or familiar in the midst of such an overpowering assortment of scents all competing with each other for dominance, the through-line seems to be a natural origin. There's nothing chemical here, or if there is, it's lost on me.

A quick scan of my surroundings further confirms this theory. Much like Selene's 'office'—if you can even call that weird room I visited that day an office—was adorned with plants and strange herbs in jars and bottles, this space is set up similarly. But judging by the sheer volume of the oddities I'm seeing right now, her office setup is just the satellite station to the main attraction here at her home. There have to be hundreds of pots, urns, bowls, and vases strewn out over the shelves along the walls, lining the boundaries where those walls meet the floor, and hanging from woven twine and rope chains dangling from the ceiling.

Smack dab in the center of the room is a tree—a literal tree—growing up and out from the floorboards. It's massive, as wide around as any tree I've ever come across, like something I've heard people talk about when they describe California redwoods and other great wooden behemoths up north. I've never seen a tree this size in Los Angeles, and I'm not sure I'm supposed to be seeing one now, either, though I'm no arborist or horticultural expert. All I can see is the trunk itself, set up like a foundational support beam between the roof and the floor. I guess the roots must stretch out in every direction below the floorboards, and any branches must be outside above the roof of the building, presumably blending in with the surrounding woods.

There are all sorts of strange carvings in the bark. Some are more recognizable than others. Really, it's just the little human figures that feel relatable. Everything else may as well be ancient runes or markings done by an alien race, since I don't know what to make of any of those symbols. It's all been done with a knife, I guess. Some carvings look older than others. Many appear discolored: red, purple, or black, like some kind of liquid or dye has been smeared into the cuts.

As was the case with her office, this room is also littered with pillows all around the floor. You'd be hard-pressed to walk across the floor from one end of the room to the other without stepping on or bumping into one. And similar to her office space, I guess this is what passes for hospitality and home décor in Selene Blackwood's estimation, since there's not a whole lot of furniture in here. She does have a plain wooden bench set up in the far corner of the room, and there's also one wooden chair facing the fireplace to my left.

It also comes as a shock that that the fireplace is lit. I stare at it for a couple seconds and blink my eyes to make sure I'm not hallucinating, but it's really happening. There's a robust woodfire burning there in the stone hearth.

And it's not the only open flame in here, either. Scores of candles burn along the walls on those same shelves that house the bottled herbs and spices… along with the books. Sooooo many books. She's got a whole private library in here of leather-bound hardcovers, some more tattered and worn than others.

Surely, there's more to this place that I'm just not seeing yet, so I quietly shut the door behind me and move further into the interior, carefully stepping over and between pillows as I round the tree trunk past the roaring fire.

Everything I'm taking in is a whole lot to process, but I just keep reminding myself that when you consider who lives here, it all tracks. Is it strange and spooky? Of course. But then again, so is Selene.

A small kitchen finally comes into view, and it's honestly like a breath of fresh air. Between all the smells, the books, and the giant fucking tree growing out of the floor, I was beginning to think I wouldn't find anything in here that actually constitutes a dwelling fit for human inhabitation in the 21st century. I never thought I'd be so relieved to see a refrigerator in my life.

Still, even the kitchen seems lacking in appliances and modern conveniences for a home on Mulholland Drive. It's minimalist at best and survivalist at worst. She has an oven but no microwave, a sink but no dishwasher, and plenty of counter space but no common appliances on top of it. Somewhere in Reseda, Sarah is brewing a fresh pot of coffee and laughing at me.

How nosy do I want to be? I'm tempted to rummage through her cabinets and drawers just to see what I might be dealing with during the time I'm staying here, but I also don't want Selene to come home and discover me doing that first thing. After all, I'm still her guest, and this is her personal space. Odd as it may seem to me, I don't need to go pushing the envelope before I've even fully settled in.

On that note, I clock a door across the way from me on the wall opposite the kitchen. It's the only door I've seen in here besides the front door that I came in through, which makes me wonder just what I might be missing still. I know she mentioned a garage and a back entrance to her home. Is that where this door leads to? And if so, what about the bedroom? Where does she sleep?

I'll just take a quick peek inside. She couldn't possibly be offended by that. After all, she's the one who told me to make myself comfortable. I'd feel a whole lot more comfortable if I knew where I'd be sleeping tonight. I don't think that's rude or an overstep on my part.

Quickly, I make my way across the wooden floorboards, careful once again to thread my feet through the narrow spaces between pillows, until I'm there at the doorway. I reach for the handle and give it a turn, but the door doesn't budge. Sure enough, when I pull my hand back, I spy a keyhole in the black iron knob that I didn't notice before.

"I wouldn't go in there if I were you."

I jump back and spin around so quickly that my foot steps on a pillow and slides out beneath me. It's a miracle I don't completely fall flat on the ground, but miraculously, I manage to somehow regain my balance just in the nick of time. There's no salvaging my inner equilibrium, however.

"Jesus, Selene!"

"That's where I keep the dead bodies."

She winks at me. I didn't hear her come in, but here she is all the same, standing in front of the closed front door with her hands on her hips and her fierce, fight-me-or-fuck-me smile on full display. Also on full display are those legs, propped up as before on black stilettos, but now just barely covered at the top by a fashionable nude-colored trench coat she has cinched at the waist and buttoned up to her collarbone.

"You scared the shit out of me."

"Aww… poor baby. Here, let me make it up to you."

My heart's still beating a mile a minute, but for different reasons now, as she slinks across the floor toward me. Even though she's got her eyes locked on mine, Selene doesn't have any issues navigating the minefield of pillows on the ground, not even in her high heels. How does she do that? How could anyone do that?

She stops just in front of me and snakes her hands up around my neck until I can feel her nails scratching along the base of my skull, and it feels like I'm home again, right where I needed to be all along. This just feels right. There's no other way to put it.

"Miss me?"

"Like you wouldn't believe."

I lean in for a kiss, but she stops my lips with a finger.

"Make me believe."

Her words are barely more than a whisper, but there's a weight to them. I can see in her eyes that she's serious. This might be a game, but she's dead-set on playing it.

I wrap my arms around her waist and pull her closer to me. She responds with a soft little grunt that empties all the blood in my body down to the one place that needs it desperately right now. Slowly, I tilt my head down so I can plant a kiss on the side of her neck.

"Is that what you missed about me?"

God, she knows how to get me going. Just her voice and the way she speaks makes me want to come.

"Yes, that, and this…"

I move up her neck to nibble on her earlobe, breathing warm, wet air into her ear as I do, knowing full well the effect it will have on her. These little tiny goosebumps of hers give me life.

"Mmm… so is that what you missed about me, then?"

This fucking creature. I want to devour her.

"It is, but it's not all…"

I take her face between my hands and kiss my way forward along her cheek and jaw until I've found the corner of her mouth. Her lips taste like heaven and hell all wrapped up in one. There's nowhere else I'd rather spend eternity.

Selene manages to get the words out, but they're almost nothing, just little gaps between our mouths where tiny gasps of air can flow like secrets meant only for us.

"What else… did you miss?"

My fingers are already working on the buttons of her rain jacket. Whatever she has on beneath it—if she has anything on beneath it at all—I need to know now. I've never had a curiosity or a hunger like this before. Her body is the only cure on Earth that can slake me.

I'm practically ripping these buttons off the thread by the time I get the last one undone, and Selene helps me by untying the belt at her waist and shrugging out of the coat so it falls on the floor around her ankles.

Mother of God. Of course she's not wearing anything beneath it. That wouldn't be her style. She is a gift, and her overcoat was just the wrapping paper she allowed me to tear off like a kid on Christmas morning. Only I've never been given anything as perfect as this present.

Selene is not entirely bare. She has a thin chain around her neck supporting a small ornament that hangs low between her breasts. At first, I think it's that silver pendant I've seen her wear on occasion before, but now that I look closer, I realize why the bauble looks so familiar. It's my grandfather's Claddagh ring.

I take it between my fingers.

"Is that—"

"Yes."

I'm surprised to see it. And I'm also ashamed to admit I'd completely forgotten about it until this very moment.

"This is my ring. Isn't it?"

"It was your ring. You gave it to me. Remember?"

I do now. In the bathroom of the movie theater. I did give it to her. The memory is hazy, but I remember taking it off and giving it to her. I don't think I've thought about it since. The silver is warm from her skin still.

"I do. I do remember. Do you wear it often?"

"Believe it or not, this is my first time. I just picked it up… from the jewelers. For the chain, you know."

She leans in so her mouth is next to my ear, takes my hand off the necklace, and moves it to her breast instead.

"Do you like it on me? It makes me feel closer to you."

Now she's the one kissing me and giving me goosebumps, and before long, I've got both hands on her chest and I'm squeezing her, and she's undoing my belt and unzipping my pants, and now we're both in a mad rush to get me undressed, as if the clothes I'm wearing are contaminated and the only hope for salvation is to feel as much of her skin against my skin as is humanly possible.

Selene pushes me down onto the pillows, and suddenly, they don't seem so out of place down here as they did before. It's perfectly normal and absolutely natural to cover your entire floor in pillows if it means you get to fuck on top of them next to a crackling fire in the middle of a cottage that may as well be in the woods. After all, I've got a real-life tree right here next to me.

"You know what else makes me feel close to you?"

This may be my new favorite angle to take in Selene. I stare up at her from the ground as she straddles a leg out on either side of my head, candles and firelight making shadows dance across the curves of her perfect figure. What did I ever do to deserve her? I'll never need anybody else.

My lips and throat are so dry I can barely speak. She literally takes my breath away.

"What?"

With an agonizing slowness, Selene begins to lower her body down into a crouch, teasing and tantalizing me with every vanishing inch of space between us, until she finally rewards my mouth with her pussy.

I close my eyes and take her in eagerly, voraciously. It may as well be the first time I've tasted her because it's been far too long since the last time, and I know that's how it will always be with us. I grasp her ass cheeks and pull her even more down into my face, and she rocks herself forward onto her hands and knees so she can give me more of what I crave.

Selene moans her approval from above, and I feel her body writhe. There are a couple soft thuds on the floor when she peels off her shoes and kicks them to the side, and then she surrenders herself even more to me now that she's completely comfortable.

Some men need food, water, air to breathe. I don't need any of that. Not anymore.

This, this right here. Selene sitting on my face, her lips on my lips, my tongue buried deep inside her. I could fucking do this forever. This is all I need in the world to survive. Take this away from me and I am nothing.

Selene's breathing intensifies, and I can sense her orgasm coming. She grips the top of my skull with the same frenzied strength I grip her ass with from behind. We both keep pushing ourselves into each other, desperately doing anything in our power to get closer, feel closer, be closer. I want her to envelop me.

"I'm coming."

I know.

And then something really strange happens. Something that's never happened to me before. I feel a surge down below about to break. My attention shifts away from the present moment, which was her and only her, to my own body and my own pleasure, and I realize with astonishment and delight that I think I'm about to come, too.

It makes no sense since she hasn't even touched me, and I don't think—no, I know that I've never in my life come like this before, with no one touching me or taking me inside them in some capacity.

And yet here I go, right along with her, and we climax at the same time. The sounds she makes and the way she tenses up on my face brings me right back up out of myself and back to her again where my focus truly belongs. I lose myself in her all over again.

For a long time, Selene and I remain like that, quivering and catching our breath. Slowly, she eases her way back from my face until she's positioned herself on my lower abdomen. She doesn't need to do this—and frankly, I'm not sure I can survive it, either—but she takes my cock in her hand and massages it from base to tip and back again, oh so slowly, drawing out and draining every last bit of reserve I have. Little aftershocks of pleasure course through me, make my toes curl, and cause my breathing to hitch.

"This is what I missed."

She brings her hand back up to her mouth, runs her tongue along a sticky finger, and swallows with a decadent purr.

Absurdly, the thought that crosses my mind in this very moment has nothing to do with how hot that just was. What I'm actually thinking right now is that I sure hope it's not the only thing she missed about me. And I know that's an insane thought to have, and it's a new thought for me to have when it comes to women, but it's as obvious and undeniable as anything I've ever experienced.

It's yet another reminder that this relationship with Selene… this is different. This is new for me. It's about more than just the sex. I actually care about her in a profound way I've never felt for anyone else before. And I can't keep pretending or ignoring the pounding truth of what that feeling is. I'm in love with this woman, and I know it.

Selene places her hands on my chest and closes her eyes. Can she read my thoughts? It's not the first time I've wondered. Did she intentionally mean to put her hand over my heart? Is this her way of signaling that she's on the same page as me, and that she's every bit as wrapped up on me and crazy about me as I am when it comes to her?

Christ, I've become one of 'those' people. Never in a million years did I ever foresee myself becoming the type of person with the constant running monologue in their head. The person who can't stop thinking about that other person, wondering what they're thinking, wondering if that person is thinking of them.

It really is a sickness. Or maybe a madness. Whatever it is, I've got it, and it's got me good. I really am fucked in all the worst ways. But again, I couldn't be any happier about it if I tried. Maybe I'm just a closet masochist.

Her lips are moving. Is she talking to me? Actually, they've been moving for some time. I've been staring in wonderment and fascination, but I haven't really processed what's been happening since I've been too busy with my own thoughts. She's mumbling something to herself, and she's been doing it ever since she shut her eyes and spread her palms out over my chest.

"What are you doing?"

Selene's eyelids flutter slightly, but she doesn't stop moving her lips.

I let out a small laugh. What she's doing is so subtle, it was easy to miss it at first. Her face is relaxed and she's so still, it almost looks like she's sleeping, except for the fact that she's sitting up and she's definitely saying something to herself. Though what it is, I have no idea, since I can't hear her.

"What are you saying? Selene?"

Is her mouth moving in a pattern? I'm watching it form shapes without sound. I try to read her lips for a while, but I don't recognize any words. Finally, I put my hands up on top of hers and lift my hips a bit beneath her in an effort to get her attention.

"You putting a spell on me or what?"

Her eyes snap open and her lips stop moving.

"Yes, actually."

She says it so matter-of-factly, like she's talking about the weather.

"You are?"

"Yes."

Selene holds my gaze, her expression perfectly neutral.

"What kind of spell?"

"A good one. Don't worry. I only have your best interests in mind. Always."

I know I should be expecting her to break into a smile or a laugh at any second now, but I'm not. Because I already know that she's not kidding around. This isn't a joke. I know it, and she knows it. It's just the first time we've talked about any of this out loud.

"So... you're a witch?"

"I am."

Again, she couldn't possibly be any more casual about this revelation. I may as well have just asked her if she's a casting director, a woman, or a homo sapien.

Selene finally blinks.

"How does that make you feel?"

Man. What a question. How does anyone respond to a question like that?

It's weird because I'm not necessarily shocked in the slightest. But I also don't know how a person is supposed to react to learning such news. There's no playbook for this kind of situation, and I certainly don't have any real-life experience to draw on.

"I mean... I don't know."

"Are you surprised?"

"No. I mean, yes, on some level... but also no."

"Are you afraid?"

Firelight gleams off her necklace. Off my ring.

"Should I be?"

"I wouldn't be if I were you."

For the first time, I realize that I've never seen a scab or a scar on her palm where she cut herself with the knife that day. And then I realize that I've never seen one on myself, either. How could I not have noticed any of this?

Selene's face softens and she rubs my chest with her perfectly unblemished hands. Is she listening to me think? How long has she been able to do that for? What's real and what's imagined?

"Let me tell you what I always tell them now."

Who are 'them?'

"Every single one of us is a witch. To some extent, that is. You close your eyes and make a wish before you blow the candles out. You kneel and offer up a prayer in a church or a temple to a god or some mythical being you've never met. You list out your New Year's resolutions, you recite your affirmations in your mind, you create a vision board, you give yourself a pep talk, you imagine the perfect job or the perfect partner or the perfect life for yourself, you manifest your dreams into reality… The list goes on and on, endlessly, for all of us and for all of time. Everything is energy, and energy is magic, so we are all practitioners of magic."

Selene winks.

"Some of us are just a bit more adept than others."

It's a lot to take in. Selene observes my expressions from above. She appears patient and perhaps sympathetic, at least in my estimation. How many times has she had this conversation before? It sounds natural, but also just the tiniest bit rehearsed.

She did say that this is what she 'always tells them now.' What does that even mean? Who are 'them?' Was that Australian guy one of 'them?' Who else?

She strokes my chin.

"How are you doing there, my love?"

It's a loaded question. I'm not freaking out, but I'm definitely processing. I think anyone in my position would be.

"How many people have you had this conversation with?"

"Are you asking me how many people know that I'm a witch? Or are you asking me how many people I've ever been in love with?"

My heart flares and swoons in my chest. Despite everything that's happening, she just said that she's in love with me. Selene Blackwood is in love with me!

Christ. It's as if all of a sudden, none of that other stuff even matters. This revelation trumps all others.

My body feels like it's on fire, and I can see in the way she's looking at me that she means it. That just makes me burn all the hotter. It's not just about the sex for her, or the acting, or the money. She feels the same way I feel. It's more than all that. She's as obsessed with me as I am with her.

Selene smiles the tenderest smile I've ever seen from her. It's a new smile, and it feels like a confirmation that I'm not wrong. That we've entered into a new phase. That I'm not alone in all this.

"Does it matter? I don't need to know your past or how many lovers you've had before me. All I need to know is that, here and now, you love me the way that I love you. What else matters but that?"

Nothing. She's right. Nothing else matters besides that.

Selene takes my hands in hers.

"What are you thinking? I can't read your mind, you know."

That's a relief, but it still makes me wonder just a bit...

"Do you love me, Lance?"

I know the answer to that question. For the very first time

in my life, I understand.

"I do."

There it is again: that smooth, warm smile that's overflowing with tenderness and adulation. It's quickly giving the fight-me-or-fuck-me smile a run for its money as my personal favorite Selene Blackwood smile.

"Good. I love you, too."

She bends forward at the hips and pulls my face into a passionate kiss. My arms curl up around her back and press her into me further.

I was beginning to believe I'd never have the 'I love you/I love you too' moment. But now that it's here and happening, it just feels right. All the stupid songs, books, movies, and TV shows just don't seem quite so stupid anymore.

It's a different kind of kiss for us. I wonder if she notices it too. It's as much a promise as it is passion, a vow we're making to each other with our words and with our bodies. And judging by the way mine is reacting, the next step surely must be to consummate it.

My hands slide down Selene's backside until my fingers find what they're looking for. I'm unsurprised to feel that she's already wet and waiting for me, just as I'm sure she's unsurprised to find me rock-hard and ready to go when she takes me in her hand. We're always ready for each other.

On some level, I think I've been ready and waiting for her my entire life. I just needed to find her first.

Selene eases herself back into my lap. Right before she guides me in, she pauses and peers deeply into my soul.

"I'll give you everything, Lance. I promise you'll never leave me."

CHAPTER 20

Hand in hand, Selene and I walk past a long row of the most massive manicured shrubs I've ever seen in my life. Dotted here and there along the top are cameras, each angled in a different direction. They're all tastefully concealed by the greenery, but they're also just visible enough to remind any casual passersby or would-be intruders that they exist to begin with.

Now this, this is what I had in mind the very first time I came up to her place, almost two full months ago now. This is the kind of ostentatious grandeur you picture in your head when people talk about Hollywood back in places like Oklahoma.

"You're sure this isn't a bad idea, coming in together like this?"

Selene scoffs without breaking stride.

"What, are you worried about the paparazzi?"

But now she stops and looks at me.

"Or are you ashamed to be seen with me?"

I laugh and pull her in close.

"I don't think it's possible for anyone to feel shame being seen with you."

We kiss. She smells especially ravishing tonight. I don't know what kind of homemade oils and elixirs she rubbed into her skin, but they're working. It will be impossible not to spend the whole night searching for a dark corner of this party to steal her away in.

"There won't be any paparazzi here. Trust me. So, you can relax, Mister Big Time."

Maybe it's shameful to admit, but I swear to God, Selene stroking my ego is just as effective at getting me hard as when she's actually stroking me physically. Worst of all, she knows it, too.

"You know what happens when you call me Big."

Selene rubs my erection through the black tuxedo pants and kisses up my neck.

"Mmmm… is that a threat?"

Jesus Christ. We're never going to make it inside at this rate. Actually, keep this up, we're bound to get cited for public indecency. Not that I'd mind normally, but that's the last thing I need right now: to end up in the tabloids during the middle of production.

With an enormous degree of difficulty and will power, I manage to extricate myself from her.

"That's my fault. I'm the one who keeps trying to make us late."

It's true. Even though the address for this place is just a short walk from our home, I've been having the hardest time keeping my hands off Selene all night. Mainly, I blame the sheer dress she chose to wear. I've already managed to take it off her twice tonight, and we haven't even made it to the party yet.

Selene smiles knowingly at me.

"There's no such thing as being late to one of these. They

go all night."

She gives me a quick kiss.

"You ready though? They're waiting for us."

"Who's 'they?'"

Selene nods behind me, and I turn. I must not have seen them before in the dim evening light, because there are two men in black suits standing just up ahead in front of a large iron gate that bifurcates the towering hedges. They look like they could be NFL linebackers, except they're dressed like they should be Men in Black or Secret Service.

"Holy shit. What kind of party is this?"

"Like no party you've ever been to. You ready?"

I guess so. At least I'm dressed the part. She made sure of that.

Besides telling me what I needed to wear, Selene hasn't given me very much information about what this party is or who the hosts are. All she's told me is that they're very important people who hold a lot of power, they like to enjoy themselves, and they're extremely private. I've also gathered that this invitation is exclusive, and that there's no way I'd normally be getting in here without Selene—not even with my burgeoning status as a Hollywood star.

Lastly, I've been warned in no uncertain terms that I need to be ready for anything and everything. This conversation also included me promising her I wouldn't say no to anything she asked me to do tonight. Literally and metaphorically, I am in her hands this evening. This is what it must mean to totally put your faith in another person and to trust them implicitly with your well-being.

Of course, it doesn't hurt if that other person practices magic, either.

The guards see us coming, and one of them turns to enter

a code on the keypad, while the other one bows slightly.

"Good evening, Miss Blackwood."

She nods at him. Of course they know her. I'm not surprised in the slightest. How could anybody forget her?

"Good evening, Mister Lonergan."

That one comes as a surprise, however. I try not to show it on my face, nodding coolly as we walk past the guards through the open gate and onto a cobblestone path that's flanked on either side by more gigantic leafy hedges.

Unlike Selene's 'path' at home, this one actually is fairly well-lit by torches that show us the way forward. It's an infinitely longer walkway than ours, though, and one that's full of twists and turns. I keep waiting for it to finally end and open up on a lawn party, but it's not happening anytime soon. We just keep walking and walking, following the lights like moths, drifting ever onward between these winding maze walls of green and black.

"Jesus Christ. Who lives here? Elon Musk?"

Selene laughs.

"Absolutely not."

"Who is it then? Is it an actor? A director?"

"Just trust me. You do trust me, don't you?"

"Of course."

"Good. Don't forget that tonight. Remember what I told you before, back home. I am going to push you tonight, but it's all part of the process. Think of it as leveling up. No matter what your mind might tell you, I want you to remember how far we've come. Remember everything we've made possible through faith, ritual, intention, and sacrifice. That voice in your head that tells you not to believe, that's just fear talking. And you don't owe it anything anymore— not now, not with me. Understand?"

"I do."

"Good boy. I love you."

"I love you, too."

With anyone else in the world, I'd maybe be nervous. You don't hear that kind of a speech normally and come out on the other side feeling full of confidence and moxie. Maybe you'd usually turn around right about now, tuck your tail between your legs, and head for the exit. It'd be hard to blame anyone for getting uneasy and apprehensive in this situation after receiving such a cryptic warning about what's still to come.

But I'm just fine. If anything, I'm curious. Excited, even. Because she's right. Look at where we are now, and look how far we've come.

Better said, look how far I've come. Selene's been attending these types of events for years now I'm sure. This is old hat for her. For me, though, this is another first taste of the high life—the kind of exalted, dreamlike, magical existence I always dreamed of having for myself as a kid.

And pinch me, because I'm actually here now, living out my dreams, stepping outside my comfort zone, and living like a god. All because I'm dating one of the most powerful people in the entertainment industry—who just so happens to also be a witch.

"Lead on."

She does.

Ever so slowly, I begin to hear the sounds of people talking in the distance. It adds to the excitement as much as it also brings a certain amount of relief, because frankly, the only thing I was really worried about was that this hedge maze would never end.

We finally do come around a corner where the greenery

grows apart and fans out on either side of us, and when it does, the tableau revealed takes my breath away and stops me cold. Selene has her face turned to me, and I can tell she's smiling at the edge of my periphery as she lets me soak in the sights. She sends a small squeeze between our hands to signal her awareness of what I'm going through.

Awe. Amazement. Disbelief. Wonder. I go through all of these emotions and more. Vaguely, I'm aware that my jaw is hanging open like a gaping fool, but I couldn't care less. Because what a spectacular scene this is to behold.

The first thing I notice is the house… because of course the first thing you have to notice is the house. Because that is not a house. That is a castle. That is a palace.

I get now why Selene laughed at the notion that Elon Musk would live here. The king and queen live here. Of what country? I don't know. It doesn't matter. If America had a king and queen, surely, they would live here. Maybe every king and every queen of every country that has royalty, they all live here together. There certainly must be space for them all. Without a doubt, that is the largest, most impressive, most beautiful home I've ever seen in real life.

Scratch that, it's also better than anything I've ever seen in the movies or on TV as well, even in fantasy. Whoever actually does live there must be richer than God.

Christ. Who does live here?

The house is far from the only remarkable sight out here, though. There's an enormous treasure trove of visual interest to take in. It's almost overwhelming, to the point where I don't even know where to begin looking.

For starters, whoever lives here appears to be some kind of collector or amateur museum curator enthusiast, because the massive yard that surrounds the castle-house is littered with all sorts of statues, fountains, sculptures, and other works of art. I can't even remember the last time I was in a museum—maybe a field trip in high school or something— so I have no idea what I'm looking at. But just based off the sheer volume of stuff there is, it's impossible not to be impressed.

The yard itself is even impressive. It's every bit as manicured and well-maintained as everything else I've come across on this sprawling property tonight. Give me a few shots of Ketel One, and I bet I'll swear that I'm in the gardens of Versailles or some French hoity-toity estate before all is said and done. We're certainly not in Kansas anymore, Toto, and I don't think we're in California anymore, either. This looks and feels like Europe. It also feels like another century, like I've stepped back through time itself.

Part of why it's so easy to recognize the size, scope, and just all-around magnificence of this lawn is thanks to the preponderance of torches stuck in it. Growing up, I remember my parents being proud of the way they brought their backyard to life at night with two or three tiki torches and a firepit. Boy, would they have something to say now. The outdoor illumination happening here would put the sun to shame.

It's not even that the torches are all stuck in the ground on top of each other, either. That's part of what makes this place so unbelievable: the torches are actually all spaced out from each other by probably a good ten or twelve feet, and yet they go on endlessly in so many different directions. I'm reminded once again just how epically large this property really is, and I wonder how long it would take a person to walk the full perimeter. I certainly can't see anything that even remotely resembles a boundary of any kind, and in any direction, for that matter.

And then, of course, there are the people.

Milling about beneath the stars and amongst these statues and flames are some of the most elegantly-dressed, physically-attractive human beings I've ever seen. Everyone looks like a movie star, even if I don't recognize any of them as being actual movie stars. This strikes me as being the same crowd you probably would find at an awards show, a banquet, or a state dinner, but not necessarily the people you'd see aping around and gawking at the cameras, desperate to be seen. These are old-money types rather than new-money. There's a certain austerity, a countenance and a calmness, that marks so many of their faces. It's obvious that they've never wanted for anything their whole lives. These are the people pulling the strings of the world.

Speaking of powerful people, I recognize one of them now as he fast approaches Selene and I. It's been months since I last saw him, but he's a face I'll never forget—though I admit it's odd to see him now with his hair slicked down, his bushy beard combed, and his hulking figure confined in an all-black three-piece suit instead of bulging out from beneath a silk kimono.

"Well, I'll be damned! You two look gorgeous together!"

I go in for a handshake, but Martin Schwartzman pulls me in for a hug. He smells like wine—surprise, surprise. The hug lasts longer than I'd like it to but also about as long as I expected. He's even so bold to plant a loud, sloppy kiss on my cheek as I draw back from him finally.

"The one that got away. And to think, I could have claimed you as my own discovery."

"Now, now, Marty. You know that he's mine."

Martin turns his hungry gaze from me to Selene.

"Selene. My darling. My everything. You are a vision, as always."

Selene allows him to embrace her. I note that he doesn't hug her nearly as long or as fiercely as he did me, but he does do something else that turns my stomach: he kisses one cheek, then the other cheek, and then—worst of all—her lips. I'm not sure if I'm about to sock him in the face or throw up first, but Selene doesn't seem to be fazed at all by his antics. She just smiles warmly and pats him on the arm.

"I hope we haven't kept everybody waiting."

"Not at all. The night is young, the crowd is lively, and the magic…"

His eyes light up as he leans forward, and his voice goes into a reverent whisper.

"…it's already happening."

Selene raises an eyebrow.

"Not without us, it's not."

Martin clears his throat, and he straightens both his spine and his bowtie at the same time.

"Of course, of course. I just mean that you both should catch up. Get on my level, you know?"

Selene nods and loops her elbow through mine.

"Point taken. Always good to see you, Marty."

I nod at him as well. There was a time not so very long ago when this man brought a great deal of anger and disappointment to me. But now that all feels like a distant memory, especially with Selene at my side, her arm interlinked with my own. I'm the one that got away, and all he can do now is rue the day that he passed on me.

"Good seeing you again, Marty."

Martin wipes a hairy, pudgy hand across his gleaming forehead.

"Be seeing more of you real soon, my lad."

Selene leads me through the throng of partygoers. I'd estimate there are maybe forty or fifty people here in total. It's certainly not a rager, not anything like the house parties I used to go to with Jared when I first got to L.A. This crowd is much more refined, though definitely not unfriendly or standoffish. Every person that Selene introduces me to is warm, loquacious, and welcoming.

The only weird thing is that I get the sense they all already know me somehow. Even though they introduce themselves and they allow me to introduce myself or allow Selene to make the introductions for all of us, there's something peculiar about the way they look at me and speak to me. It's almost like they were expecting me, or expecting this encounter, or generally just like we've met before at some point, and this meeting is more a reunion or a rekindling than a true first introduction.

And then it finally dawns on me: this is what it feels like to be famous. Even though I've never actually met any of these people before, of course they're acting like they know me already. It's because they know of me already. Whether that's from the trades, the news, industry gossip, social media, or even just from all running in the same circles, it's no wonder I'm picking up on a more heightened sense of familiarity from these strangers than I should be.

After a dozen or so introductions, I run into a truly familiar face.

"Gilda! What are you doing here?"

Gilda Fontenoy stands with two other women who look to be of a similar age to her, somewhere in their late fifties or early sixties. It's impossible not to notice right away that all three women are dressed from head to toe in black—

though only Gilda is in a pantsuit, per usual. At least she's not wearing sunglasses at night on this particular occasion, I notice with a grin.

Gilda gives me a tight, close-lipped smile and a curt nod, none of which surprises me. We worked well together while shooting, but for whatever reason, we never necessarily grew close. I have all the respect in the world for her, though, and I know the feeling is mutual.

"What am I doing here? I wouldn't miss it, of course."

If our relationship is professional, her relationship with Selene is exponentially more personal. To be fair, it goes back a hell of a lot longer, and she told me they were good friends the night I first met her. That's why I guess I'm less surprised to see the two women lock lips right in front of me after they embrace. It's not a long kiss, but it's not a short kiss, either. At least it doesn't bother me to the same degree that Martin's did. I suppose that's a win.

"Selene."

"Gilda."

Selene turns to the other two women, greeting each in turn and in a similar fashion: name, hug, kiss, name, hug, kiss. She introduces them both to me afterward, and I'm not sure what I'm supposed to do for a minute. Thankfully, Selene keeps me pressed close to her side, almost as if she's pinning me with her arm to save me from any unintentional social blunders.

Gilda's two companions smile and nod in much the same way that Gilda did. The three women really could be triplets. It's almost eerie.

"Are you ready, Lance?"

I blink vacantly in Gilda's direction.

"Ready for what?"

Selene pulls me in even closer to her side and pats my arm.

"He doesn't know. For now, let it be a surprise."

Gilda processes this information.

"Of course. Better that way, sometimes."

I turn to look at Selene. She reads my expression.

"Should we get a drink?"

"Sure."

Selene glides us past Gilda and the two other women.

"Excuse us, sisters."

"Of course. Till then."

I mumble something like 'excuse me' as I pass them, but my mind is elsewhere. Why does it feel like everyone here is in on some secret except me? Did I miss a memo? Maybe Selene said something earlier tonight back at home, or even on our way up here or while we were walking through that maze, that I'm just not remembering right now.

"Am I missing something?"

"What are you talking about?"

She leads us to a large marble archway that looks like it's been converted for the evening into a makeshift bar front. Of course, because it's part of this particular party at this particular estate, there's really nothing 'makeshift' about it. The setup here puts Jared's setup at Royalties to shame. Unsurprisingly, they only have top-shelf brands. Some of the bottles I don't even recognize, and many don't have labels at all.

"Why did Gilda ask if I was ready? Ready for what?"

Selene pulls out a pack of cigarettes from her clutch. Though she obviously doesn't need my help, she allows me to be chivalrous and light one up for her. When I'm done, I pass her back the lighter, and she takes a lengthy drag, staring at nothing in particular. She looks just the tiniest bit vexed.

"Everyone's just excited. That's all."

"Excited for what?"

Selene forces a smile before exhaling a thin tendril of smoke in my direction.

"The main event."

"Which is what?"

She takes a step closer and places her hand on my cheek.

"Remember earlier. You said you would trust me."

"I know."

"You said you wouldn't fear."

"I know, and I don't. But can't you tell me what's going on at all?"

She runs her thumb slowly across my lips.

"And ruin all the fun? Of course not."

Selene has barely had any of her cigarette, but she stubs it out and disposes of it in a waste bin near the bar.

Out of nowhere, a person has materialized beneath the arch in front of the bottles. There was no one there a second ago when we first walked up, but now there's a man in a suit standing there silently watching us.

This is only the second-creepiest aspect of the moment. Creepier still is the fact that his entire face is obscured by a mask. It's nothing fancy: just a plain white mask, that of a man, with neutral features. But it feels like it belongs in another time period, along with so much else of what I've already seen tonight.

Selene turns back to me. If the man's sudden appearance startled her at all, she certainly isn't showing it. Maybe she knows the guy already, and this is his schtick or something.

"Drink?"

Couldn't hurt. It's probably a great idea at this point.

"Yeah. I'll do a whiskey sour."

Selene takes my hands in hers.

"Hey. Are you here with me?"

"Of course. What kind of question is that?"

"You trust me."

That one wasn't a question. But I do.

"Yes."

"You love me."

"Yes."

"You said you'd do whatever I told you to do without saying no."

"I did."

"Then drink this."

She turns and reaches out toward the man in the mask.

Holy shit. Whoever he is, now he's got two glasses of what looks like red wine in his hands. I wasn't paying close attention, but I swear I didn't see him move a single muscle out of my periphery.

This guy appears out of thin air, and then because that's not good enough, he makes two glasses of wine appear out of thin air as well. I glance around at the bottles behind him to see if I can connect the dots between what he has in his hands and where it might have come from, but there's no obvious correlation.

Selene takes one glass and passes it to me, and then she takes the other from the masked bartender. His hands empty, the silent figure slowly bows to us, his duty evidently fulfilled. And then he turns and starts walking off along a row of torches toward the house without another word.

I watch him go until he finally disappears completely from my sight. When I turn back to Selene, she's watching me every bit as intently as I just watched the man. Again, I find that my jaw is having a hard time staying up tonight.

"What the fuck was that?"

Selene is so utterly unfazed.

"I thought you used to be that."

"What? A catering worker? Yeah, I mean—I did all sorts of gigs, but not like that. That was just... weird. Like, with the mask, and the whole silent thing? Do you know that guy? So weird. What was up with that?"

"Are you offended?"

"What? No, I'm not offended. I just... you didn't think that was weird?"

"Lance."

Selene commands my complete and undivided attention.

"You want answers, so I'm going to give them to you. Because I love you, and because that's what you deserve. Okay?"

"Okay."

She holds up her glass between us, and I watch the dark red liquid inside catch the light from all the torches surrounding us.

"Raise your glass."

It's another command, but it's a gentle one. I only slightly feel the invisible forces tugging at my muscles, bones, and blood, dragging my arm up from my side into the air until my glass is level with hers. At this point in our relationship, the experience is about as ordinary for me as I imagine it must be to wish your partner pleasant dreams before sleep, or to give them a kiss for greeting when you or they first walk in through the front door. It's just a part of who we are as a couple.

"Tonight, we drink not the poison of man, but the nectar of the Goddess eternal. Let this, the acolytes' ambrosia, quiet your mind, open your heart, stiffen your manhood, and surrender your soul."

Selene stares at me knowingly, waiting.

"It's more than wine… right?"

I feel like an idiot even asking the question after hearing her incite that toast or prayer or spell, whatever it was. But I have still to ask, for some asinine reason or another.

She gives me 'the smile'—the one smile she knows I can't resist; the original smile between us that leveled mountains and boiled oceans.

"So much more. Provisions for the journey you're about to take."

Selene waits but doesn't wait long. With a deep breath, I tilt the contents of the glass back into my mouth and drain the whole concoction down in one long, gulping swig.

It doesn't taste nearly as bad as I thought it would. Does it taste like wine? Definitely not. But I've also tried worse things in my life. There's a faint bitterness on my tongue once I've finished, almost like a chalky aftertaste, but I put it out of mind and memory with a couple quick swallows of my own saliva.

Truth be told, it's probably the same weird homemade concoction Martin Schwartzman was peddling back at his house that day. Maybe this is his side hustle or passion project, making wines for his rich celebrity friends and then spiking them with psychoactive substances. It wouldn't surprise me.

What's done is done. I set the empty glass on the ground near the base of the arch.

When I turn back toward Selene, I see that she's done the same. Her glass is empty and resting near the other end of the arch, and she's observing me closely.

"That's a good boy. The best is yet to come, I assure you."

I'm no stranger to drugs, but at least I usually know what I'm taking before putting a strange substance into my body. This is the second time I've found myself in this kind of situation. I'm not panicking or anxious, but I'd also be lying if I said I'm completely at ease with everything that's unfolding this evening.

"Are you going to tell me what was in that?"

Selene smirks and wraps her arms around the back of my neck. She smells so rich, so divine, it's impossible to focus on anything else.

"What do you think?"

Why did I even ask? She's right. I already knew the answer.

"How long is it going to take… for whatever it is to kick in?"

She plants a soft kiss on my lips. I can still taste the residue of our drinks on her mouth, but I'll be damned if I care. Every time she kisses me—every single time—she makes me want to melt into the earth.

"It is already begun. Come. Follow me."

Selene threads her fingers through mine and leads me off in the direction the bartender went toward the house. The soft sounds of the party begin to recede in the distance behind us as we move through the grass alongside a long line of torches.

"Where are we going?"

Selene stops and turns to me. Again, her expression conveys a mild annoyance or impatience, even if she appears to be working hard to mask it.

"So many questions. I'd cast a spell to keep you tongue-tied if I didn't already have better plans for how to use it tonight."

She kicks off her shoes so that she's barefoot.

"You know what I do when I find that my mind is whirring unnecessarily? I reconnect with where I came from. With where we all came from. Mother Earth."

Her toes wiggle in the grass, and now she's bending down to untie my shoes for me.

"People don't want to believe in magic anymore, even though it's all around us all the time. There's so much untapped energy and lifeforce, right here beneath us, and yet people go to such great lengths to cut themselves off from it, to forget it all, to lose themselves in the banal trivialities of what they consider existence."

She lifts each of my legs in turn to remove my shoes and socks until I'm also barefoot in the grass.

"Feel that? That is true existence. Solid ground beneath your feet. Blades of grass poking up between your toes. Billions upon billions of atoms teeming and twirling together into an illusory series of shapes and hallucinations that we call reality. There's so much more than meets the eye everywhere you look, so why seek answers to questions that aren't important? Everything is what you make of it. So, what are you making, Lance?"

She rises and touches her index finger to my temple.

"Are you making up reasons in your brain to be anxious or afraid?"

Her hand slips lower until it covers my heart.

"Are you making your dreams come true and following your heart?"

And then she slides it even further down until she has my manhood in her grasp, and now her voice is a breathy whisper, and her eyes are as wide and inviting as the moon.

"Are you making love?"

Selene leans in closer and kisses up my neck as she

massages my erection into being.

"Are you making love to me?"

Her kisses trail ever higher along my jawline as I pull her body flush against my own. My head is light, but all I know is that she's never felt better beneath my touch than now.

"Are you making love to me, here, tonight?"

Selene's fingers undo my belt buckle. Before I know what's really happening, we're making out like we've never made out before. We kiss and embrace with a desperate, thirsty urgency, like this is all new and like we've never done any of this before. Because we haven't, at least not like this.

Her hands and lips are everywhere on me at once in an impossible way that doesn't make sense, but I don't care. Why would I? This is orgasmic and incredible. So what if it's not normal or even natural? Once again, she's right about everything. 'Normal' and 'natural' don't exist, not really. Or if they do, they're subjective states, and they're unlike anything I've ever previously considered them to be, anyway.

My body is tingling as much as my brain. I'm vaguely aware that my pants are at my ankles along with my underwear, and Selene is making quick work of my shirt, jacket, and tie as well. I don't know if I've ever gotten naked so quickly in my life. I've certainly never gotten naked with so little thought or action of my own.

From somewhere deep and distant within a faraway, forgotten corner of my mind that I've all but forever abandoned, there comes the faintest recollection of a memory. In between a million kisses and gasps, I attempt to let it out.

"Selene… the party…"

"Mmmmm…"

It's fading fast. I'm not convinced I still care enough to

try for this, but I feel like I should. At least one more time, before it's too late. Before my mind is mush… if it isn't already.

I… I think it actually is already. It might already be too late. My brain is melting. But at the same time, it's unbelievably pleasant. Truly. The most gratifying, spine-shivering, breathless kind of sensation I've ever experienced.

There's that small fleck of a thought again…

"People will see—"

"Let them see."

She places my hands on her breasts—which are bare not just to me, but to the whole world. Where her dress has gone is anybody's guess. In between lucid moments of focus on various parts of her body, my eyes catch a glimpse here or there of the grass beneath and all around us. Nowhere to be found are her shoes, my shoes, my socks, my pants, my shirt, my tie, my jacket, her dress.

It's all gone, gone, gone. Just like my mind. And also, just like my worries. I can't help but laugh a little at my own calm resignation. Already, any trace of alarm that sounded even seconds ago feels comical to me now.

Because she's right: this is how it's supposed to be. This, this is natural. Like Adam and Eve in the Garden of Eden, this is how humanity began. Naked is the way we came into this world. Why should it be any other way after we're born? I'm not ashamed. What is shame anyway but a manmade objection—some ill-conceived, hive-mind notion cooked up by a brainwashed society that's forgotten what it means to truly be alive?

"Get out of your head… and get into my body."

Selene knows all the right things to say to me in this state. It doesn't matter if it's a suggestion or a command.

Not anymore. All that matters is that I agree with her wholeheartedly.

Time spent doing anything other than absolutely savoring every second of existence with this perfect being is time wasted, especially given all the heightened filters and sensations I'm experiencing right now. Best to take advantage of the moment while the moment lasts, because who knows how long we'll have. Who, after all, knows how long any of us really has?

She's gentle in guiding me all the way down through the cool, pregnant air, until we finally reach the solid ground. I'm resting on my back in the grass and she's straddling me with a knee planted on either side of my hips. There's a moistness on the earth that could be dew or could be from us. I'm not sure.

To be honest, I'm not really sure of much anymore. My head is swimming.

That's not true. There is one thing I'm sure of: Selene. I'm sure that this is a good thing, this is a great thing, and this is the only thing. Nothing else matters. Without her, I was nothing. With her, I am everything. I have everything. It's exactly as she said it would be.

No—it's better, actually. Beyond my wildest dreams. This feeling that's coursing through my veins like a radioactive riptide. I've never felt this way before. Every pore in my skin is open and soaking up the mysteries of the universe. I find myself engorged with the fat of creation, and I never want to feel any other way again. Please don't ever let this stop.

With a gorgeously slow smoothness, Selene slides down onto me, reveling in how we conjoin together centimeter by centimeter, getting deeper, warmer, wetter, fuller, closer as we go.

I swear the torches around us just got brighter and then dimmed out again, but maybe that's just my eyesight failing in the dark. Certain senses are dulled while others have never been more heightened. Touch is everything in the world to me in this moment. So long as I can feel her tightening around me, I am home.

Selene moans, and I moan with her, until our sounds congeal into one sound, and with it, we become one body.

Something is happening. I'm losing my sense of dimension. The lines are blurring between her and me, just as they are with other elements, such as light and dark, fire and night, earth and sky. She moans again and I moan again. Selene is riding me, but I've never gone this deep before. I can feel her heart beating inside my rib cage. My vision shimmers.

Even if I wanted to say something, and I don't, there wouldn't be anything left to say. There comes a point where words fail to describe the transcendental experience. I am aware of myself as a person in a physical sense, but on a grander, more cosmic plane, I am aware of the energy exchange between us. Selene has given me so much… so much. I owe her everything. Whatever she needs from me, it is hers. I cannot offer it to her more freely.

Selene throws her head back violently, and her hair flutters out behind her and then floats suspended in the air, changing colors and behaving as if she were underwater. She squeezes me tighter between her powerful legs, wrenching me upward and further into her space, even though I would have once thought that impossible. Such a communion between souls and bodies can only be possible when you suspend your disbelief and truly surrender yourself to the awesome magic and power of life, I realize with tears in my eyes.

More energy gathers between us. It seems to be pooling and storing there where the connection is the most potent, like the heart of the sun. My fingers and toes are trembling as she summons more and more vitality to the nexus of us, drawing it all in from my extremities so it can be repurposed and repackaged to better our lovemaking. Selene's moans have become gasping exaltations, what would sound like gibberish to any ear but mine. But because I know her, I know that nothing is as it seems with this woman divine.

There are other voices, too, joining in the congregation. At first, they're merely murmurs—indistinguishable, really, from the crickets and the toads, the music of the night. Gradually, they build into what could maybe be labeled human. Though I think these sounds are like none I've heard before from humankind. They're all around us now, a ring of incantation, urging us onward and lending an impassioned blessing to the magic of our sex.

Selene rakes her nails without warning along my chest, but the pain is pleasure, and I've never felt more alive. She smears what must be my blood up along her thighs, stomach, breasts, and neck. Finally, she brings it to her mouth and tastes me.

Then she sort of shudders, and that movement alone is enough to nearly make me lose myself. It's only because she isn't ready for me yet that I'm not ready yet, because we have never been more intertwined than we are now, literally and spiritually. We will have the little death together tonight before it all ends.

My vision shimmers. The earth has fallen away from us, but the voices are still there, even closer now than they were before. Gone, too, is the moisture on my back, as well as the mild, pinpricked coolness of the dewy grass scratching against my skin. In their place is solid air, a carpet of charged ionic particles that lift us further and further from the ground, until I can feel the lick of fire below me, and I know we've just risen above the torches.

The voices intensify until it's no longer mere incantation. It's singing now, a chorus of upturned individual spirits merging into one unified mass. I know without trying to know that they are celebrating what's happening here, and that this is what they've been waiting for this whole time.

Silently, I thank Selene for not ruining the surprise. She's right once again, as always. It is so much better this way. I needed to experience this for myself. No one could have explained it to me otherwise. I'm so immensely, unbearably grateful, my heart swells up within my chest and threatens to burst. I can feel it thumping its way right out of me.

And so can Selene, because she holds out a hand to receive it as she smiles my favorite smile down at me, her hair still floating out behind her in the night sky, her pupils haloed now in golden flame.

Tears of iron are streaming down my face because I'm just so very grateful. So honored to be chosen and to be worthy. To have made it. To have finally, finally made it. I cannot stop crying. It's the greatest release of my life. Everything within me is pouring out, and she, Selene, is absorbing it all.

And just when I think I can give her no more, she suddenly climaxes with a scream, and so do I, and so does everyone else. The whole universe shakes around us for a moment, and then the moment's gone, and it all goes dark.

Acknowledgements

First and foremost, I want to thank you as the reader for picking this book and giving it a read. I truly hope you enjoyed reading it as much as I enjoyed writing it.

I also want to thank my family members--and specifically, John, Sue, Megan, and Paul--for their unconditional and unwavering support. Unlike the main character in this story, I am beyond blessed to have always had the most loving and encouraging family an aspiring artist could ever hope for. Please don't disown me for writing such an explicit book.

I'd also like to extend my deepest gratitude to all of my wonderful friends. You guys mean so much to me, and I appreciate the light, love, and laughter you bring into my life. Specific thanks to you, Kasey Dailey, for never holding back and giving me unfiltered, honest, and amazing advice on this one.

Thanks to Christopher Bailey and Phase Publishing for taking a chance on me three years ago and showing me the ropes of this industry. I am so very appreciative of the belief and support you've always instilled in my writing.

Special thanks to Tim Wood, a modern-day patron of the arts if there ever was one. I'm so thankful our paths crossed. Your generosity of spirit knows no bounds.

Thank you, Kayle Hill, for inadvertently giving me

the title to this book over beers and pizza that one time.

Finally, I'd like to thank my fellow author and friend, Alejandra Andrade, for her immeasurable contributions to this work.

About The Author

Patrick Morgan is a writer, dog dad, and hammock enthusiast who currently resides in Los Angeles, California.

He is also the author of Hope's Last Refuge, Viaticum, Realms, and Apparent Horizon.

When not writing books, Patrick enjoys spending time with friends and family. He is a big fan of the ocean, the beach in general, plants, nature, the New England Patriots, and Nacho Cheese Doritos dipped in cold Tostitos Salsa Con Queso (don't knock it till you've tried it).

You can contact him via his website at:
www.patrickmorganonline.com